A VICKY HILL MYSTERY
ACCUSED!

Murder is in the air when hedge-jumping champ Dave Randall accuses his arch enemy, Jack Webster, of sabotaging his dream to compete at the upcoming European Games. Vicky is used to Dave's histrionics and she turns a blind eye. After all, she has bigger fish to fry – namely solving the mysterious death of worm-charming diva, Ruth Reeves, whose sudden inheritance has made her very unpopular with old friends and neighbours alike. But when Jack Webster ends up dead, too, there seems to be a strange connection between the pair and Dave becomes the prime suspect.

A VICKY HILL MYSTERY
ACCUSED!

A VICKY HILL MYSTERY ACCUSED!

by

Hannah Dennison

Magna Large Print Books
Long Preston, North Yorkshire,
BD23 4ND, England.

British Library Cataloguing in Publication Data.

Dennison, Hannah
    A Vicky Hill mystery accused!

    A catalogue record of this book is
    available from the British Library

    ISBN   978-0-7505-4276-0

First published in Great Britain in 2015 by Constable

Published in Large Print 2016 by arrangement with
Little, Brown Book Group

Magna Large Print is an imprint of Library Magna Books Ltd.

Printed and bound in Great Britain by
T.J. (International) Ltd., Cornwall, PL28 8RW

For Claire Carmichael

Mentor and treasured friend

Chapter One

'Vicky! Help, *help!*' Dave Randall yelled on the other end of the line. 'Jack Webster is trying to kill me!'

'Call the police,' I said wearily. 'I'm busy.' And I was. In fact, I was sitting in my car on a mission of vital importance, namely a lunchtime stake-out. 'I've got to go.'

'Don't hang up!' Dave sounded desperate. 'Wait! Get away from there, you bastard! Vicky – don't hang up, *please.*'

'Fine.' I hit speakerphone. 'I'm listening but it had better be worth it.'

Was I becoming jaded already? In the old days, Dave's pleas for help would have turned my reporter instincts onto high alert – a murder always made headlines – but not any more. Experience had shown that Dave Randall, hedge-jumping champion extraordinaire, was crying wolf. Again.

'Don't go in there!' Dave's voice shot up an octave. 'No!' There was the sound of breaking glass followed by an ominous silence.

'Nice try, Dave.' He'd used the broken-glass ploy before – an empty milk bottle thrown against a dry stone wall – but to quote another cliché, once bitten, twice shy.

'Oh Vicky!' There was an anguished sob. 'Jack's gone mental. It's different this time, I swear to God. You've got to come quickly.'

'Do you want me to call the police?' Of course I had no intention of doing such a thing. As the daughter of The Fog – one of the top ten most-wanted criminals in the world – I'd rather die than phone a copper.

'No! No police!'

This didn't surprise me. The police were just as fed up with Dave and his ongoing feud with hedge-cutter Jack Webster as I was.

'Please come. *Please.*'

'Nope,' I said firmly. 'This time you boys will have to sort it out yourselves.' I disconnected the line and checked my watch.

Why hadn't he called? The suspense was killing me. I stared at the old red telephone box – one of the few working and untraceable payphones in the whole town of Gipping-on-Plym – and willed it to ring.

As per my orders from Chuffy McSnatch, Dad's right-hand man, I was to wait at Ponsford Cross to receive 'further instructions' on Operation George. For the last seven days I'd done just that, but to no avail.

At least the priceless 'Spat' Georgian urns that had been mysteriously thrust into my safekeeping were safely buried in my landlady's vegetable garden, where they were unlikely to be discovered, but people – namely my co-workers – were beginning to talk. My disappearance between the hours of twelve thirty and two fifteen was being noticed.

I pushed Dave and his drama out of my mind and turned my attention to this afternoon's 'Day in the Life' assignment. This week's guest was champion worm-charmer Ruth M. Reeves. For the past nine years she had taken home the Tre-wallyn Charmer's Chalice, and she was due to defend her title this coming Sunday.

Frankly, I thought my readers would be far more interested in hearing about her husband's unexpected inheritance, but when I'd called to set up an interview, Ruth had made it clear that the topic was off-limits because she didn't want to get 'begging letters' or 'make people jealous' about their new-found good fortune.

My iPhone rang again.

The caller ID flashed up the name 'Pete Chambers' and my stomach turned over. Our chief reporter never called me unless there was an emergency.

'Where are you?' he barked.

'Just on my way to do the worm-charming feature with–'

'Ruth Reeves will have to wait,' said Pete. 'Got a call about a fight between Dave Randall and Jack Webster.'

'Oh *that*,' I said airily. 'It's nothing. You know what they're like.'

'This time it's serious,' said Pete.

'It's always serious,' I protested. 'I'm seeing Ruth Reeves at two thirty and I'm nowhere near Pennymoor Jump. Can't someone else go?'

'Randall and Webster aren't at Pennymoor Jump,' said Pete. 'Cut the crap, Vicky. Where are you?'

'Why?'

'Where?' Pete demanded again.

'I thought this was a free country.'

'Do I have to put a tracker on your phone?'

13

I hesitated but decided to come clean. 'I'm at Ponsford Cross.'

'What the hell are you doing up there?'

'Eating my lunch and enjoying the view.' And waiting for the phone to ring. Although the view was spectacular: Ponsford Cross sat at one end of Ponsford Ridge, one of the highest points in Devon. On a clear day, you could even see the English Channel!

'Good because you're just minutes away,' said Pete. 'Those idiots were seen scrapping on Grange land by Hugh's Folly.'

'Jack Webster is on Grange land?' I stifled a rush of annoyance. This put a totally different spin on things. If Dave had thought to tell me that Jack was trespassing on Grange land, I might have taken his plea for help a little more seriously.

I had just broken one of the golden rules of journalism. Never assume!

'How did you find out?' I asked.

'That old biddy with the purple hair–' said Pete, 'the one doing the turbine petition – called it in.'

I knew exactly who that 'old biddy' was. The odious Eunice W. Pratt, who lived in Dairy Cottage and who, for all of five minutes, could have been my aunt-in-law.

'Webster is banned from going anywhere near Randall,' Pete went on.

'And vice versa,' I pointed out.

Dave was the resident gamekeeper at The Grange, while Jack Webster lived on neighbouring Brooke Farm. The last time the two men had gone up before the local magistrate for disturbing the peace they'd been ordered to keep off each other's property.

'It takes balls to defy a court order,' said Pete.

And those I didn't think Dave had.

I checked my watch. It was just gone two. 'OK. I'll be there in twenty minutes.'

'Twenty?' Pete shouted. 'You're only minutes away. And don't forget–'

'I know: facts, photos, evidence.'

'And Vicky...' There was a pause. 'What the hell are you up to? Really?'

'Aren't I entitled to a lunch hour?'

There was another pause and then Pete gave a dirty laugh. 'Well, well, well. So the rumour's true. Our Vicky is having a bit of lunchtime nooky.'

I wanted to say that if anyone knew about lunchtime nooky it was my lascivious boss, but instead I fell back on my usual trick: telephone static. 'Hello? Can't. Hear. You. Weird. Line,' and rang off.

Lunchtime nooky? Nothing could be further from the truth. I despaired of ever having any nooky at lunchtime, or ever for that matter.

Suddenly, a sleek red Audi TT Quattro with the personalized number plate GRN RPR pulled up in front of the telephone box just yards from where I was parked, and a tall, thin woman got out.

She was somewhere in her mid-fifties and sported a stylish pixie cut that had been gelled to within an inch of its life. Dressed in a tailored tweed jacket over navy jeans and tan leather boots, she oozed money, which meant she was probably a tourist.

Somewhere a phone began to ring, and I realized with a sickening sensation that it was

15

coming from the telephone box.

I leapt out of the car shouting, 'Wait! That's for me!' but it was too late. The stranger had beaten me to it.

Time stood still.

Everything happened in slow motion as I watched her expression through the glass and saw her mouth the words, 'Hel-lo? Hel-lo? Whooooooo?'

Then time speeded up and I watched, horrified, as she banged the receiver on the metal shelf three times and slammed it back into the cradle.

Her eyes met mine but I swiftly turned on my heel and trotted back to my Fiat Sisley Panda.

Blast! Blast! Blast!

Chuffy McSnatch would never call me now. Our one and only form of communication, via the old payphone, had been compromised and it was my fault. I was furious. It had taken me *weeks* to make contact with the ridiculously over-cautious Chuffy using a system worthy of MI5.

I turned on the ignition and was about to pull away when the woman materialized alongside my car and rapped on my window, gesturing for me to open up.

'Hello,' I said politely. 'Are you lost?'

She was much older than I'd first thought, with a heavily tanned face and deep lines, especially around her mouth – the signs of a heavy smoker.

'I think that phone call was meant for you, dear. I am sorry.'

'Phone call?' I acted surprised. 'Me? I wasn't waiting for a phone call. I pointed to the empty Tupperware box on the passenger seat. 'I always

16

come up here to enjoy my lunch.'

'If you say so.' To my astonishment, she winked. 'Married is he? Don't worry. We were all young once. I'm Elaine Tully. I've just moved back to Gipping-on-Plym with my son Keith. I've been away for over forty years and this place hasn't changed a bit – wait!' Elaine snapped her fingers. *'Gipping Gazette*. I thought I recognized you. You're Vicky Hill, the obit girl.'

'I'm not *just* the obituary writer,' I said. 'I do other things, too.' I wanted to add that I'd had four front-page exclusives in the past year, but I was never one to brag.

'You write that column: "On the Cemetery Circuit with Vicky". My son is one of your biggest fans.'

'One can never have enough fans,' I joked.

It was true that my weekly column was becoming popular – so much so that Wilf Veysey, our illustrious editor, had finally moved into the twenty-first century and given the column its own Facebook Page, where mourners could 'like' posts and upload photographs of their favourite funerals. At the moment I had forty-nine 'likes'.

'Herman speaks very highly of you,' Elaine went on.

'That's nice of Herman.' I wracked my brains. Herman. *Herman?* I knew every single citizen in Gipping-on-Plym, but there was definitely no Herman.

'The *vicar.*' Elaine gave a laugh tinged with scorn. 'You don't know the name of your own vicar and you're the *obituary* writer?'

'Oh, *that* Herman!' I laughed but felt my face

17

redden with embarrassment. The truth was that the Reverend Whittler always said, 'Just call me Whittler,' so we did.

Seeing my confusion, Elaine added. 'Herman and I go back decades. We bumped into each other in Disney World. I'd just lost Carlos, my fifth husband–'

'I'm sorry for your loss,' I said automatically. Good grief! *Fifth* husband? 'Well, nice to meet you. Must go. Bye.'

'Wait!' Elaine thrust a coloured photograph through the window. 'Can you tell me if this picture was taken around here?'

The photograph showed a bird's-eye view of a sparkling river running through a field of wild flowers, flanked by blossoming almond trees. Its beauty was marred, however, by five enormous wind turbines on the horizon. Eunice Pratt was right to conduct her petitions to stop these monstrosities from being built.

I shook my head. 'No. Sorry. That's not from around here.'

A flash of annoyance crossed Elaine's features. 'I see. Then perhaps you can tell me if Jack Webster has moved?'

'Jack Webster?' I said, surprised. 'No. Why?'

'No reason.' She reached in and snatched back the photograph, shoving it savagely back into her handbag.

'Did you try calling him?'

'I just tried using that old phone,' said Elaine. 'I lost my iPhone and I'm waiting for a replacement.'

Now my curiosity was piqued. 'Brooke Farm is only at the end of Honeysuckle Lane.' I pointed

18

to one of the four roads that converged at Pons-ford Cross.

'I know where it is,' she said.

'Although Jack might be out,' I added, knowing full well that he was probably beating Dave Randall to a pulp at that very minute. 'But I'm sure his wife Amelia is home.'

Elaine's eyes widened. 'Seriously? They're still married?'

'It would seem so,' I said.

'Well, thanks anyway.'

And with that, Elaine gave a curt nod and strode back to her fancy car.

I felt uneasy as I watched the Audi roar away. Who was this newcomer to Gipping-on-Plym? Was she on the hunt for husband number six? And what could she possibly want with Jack Webster, the most obnoxious person in the whole of Devon-shire?

At least Elaine had mistaken Chuffy McSnatch's real reason for calling. In fact, she had given me a brilliant idea. Why not invent an affair? I was weary of being teased mercilessly about my vir-ginal status.

Why on earth hadn't I thought of it before! It could come in handy, to say nothing of being a bit of a laugh. I might even give my imaginary lover a Ferrari, just to make my frenemy Annabel Lake pea-green with envy.

Buoyed up by my new plan, I set off for Hugh's Folly to attend to some bruised male egos.

Chapter Two

Flanked by high Devon hedges, Honeysuckle Lane marked the northern perimeter of the vast Grange estate, the seat of the ancient Trewallyn dynasty.

The current owner of The Grange, Lady Ethel Turberville-Spat – or Topaz Potter, aspiring undercover reporter to yours truly – was eccentric and paranoid at the best of times, but today it would appear her paranoia had reached new heights. Even I was surprised at the number of hand-painted signs liberally daubed with skull and crossbones saying, 'Trespassers Will Be Prosecuted', which were dotted along the boundary. But before I could dwell further on what went through Topaz's peculiar mind, Eunice Pratt leapt in front of my car, waving a clipboard.

With a yelp, I hit the brakes, fishtailing dangerously on the mud-slicked road and pulling up within a millimeter of Eunice's outstretched hand as she stood there, without so much as a quiver.

'Finally!' she shouted and slammed her clipboard onto the bonnet of my car with a deafening crash.

Here we go, I thought as Eunice stormed over to my window. She was wearing her usual head-scarf over a lavender-coloured perm and brown tweed coat with a dozen badges marking her numerous causes and petitions. I noted two new ones: 'Say No to Turbines!' and another sporting the recently formed Citizens' Patrol slogan, 'I'm Watching You!'

The whole Citizens' Patrol thing was silly given that there were precisely three houses in the vicinity – one being Dairy Cottage, which Eunice shared with her sister-in-law Mary F. Berry. The other two properties were Brooke Farm, home to the infamous man of the hour, Jack Webster, and his wife, Amelia, and John and Ruth Reeves of Reeves Roost.

I opened my window a crack and braced myself for Eunice's usual spite.

'I've been waiting for you for *hours!*' she snapped. 'What took you so long?'

'Where's the action, Mrs P?' I said mildly. Now that I was no longer interested in having a romantic future with her nautical nephew, I didn't feel the need to go out of my way to curry favour with the old bag.

'How are you Mrs P?' I said warmly.

'The police are here already.' Eunice gestured to the open five-bar gate a few yards further up the road. 'In the top field. This time, they'll put Randall behind bars. Good riddance to bad rubbish.'

'Do you know what happened?' I asked.

'Poor Jack was just picking blackberries–'

'Picking *blackberries?*' I didn't believe *that* for a second. 'That would be trespassing and Dave Randall was within his rights to order him off the property.'

Eunice looked startled for a moment. 'No. Jack mentioned that her ladyship said all her people were welcome to the Trewallyn blackberries,' she

21

declared. 'Randall just attacked him. Knocked him out cold.'

'And you saw this?'

Eunice reddened. 'I'd been to see her ladyship to get her to sign my turbine petition, but she wasn't home. On my way back I heard the ker-fuffle, so I called the police.'

'So you didn't actually *see* Dave Randall hit Jack Webster?'

'Are you calling me a liar?'

'No. But you might be called upon as a wit-ness.'

'Good,' said Eunice with relish. 'As the founding member of Citizens' Patrol it's my duty to report any trouble in the neighbourhood. I suppose you've heard about Ruth's prizewinning sun-flowers?'

I hadn't and said so.

'Slashed to ribbons, they were. Crime is on the rise in this area,' Eunice declared. 'We need to be extra vigilant.'

'Hence the reason for all the new trespassing signs?' I suggested.

'I'm glad her ladyship listened to me,' said Eun-ice. 'What with the Spat urns still being missing—'

'I'm sure they'll have left the country by now,' I lied.

'And of course, Amelia was robbed.'

'Amelia was robbed?' I exclaimed. 'When?'

'She can't remember,' said Eunice. 'She said she was looking for her silver punchbowl this morning and realized that a few pillboxes and a pair of candlesticks were missing.'

'Did she tell the police?'

'She's going to,' said Eunice. 'These are dark days in Gipping-on-Plym. Mary's been oiling the twelve-bore. Of course, we all know who's responsible.'

'You think Dave Randall is a thief?'

'Not *Randall!*' Eunice spat. 'Although I wouldn't put it past him. No, that chappy – the famous burglar. What's his name? The Fug.'

I hoped my face didn't betray my shock. 'You mean The Fog.'

'That's the one. He held up a bank and shot all the hostages.'

'No he did not!' I exclaimed. 'Where on earth did you hear that?'

'*The Daily Mail Online.*' Eunice nodded. 'Oh yes, we've got the Internet now.'

'*The Daily Mail Online* is misinformed,' I said. 'It was a security guard and his own gun accidentally went off in its holster. He's supposed to make a full recovery.' I knew this for a fact because say what you like about my dad, he was not a violent man.

Eunice just waved away my comment. 'There was no sign of a break-in at Brooke Farm,' she went on. 'Just like that stealth robbery at The Grange.'

My heart began to race erratically. Dad had earned the nickname The Fog because he materialized out of thin air and disappeared without a trace. Often, his victims didn't even know they'd been burgled, thanks to his knack of selecting valuable but obscure pieces and then rearranging the silver cabinet. I had to admit it bore all the trademarks of my father's fair hand.

Eunice slammed her clipboard on top of my roof, putting an end to my musings. 'Did you hear what I said?' she demanded. 'I told the red-headed copper all about Amelia's punchbowl and he was most interested.'

My stomach gave a jolt. 'Redheaded copper? You mean the one with the freckles– ?'

'And teeth like a shark. Yes. *Him.*' Eunice pulled a face. *'Probes.* I thought he'd gone for good.'

As did I! I couldn't believe it. Detective Inspector Colin Probes was back in the fold after weeks and weeks away. Wait! Was he back because he'd heard something about my dad?

'And you mentioned ... The Fog to the police officer?' I ventured.

'Who? No!' said Eunice. 'We've got more important things to worry about. Randall is after Jack's blood. Mark my words. You write *that* in your paper. And you tell *them* that you heard it from Eunice Pratt first when poor Jack ends up dead in a ditch.'

As Eunice raged on about Dave Randall's short-comings and that England should bring back hanging, Dad was forgotten. Instead I was consumed with the memory of my last conversation with the redheaded policeman – it was one I knew off by heart.

'Vicky.' he'd said. 'I don't care who your father is. None of us can choose our parents.' I *knew* that he was about to declare his feelings for me, but I'd panicked, made my excuses and rushed off. The next thing I heard was that Probes had gone away to work on a drug case with 'inter-national' connections and wasn't expected to return for months.

Dad always said that the only good copper was a dead copper, but I'd had time to think about it. History was dotted with tragic love affairs – Romeo and Juliet, Heathcliff and Cathy, our receptionist Barbara Meadows and editor Wilf Veysey, to name just a few. Wasn't I entitled to my own Romeo? Surely Fate wouldn't be so cruel as to deny me those feelings of passion and desire – even if it did end badly? Was I destined to remain a dried-up old spinster?

I could see it all now. I would be at the altar, dressed in white – no wait. I wouldn't want to be a virgin on my wedding day; I'd wear ivory and a circlet of roses in my hair – while Colin would be in a matching suit. Reverend Whittler – Herman – would announce us as man and wife, but as we embraced, my father would burst in and–'

'Did you hear what I said?' Eunice banged her clipboard again.

'Of course,' I said, all business. 'I'd best go and see what's happening.'

'I'll be expecting your call,' Eunice said. 'And make sure you take a photograph of poor Jack's skull for the paper before that chubby chap bandages it up.'

'The ambulance is there?' The only chubby chap I knew was paramedic Steve Burrows. Steve, who was determined to pursue me to the ends of the earth so that he could, in his words, 'make you mine'.

This was awkward, because by some horrible stroke of luck, every time I'd got close to having a meaningful conversation with the aloof Detective

25

Probes, Steve had managed to sabotage the moment.

Waving Eunice Pratt a cheery goodbye I drove the few yards up to the open gate just as a police Panda car emerged, greeting me with several loud parps on the horn that intimated 'get out of the way'. My stomach flipped as I recognized the timid, young Detective Constable Kelvin Bond in the driving seat, with Probes riding shotgun.

Our eyes met. I felt my face grow hot as I wound down the window, steadying myself for a polite hello. Since our last conversation, he'd grown more attractive in my imagination. I'd even got as far as picking my night-time negligee.

I waved and offered a warm smile, but Probes had other ideas.

Without even acknowledging my presence, he turned to his colleague and made some remark that caused the younger copper to hoot with laughter. I wondered if they were talking about me.

And then they were gone.

As I watched the Panda car disappear from view my disappointment turned to a peculiar sense of relief. Those weeks of longing had made me restless and oddly vulnerable and, as we all know, there's no room for vulnerability in the cut-throat world of investigative journalism.

I'd never been one to pine and mope and I wasn't about to start now. I thought of Barbara, our receptionist, whose love life lay in tatters, or Annabel and her obsession with married men and their cars. My infatuation with the copper had been a temporary indulgence and one I was determined not to repeat. What had I been thinking? A daughter of Harold Hill cavorting with the enemy?

Focus, Vicky, focus! Right now I had a story to write. In fact, I had three!

First, find out the real reason why Jack Webster had strayed onto Grange land. Was he really picking blackberries, or was he out to kill Dave Randall? Second, interview Ruth Reeves and question her about her slashed sunflowers. Was she right in claiming that their new-found good fortune had spawned jealous neighbours?

There was also the mysterious Elaine Tully to consider, and why, after forty years she had suddenly decided to move back to Gipping-on-Plym. What was the connection between the turbine photograph and Jack Webster?

Call it my reporter instinct, but something told me that life in Gipping-on-Plym was about to get lively.

Chapter Three

Steve's ambulance was parked alongside a dirty green Land Rover at the bottom of the field in front of a stone byre. Behind it stood the crenellated turret of Hugh's Folly peeping through the trees. Standing 30 feet high and with a tiny window up top, the tower smacked of Rapunzel's prison from *Grimm's Fairy Tales*.

There was no sign of Dave Randall.

27

I assumed this vehicle must belong to Jack Webster since Dave's Land Rover was distinguished by the hand-painted logo on the driver's side: 'Jump Azberjam 2016' with Azerbaijan spelled wrongly, of course.

Ever since the sport of hedge-jumping had been excluded from the Olympic games, Dave was a changed man.

Dave had campaigned hard for 'Team GB 2012: Let's Jump' and many private citizens and small-business owners had donated their hard-earned cash and held fundraisers for extra training. Even my landlady Mrs Evans had helped sew the custom-made logos onto dozens of pairs of moleskin trousers. When news that hedge-jumping did not meet the global qualifications needed to be a sport 'accessible by all', things had turned nasty. Investors wanted their money back – with interest – but it was too late. Dave had spent the lot.

It was only when he learned that the Inter-Continental Games was to be held in Azerbaijan in 2016 that Dave pulled himself together and made a last-ditch attempt to get hedge-jumping back on the competitive map. To say he was obsessed would be putting it mildly. He'd become repeatedly paranoid that Jack was out to sabotage his life-long dream and, given Jack's illegal presence this afternoon, Dave might have a point.

The snag was that Dave's hedge-jumping course was located a few miles away at Pennymoor Jump. It was not on Grange land.

Maybe Eunice was right and Jack really *had* been picking blackberries.

Suddenly Jack emerged from behind the

ambulance holding an icepack to his forehead.

Steve followed, carrying a spiked shooting stick. He wore his usual white medic's coat which, despite Eunice's cruel comments about Steve being chubby, didn't look as tight as usual.

'Good afternoon, gents.' I braced myself for Steve's usual onslaught of flattery.

'Can I help you?' Steve's sparkling blue eyes seemed puzzled.

'Hi Steve,' I said.

Steve jabbed the spike into the ground and opened the aluminum handles with a snap. 'There you go, Mr Webster. Take a pew and sit down for a moment.'

Jack duly did as he was told, although those portable seats aren't the most stable.

Steve turned to me with a frown. 'Have we met before?'

'Very funny, Steve,' I said.

He snapped his fingers. 'Oh yes. Vicky, isn't it? That's right. I didn't recognize you. Excuse me.'

Steve retreated to the ambulance, leaving me more than a little miffed.

What wasn't there to recognize? I'd only seen Steve three weeks ago. I was dressed in my trademark Christiane Amanpour safari jacket, my hair was its usual shoulder-length bob and I had given up wearing contact lenses to disguise the true colour of my sapphire-blue eyes, which Steve claimed he could 'drown in, doll'.

True, I never returned any of his phone calls – unless it was something to do with the morgue – so obviously Steve was trying the old reverse-psychology ploy. How childish.

Turning my attention to the injured party I said, 'Are you hurt, Mr Webster?'

With his bright red nose and a map of capillary veins stretching over his cheeks, Jack bore all the signs of a heavy drinker, and he'd clearly been drinking today.

The farmer removed the icepack. 'What do you think?' He pointed to a deep gash on his forehead that was matted with congealed blood.

'That looks painful.'

'Randall hit me on the head with a bloody rock,' he said.

I pulled out my notebook. 'Where *is* Mr Randall?'

'Bloody coward skedaddled the moment the cops turned up,' grumbled Jack. 'Bloody Eunice and her Citizens' Patrol. She should have kept her mouth shut.'

'Why can't you boys get along,' I scolded. 'Live and let live.'

'It's barbaric, that's why!' Jack fumed. 'We've got to preserve our heritage!'

For the average layman, it would seem that since the two sports shared a common interest – namely, hedges – they should be able to coexist quite happily. Cutters took care to craft and build the Devon hedge-bank for various competitions, as did the jumpers. The disagreement between the two came from one basic fact: many of Dave's hedges were inadvertently destroyed during practice. To Jack, this was a crime against nature; to Dave, it was all part of the fun.

Privately, I agreed with Jack Webster, but it was a reporter's job to remain impartial.

'What were you doing trespassing on Grange land anyway?' I demanded.

'Eh?'

'Why is your Land Rover parked in this field?'

'Eh?'

'Why you were here in the first place, Mr Webster?'

'Blackberries,' said Jack suddenly. 'I was picking them for Amelia, like. Ask Eunice; she'll vouch for me.'

'You drove your Land Rover to pick blackberries.' I considered the nearby hedge-bank. With my practiced eye I could identify every hedge species, and the one enclosing this field was a mixture of hawthorn, laurel and beech. There wasn't a blackberry to be seen.

'Where were you picking blackberries?'

'What are you? The police?' Jack said angrily.

'The police were here,' I said. 'Our newspaper was informed. I am only doing my job. If you want your story to appear in print, I need to hear your side.'

'I'll tell you what I told the cops,' said Jack. 'I don't want to press charges.'

'What?' I exclaimed. 'But you said Dave struck you!'

'Yeah well, accidents happen.'

This was highly unusual. Here was Jack Webster's chance to ruin Dave's life – just as Dave had feared – and for some reason Jack had decided not to. Clearly the blow to his head had affected him more than he realized.

'Time to stitch you up, Mr Webster.' Steve reappeared holding the biggest needle I'd ever seen.

Jack's eyes bulged in horror. 'What the hell? You keep away from me, you big fat idiot!'

Steve sucked in his stomach. 'Suit yourself. It's your funeral,' he said. Then, to my surprise, he abruptly shoved Jack Webster off the shooting stick and sent him toppling onto the grass.

Steve folded the contraption, tossed it into the rear of the ambulance, slammed the doors, stormed around to the cab and got in. Moments later, he started the engine and began the slow climb back up the hill to the five-bar gate and Honeysuckle Lane.

I was rather surprised by Steve's uncharacteristic rudeness. He hadn't even said goodbye.

Cursing, Jack got to his feet.

Recalling my instructions to get 'facts, photos, evidence', I brought out my iPhone and scrolled to the camera feature.

Jack's hands flew to cover his injured face. 'No photos,' he cried.

'My boss will kill me if I don't get at least one.'

'Vicky – please luv.' Jack mumbled through his fingers, all bluster gone. 'Keep this quiet. Just this once, will you?'

I wondered if Jack had concussion. For starters, he always wanted any spat – especially one involving Dave Randall – reported in the papers, and secondly, he had never ever addressed me as 'luv'.

'Well, I'll need to talk to Dave,' I said.

'Please don't, Vicky … it's Amelia,' said Jack urgently. 'She doesn't like Randall and, well, this will only upset her. I don't want her to know about any of this because....' he thought so hard I could almost hear his brain whirring, 'she's got a weak heart.'

Pointing to Jack's head wound I said, 'How do you plan on explaining away that?'

'I walked into a door.'

Typical! How many times had Amelia said the very same thing when sporting a telltale bruise on her face – and then I had a hunch. Jack Webster was up to something, and it wasn't just picking blackberries.

'Oh, someone was looking for you earlier,' I said, feigning innocence. 'Do you remember an Elaine Tully?'

'Eh?'

'She's moved back to Gipping-on-Plym and was asking after you.'

All the blood drained out of Jack's face. 'What ... what did you tell her?'

'Nothing, but she did try calling you. Apparently your phone is out of order.'

'That's right.' Jack Webster nervously licked his lips. 'Did she say anything else?'

'She showed me a photograph of wind turbines.'

'You don't know what you're talking about!' Drawing up to his full height he shouted, 'You mind your own bloody business, do you hear me? Interfering little busybody.'

Astonished, I could only watch him storm back to his Land Rover – just as Steve had done moments earlier – start the engine and struggle up the hill in the ambulance's wake.

There was a rustling of leaves as Dave Randall scrambled out from the interior of the hedge where he'd obviously been eavesdropping.

'Has he gone?'

Dave was wearing a pair of brown moleskin trousers and a matching brown sweatshirt sporting the Jump Azberjam 2016 logo.

'Yes. He's gone.'

Dave's handsome face was smudged with dirt. 'Vicky, I'm so glad you're here. I told you Webster was out to get me.'

Dave dragged off his knitted beanie and ran his fingers through his dark curly hair, making it stand on end. He seemed so emotional I could almost swear I saw tears in his eyes.

'I'm ruined,' he whispered. 'It's all over.'

'I think you'd better start at the beginning,' I replied.

Chapter Four

'But I swear he lied!' Dave exclaimed. 'I never touched him.'

'Jack Webster claimed you hit him with a rock.'

'I threw it as a warning, like,' Dave said defiantly. 'It didn't even hit him. It hit that wall.' He pointed to the byre. 'But Jack went mental and then he attacked me with a bottle.'

I recalled the sound of breaking glass. 'Go on.'

'You don't believe me, do you?' Dave grabbed my hand – his were rough and calloused – and steered me over to the side of the byre, pointing to a mound of broken glass that lay in pieces on the grass. 'See! See!' he cried. 'He threw that at me!'

'And he missed,' I said.

'What a waste of scrumpy,' he said with disgust.

I poked the shards with the tip of my boot and was surprised to see that instead of the usual thick brown glass of Sandford Orchards – a local favourite – this bottle was green. I bent down and carefully picked up a large chunk. The label bore the name Asti Spumante.

What on earth was Jack Webster doing picking blackberries with a bottle of Asti Spumante on a Wednesday afternoon?

'I caught Webster red-handed,' said Dave. 'He was trying to break in.'

There was a shiny brass padlock fixed to the old byre door.

'Where were you at the time?' I asked.

Dave pointed to a patch of scrubland where I could see his Land Rover parked. 'I was checking fences and the like and I saw him drive down the hill.'

'And then what?'

'I watched him, didn't I?' said Dave. 'He got out and tried to open the byre door, but I'd just put on a padlock because I've seen him snooping around here a lot recently.'

'And then what?' I said again.

'Jack went back to his Land Rover to get a pair of loppers.'

'Was he holding the bottle of Asti Spumante?'

'Yeah.'

'But surely he couldn't hold the loppers and the Asti Spumante,' I pointed out.

Dave shrugged.

'So you didn't *see* Jack Webster with the loppers,' I said. 'And the padlock was never broken.'

'Yeah but...' Dave swallowed hard. 'Then he turned on me something wicked, told me he'd make me sorry–'

'And that's when you threw the rock?'

'And he threw the bottle.'

'And that's when you called me?'

'Yeah. And then bloody Eunice Pratt phoned the cops.'

'It's a tough one, Dave,' I said. 'Webster was trespassing but he didn't actually break into the byre.'

'He was going to.'

'That's your word against his, and you know Eunice won't side with you. You also attacked Jack first.'

Dave sank onto the edge of the water trough and put his head in his hands. 'This is the worst day of my life.'

Much as I felt for Dave's predicament, he could be so melodramatic.

'Why do you suppose Jack wanted to break into the byre?' I asked.

'Oh Vicky, swear to God and hope to die that if I tell you, you will never repeat it.'

I crossed my fingers behind my back. 'You can trust me, Dave.'

Dave shot me a look of pure agony. 'You know what happened after the Olympic fiasco,' he said miserably. 'When Quentin Goss screwed us over?'

I hardly thought that was fair. Quentin Goss's Leviathan farm machinery company had been one of Dave's sponsors and, quite reasonably, they had requested their money be returned.

'The Inter-Continental selection committee is coming next Wednesday to inspect the course.'

'At Pennymoor Jump,' I said.

Dave shook his head. 'No.' He jabbed a thumb at the wood behind. 'Down yonder at Boggins Leap. Her ladyship gave me permission. Sir Hugh Trewallyn used to jump there in the '60s but he abandoned it in favour of the park.'

I should have realized that Topaz's great-uncle – founder of the sport of hedge-jumping and Dave's mentor – would have had several hedge-jumping courses on The Grange estate.

'Boggins Leap was in a bad state,' Dave went on, 'but I've been rebuilding it on the quiet, like. And now Webster has found out.'

'Why didn't you build it at Pennymoor Jump where you've already got tight security?' In fact, the last time I had visited Pennymoor Jump, all the electric fencing and razor wire reminded me of one of Dad's many stints as a guest at Her Majesty's pleasure.

'You don't understand. The course has got to be pristine. Perfect.' Dave's mood turned to one of despair. 'But what does it matter now? Jack has destroyed me.'

'What are you talking about?'

Dave's eyes brimmed with tears. 'Remember that scandal with the Olympic swimmer Michael Phelps? Remember when he was caught smoking illegal drugs?'

It was hardly in the same league as hedge-jumping, I thought, but said, 'You haven't been smoking illegal drugs, Dave.'

'You don't understand!' he said again and gave a tiny sob. 'The committee won't tolerate violence or a police record. So you see, I'm finished.

Damn Jack bloody Webster!'

'Well, guess what, Dave,' I said. 'The good news is that Jack Webster isn't pressing charges.'

'But ... but ... I saw the police. They were here!'

'It's your lucky day. Jack – for whatever reason – sent them away.'

Dave's jaw dropped. For about ten seconds he said nothing, then he pulled me into his arms. 'Oh Vicky, Vicky. Thank you – but why?' He thrust me away. 'No. *No!* He's up to something. I don't trust him. He's got another plan.'

'Let's cross that bridge when we come to it,' I said. 'You still haven't told me why you think Webster wanted to break into the byre.'

'My equipment is in there – loppers, axe, bill-hook and a brand-new chainsaw,' said Dave. 'Can't get my Land Rover down to Boggins Leap. I've got to go in on foot, so I keep all my stuff here, see?'

And I did. Maybe Dave was right about Jack, after all.

'Do you want to come and see Boggins Leap?' said Dave shyly.

I checked my watch. I was already half an hour late for Ruth Reeves, but Pete had wanted a story and I had one right here – it wasn't the one Pete expected, but it was a story nonetheless.

'Lead the way,' I said.

Dave skirted the byre and clambered over the wooden stile in the corner of the field – I noted that he didn't help me up, over or down. The age of chivalry was, indeed, dead.

'Which way is The Grange?' I asked.

'About twenty minutes' walk that way.' Dave

38

pointed to a leafy tunnel that disappeared into Trewallyn Woods. 'And over there—' he gestured to another wooden stile on the opposite side of the footpath, 'eventually takes you up to Honeysuckle Lane.'

And Dairy Cottage – Eunice Pratt's humble abode – Brooke Farm and Reeves Roost.

'But *this* is the way to Boggins Leap,' Dave declared with a hint of pride. I followed him around the small circular tower of Hugh's Folly until he stopped at a pile of brushwood and branches.

Dave removed several and revealed a narrow entrance to an animal track. 'Down here,' he said. 'I keep it covered up, like.'

The first thing I noticed were the number of trees daubed with blue paint marking our way – so much for a secret location. Dave may as well have written, 'This Way To Boggins Leap.'

Ten minutes later, after much ducking under low branches, battles with brambles and muddy puddles, we emerged into a grassy clearing.

'Wow!' I exclaimed. 'This is incredible.'

Dave turned to me, beaming with pleasure. 'I know.'

The course was just like Pennymoor Jump, but on a much smaller scale. Just like the coded runs in a ski resort, the area was divided into coloured zones according to skill. The green zone was easy to jump and comprised of low-growing hedges like dwarf box and privet. Blue ranged from leyland cypress and spotted laurel to copper beech. The red zone provided splendid hedges of yew and black, and double black diamond was on a slope and incorporated the treacherous Boggins bog at the bottom of the field.

Dave had done an excellent job of showing every single jumper's hazard – including marshland, water obstacles, vicious thorns and sharp objects hidden in the foliage. There were even inflatable coloured bags set on a timer to throw a jumper off mid-stride.

'I can't believe you built all this yourself,' I exclaimed. 'I want to take some photos.'

I already had a few headlines: RANDALL RISES AGAIN! A VICKY HILL EXCLUSIVE! or LEGENDARY LEAP FEAT! A VICKY HILL EXCLUSIVE!

'But you can't tell anyone about this until after Wednesday. Promise?'

'Promise,' I said. 'You have my word.'

I wandered around taking photographs on my iPhone whilst Dave lovingly adjusted a sprig here and there.

'I've got to go,' I said. 'I think I can find my own way back.'

Dave stood there staring at me.

'Are you OK?'

'I think I love you,' he blurted out and pulled me into his arms for the second time that afternoon.

'Dave!' I protested as his lips tried to find mine. I inhaled the smell of earth and damp leaves and tried to push him off. How ironic that a mere twelve months earlier Dave's declaration of love would have been music to my ears, but not any more.

'Dave, please–'

Suddenly his lips clamped onto mine and his

tongue began to poke around in my mouth, reminding me of our one and only, highly unpleasant kiss in the past. Someone needed to give him lessons and point out that he wasn't drilling for oil.

I stamped on Dave's foot.

Dave yelped. 'Ouch! That *really* hurt!'

'I've got a boyfriend!'

'What do you mean? A boyfriend? You said you'd wait for me.'

'No, I didn't,' I exclaimed, thinking I should have played the boyfriend card before.

Dave scratched his head. 'But ... but ... I've always loved you, Vicky.'

'What about your girlfriend Loretta Lovedale?' I demanded.

'A transitory object who didn't understand the importance of my dream,' said Dave, grabbing my hands and drawing me close. 'But you always have. You always knew that hedge-jumping came first. You knew that once it was all over and I was the world champion, we'd have a future together.'

Surely he couldn't be serious!

'Dave, the thing is–'

'Wait! Oh no!' Dave pushed me aside. 'Who is it? Who is this boyfriend? Not Steve Burrows? Tell me it's not him.'

'No, it's not Steve Burrows,' I said wearily. 'You don't know who it is. He doesn't live around here. Dave, you don't need any distractions. As you said, you've got to focus on your dream. Believe me, it's better this way.'

'Fine.' Dave turned his back on me, removed a pair of secateurs from his pocket – I'd wondered what had been pressing against my leg – and began to viciously trim some brambles.

'Bye!' I said, but he didn't answer.

As I wound my way back to my car, I thought how strange men were. Barbara maintained that they were only keen when the woman in question wasn't interested, and it would seem that she was right.

Speaking of women being interested, my thoughts turned to Jack and his presence at Dave's byre this afternoon. I thought of that telltale bottle of Asti Spumante and how he'd reacted with obvious panic when I'd mentioned that Elaine Tully had returned home to roost. I recalled Jack's sudden concern with his wife Amelia's health.

Something was definitely going on – although the thought of anyone indulging in a bit of hanky-panky with Jack Webster was something that filled me with revulsion and which I instantly pushed to the back of my mind. Besides, it was none of my business. I was a serious reporter and right now I had an important story to record for posterity: Ruth Reeves was about to share the secret to her worm-charming success. Not only that, if the rumour about her slashed sunflowers proved to be true, the act may not be the murder that Pete had hoped for this week's front page, but it would definitely be news!

Chapter Five

I pulled into Reeves Roost and was astonished to find it jam-packed with luxury toys – a monstrous Safari Cheetah RV, a sleek Cobalt A25 powerboat christened 'Ruthie Baby', and a brand-new top-of-the-line John Deere tractor.

The exact amount of John Reeves's inheritance was a closely guarded secret, but rumour had it that it was in excess of five million pounds. It was little wonder that Ruth hadn't wanted their wealth broadcast in the *Gipping Gazette*.

The next thing I noticed was that the old farmhouse had had a new lick of paint. Even the farm buildings that enclosed the cobbled courtyard had been repointed and given brand-new doors and windows.

I headed for the new front door and rapped the new brass knocker but, after waiting for at least five minutes, I realized no one was home.

A quick scan of the yard confirmed there were no cars parked there either. Blast! All that dilly-dallying with Dave had cost me the interview.

Irritated, I was about to head back to my Fiat when I heard the distant sounds of Mick Jagger on the radio getting no satisfaction. As the song grew louder I became aware of an accompanying nail-biting sound of metal striking tarmac. There was also a smell of burning rubber.

A pink Mercedes SLS class roadster with the top

down turned into the farmyard. Ruth Reeves was at the wheel, waving gaily as she trundled by, seemingly oblivious to the state of her two flat tyres and the rash of sparks flying from the wheels.

I decided – quite selfishly – that I didn't want to be the one to tell her in case her distress jeopardized my interview.

Ruth parked behind the powerboat – I noted that her £100,000 car bore a similar personal plate: RTHY-BBY – and switched off the engine. Mick Jagger fell silent.

'Vicky, dear!' Ruth got out of the car. 'I'm so sorry I'm late. My hair appointment took longer than I'd thought.'

I hardly recognized the reigning champion of the Trewallyn Chalice and the head of Gipping Women's Institute Refreshment Committee. She wore a leopard-print jacket and tight leather trousers that did nothing for her ample behind. Despite the fact that Ruth still couldn't master the art of lipstick application without a mirror, she had reinvented herself in a way that would make Madonna turn green.

Ruth's neatly cropped grey hair had morphed into a blond chiselled bob with caramel highlights; her NHS wire-rimmed eyeglasses – so often fixed with Sellotape – had been replaced by a pair of piercing green eyes that I knew for a fact were tinted contacts. Gold bracelets clattered on her wrists and she even wore one on her ankle.

'Welcome to Reeves Roost!' Ruth beamed. 'Let's go inside and have a glass of champagne.'

Champagne? At three thirty on a Wednesday afternoon! But of course it'd be rude to refuse.

I stepped into the hallway of the farmhouse, which smelled of fresh paint and newly varnished hardwood floors.

'Lovely day, isn't it?' She beamed again.

Ruth's good spirits threw me off-kilter. 'I'm sorry about your sunflowers.'

A puzzled expression crossed Ruth's face and then she said, 'Oh, *those*. Yes – all very upsetting. I'm giving up all that flower and vegetable competition nonsense anyway.'

This was definitely news. 'I hope your decision doesn't extend to worm-charming,' I said. 'You've held the Trewallyn Chalice for nine years running.'

'I'm afraid so,' said Ruth. 'This will be my last year. John and I have bought a villa in Majorca and we'll be spending more time overseas. Oh,' she pointed to my feet. 'Do you mind taking off your shoes? New carpets.'

I did mind. Especially since the toe had gone in one of my socks, but naturally I said, 'Happy to.'

I removed my trainers and allowed Ruth – who had changed into white slippers made from soft calfskin – to bear them off to a little custom-made cupboard marked SHOES.

Of course I'd heard all about how much money the Reeves's had lavished on their renovations. For months the cost had gripped the senior community – especially our receptionist, Barbara Meadows, who knew all the details. Builders had been brought in from Plymouth. Stone had been flown in from Italy. Floors had been cut from the Amazon rain forests – although I suspected that was just malicious gossip. It was even rumoured that they'd hired an interior decorator from

Milan and shunned Gillian Briggs, who could always be counted on to run up a few curtains.

'Let's go into my new kitchen,' Ruth said. 'We knocked a few of the interior walls down and it's so much brighter now.'

I followed her into an enormous open-plan living area with exposed beams. Leather sofas in white and beige were dotted throughout the room, artfully arranged around matching rugs that I'd heard were custom-made to incorporate John and Ruth's initials in the border.

'What an amazing place!' I said and it was – it looked like it belonged in a magazine. Somehow I couldn't imagine her burly husband John and his hedge-cutting cronies sitting around in their farm clothes drinking scrumpy and discussing the price of silage in such pristine surroundings.

One entire wall featured floor-to-ceiling glass with a panoramic view of the rolling countryside, interspersed with woodland and a patchwork of fields enclosed by the hedge-banks that made Devon famous.

I gazed out of the window. Across the valley on my right stood a cluster of farm buildings, the Webster's Brooke Farm.

'I didn't think I'd like the changes at all,' Ruth went on, 'but it's wonderful having central heating, endless hot water and a five-speed power shower.'

I had to envy her on the last point. My landlady's shower was handheld and dribbled at the best of times.

'Do sit down,' she said. 'I'll grab a bottle of Bolly and some nibbly things.'

Bolly! Real champagne! No cheap Asti Spumante for Ruth Reeves.

I took in my surroundings, the custom-made cabinets and granite counters, a luxury Aga (white), an American-style double-fridge and a temperature-gauged wine cooler. There was a lot of Pampas grass stuck into urns and odd bits of kitchenware (all white) that seemed to have been deliberately positioned for decorative, not practical, purposes.

Even the old chipped Brown Betty teapot – a customary sight in all farmhouse kitchens – had been banished from Ruth's new home. So the sight of a particularly ugly red fluted pie dish with a raised chicken's head on the rim looked completely out of place on the countertop.

'Is that one of your savoury tarts?' If I was going to have a glass of Bolly I needed more than the egg sandwich I'd eaten for lunch to line my stomach. My question was rendered inaudible by the sound of a popping cork. Ruth poured the nectar of the gods into a pair of crystal champagne flutes and handed one to me.

'Bottoms up!' she said as we clinked glasses and took a swig.

The bubbles went straight to my head.

'I'm so glad they sent you and not that red-headed girl,' Ruth declared.

'Why?' I asked. 'Don't you like her?' Any negative comments about my nemesis, Annabel Lake, always made my day.

'I thought she did the features,' said Ruth.

'I don't just write the obituary column,' I said, taking another sip of champagne. 'I've been doing the 'Day in the Life' column for months. And besides, Annabel is busy being the new wedding correspondent.'

'*Wedding* correspondent?' Ruth's eyes widened in surprise. 'What an odd choice!'

I knew exactly what she meant. Annabel's reputation as a home-wrecker still struck fear into the hearts of every woman in the area, no matter their age or the physical condition of their husbands.

'Still,' Ruth mused, 'perhaps Annabel will learn a thing or two about what it takes to keep a good marriage going.' She pointed to a side table, where I realized that a large fancy square box was actually a revolving photograph album showing happy scenes from Ruth and John's life together over the years.

'Like *your* marriage,' I said, feeling a sudden rush of affection for Ruth and thinking that there was some advantage to still being pure and unsullied in the romance department. The ladies of Gipping-on-Plym trusted me with their menfolk – not that any of them were attractive enough, or young enough, to lead me astray.

Ruth took another gulp of Bolly, leaned over and patted my arm. 'At least we never feel threatened by you, dear.'

It was a backhanded compliment, but I smiled all the same. 'Thanks.' I pulled out my notebook. 'Let's start with the slashed sunflowers, shall we? According to Eunice Pratt, crime is on the rise in the neighbourhood.'

A shadow passed over Ruth's flushed complexion. 'I don't want to talk about the sunflowers.

I don't want to talk about John's inheritance either,' she said firmly. 'I'll talk about my worm-charming secrets, but that's it.'

This was annoying, especially as I already had a good headline. SUNFLOWER SLASHER SHOCKER! A VICKY HILL EXCLUSIVE!

'But our readers–'

'I don't care about your readers! Really, Vicky, let it go, dear.' Ruth poured herself another glass. 'A quick top-up? More champagne?'

'Eunice mentioned vandalism and–'

'Vicky! You are a naughty, naughty girl,' Ruth scolded. 'I've already said I don't want to talk about it and I mean it.'

I was shocked by Ruth's anger and felt my face grow hot. I hadn't been called a naughty girl since I was ten, when I was caught stealing sweets from the local newsagent in Newcastle.

'I'm just doing my job,' I mumbled.

'I already told your chief reporter that I was *only* answering questions about my worm-charming secrets.'

'I didn't get the message,' I lied. 'Sorry.'

'In fact, I'll go and get it right now.' Ruth jumped somewhat unsteadily to her feet and disappeared through an archway that presumably led to a walk-in-pantry or laundry room or some such area where things like food and vacuum cleaners were kept.

Although I understood why Ruth wouldn't want to talk about her new-found wealth I couldn't understand her reaction to the stupid sunflowers.

There came the sound of a flushing loo and Amelia Webster walked into the kitchen. She was holding a pair of sturdy lace-up shoes in one hand and trying to adjust her clothing in the other. 'Vicky!' she gave a squeak of surprise. 'What are you doing here?'

'Vicky's come to interview me for the newspaper,' Ruth said, following up behind her. 'I told you yesterday. Remember?' Ruth was holding a white hand-sized object shaped like a curve shell and dotted with holes.

'Did you?' Amelia gave a nervous laugh and pointed to her sock-clad feet. 'I took my shoes off.'

'And I do wish you wouldn't just sneak in the back door like that.' Ruth seemed genuinely annoyed, which surprised me given that the two of them were firm friends.

'I came to collect my pie dish,' said Amelia.

'I haven't finished it yet,' said Ruth.

'Oh, *you* made the tart, Mrs Webster?' Stifling a wave of nausea I couldn't help but think what a lucky escape. Whereas Ruth's cooking was good but plain, Amelia's was inedible. I still gagged over the memory of her anchovy and gherkin piccalilli.

Amelia spotted the tart on the counter. 'You've hardly touched it!'

'It's a big tart,' said Ruth. 'But if you really want the pie dish back now, I'll put it into something else.' Ruth stomped over to the counter with a great degree of huffing and puffing.

'No, it's all right,' said Amelia. 'I know you'll return the pie dish.' She turned to me, adding apologetically, 'It belonged to my mother.'

It had to be one of the ugliest pie dishes I'd ever seen. 'It's very distinctive.'

'There was a set of three but Jack ... well, I've

50

only got one left now.' Amelia gave a brave smile.

'At least you've still got one.' Ruth seemed to soften towards her friend. We all knew what Amelia was implying. It was no secret that unlike John and Ruth Reeves, who were regarded as the perfect married couple, Amelia endured a miserable marriage. Jack's drunken rages were legendary, but Amelia continued to defend him, claiming he'd had a difficult childhood. *Haven't we all?* I bet Jack's father hadn't spent years in one of Her Majesty's prisons, but look at me! I turned out all right.

'What are you drinking?' Amelia squinted at the label on the bottle.

'You really should get contact lenses like mine,' said Ruth.

'Is that Asti Spumante?'

Ruth pulled a face. 'Not likely. Horrible muck. This is Bollinger.'

'Not everyone can afford proper champagne,' said Amelia coldly.

And that included her husband, Jack, confirming my suspicion that he'd been up to mischief.

Ruth sat down, clutching the large shell as Amelia hovered over the table. 'Are you going to sit down?' said Ruth.

'No,' said Amelia. 'I just want to know if Vicky's going to write about your poor sunflowers. It was terrible, Vicky! They were scattered all over the back path in pieces.'

'Was it you who told Eunice this morning?' Ruth demanded.

Amelia reddened. 'No. Everyone is talking about it! You must put it in the paper, Vicky. You must!'

'I've told you I don't want to talk about it,' Ruth cried.

'It starts with a few sunflowers and then moves on to something really violent,' said Amelia. 'Did she also tell you that someone stole her bicycle?'

'No,' I said.

'Stop *fussing*, Amelia, for heaven's sakes!'

'And that squashed worm.' Amelia shivered with disgust. 'It was left on the doorstep a week ago.'

'That's terrible!' I gasped. And it was. I jotted down 'bicycle–sunflower–squashed worm' on my notepad. It looked like Eunice Pratt was right about crime being on the rise.

'Was your bicycle stolen from here?' I asked.

'I don't remember,' said Ruth.

'You told me it happened at the pannier market,' Amelia declared.

'I *don't* want to talk about my bicycle and I *don't* want to talk about my sunflowers!' Ruth cried.

'It's a hate crime.' Amelia shot me a knowing look.

My ears pricked up. She could be right – what if the flat tyres on Ruth's car were not the result of a puncture but had been made deliberately!

'No it's not,' Ruth shouted. 'It's because I'm *rich!*' She downed the last of the champagne and slammed the glass on the table crying, 'I'm *rich!* I'm *rich!* And everyone is jealous!'

Amelia shot me a worried look and mouthed the word, 'Drunk!'

I was inclined to agree. 'Well, let's talk about your worm-charming...'

'I bet Dave Randall's got something to do with it,' Amelia broke in. 'The sunflowers! The dead worm! The bicycle!'

'I don't want to talk about my bicycle!' Ruth was practically hysterical. I want to talk about my ocarina!' She brandished the large shell. 'This is my secret weapon! Worms *love* it!'

'Maybe the newspaper could offer a reward?' Amelia suggested, clearly determined not to let it go. 'Get the anonymous caller to step forward?'

'Really Amelia?' said Ruth. 'You think I don't know who slashed my sunflowers?'

A tide of red rushed up Amelia's neck and flooded her face.

There was an awkward silence. 'Shall we all have a nice cup of tea?' I suggested.

'Thank you, but no,' said Amelia briskly. 'I must go and meet Jack. It's our ruby wedding anniversary–'

'But that's not until Saturday,' said Ruth.

'I know but we're starting early,' said Amelia. 'There aren't many of us who have celebrated forty years of marriage.'

'John and I have. Last month. You've obviously forgotten.'

'Congratulations to everyone.' I was getting weary of their bickering. Anyone would think they were teenagers instead of women in their mid-sixties. 'Wait. Does Annabel know about your anniversary, Mrs Webster?' I distinctly remembered looking in the office diary and I didn't recall seeing any upcoming milestone anniversaries.

'Oh, Jack doesn't like fuss,' said Amelia quickly.

'I don't know why you put up with his tantrums,' Ruth said. 'You *both* must be interviewed for the newspaper. Don't you agree, Vicky?'

'Jack doesn't like his photograph being taken,' said Amelia. 'He says he looks fat.'

'He *is* fat,' Ruth said unkindly. 'And you shouldn't let him boss you about. Stop being so pathetic.'

Amelia opened her mouth and promptly shut it again.

I looked at the two friends. There was tension between them and I suspected it had something to do with Ruth's bulging bank account. I'd visited both farms countless times and they had seemed to share the same financial woes that most British farmers suffer in today's modern world of rules, regulations and EU stipulations, but not any more. It wouldn't be the first time that money had destroyed a friendship.

'I've got the perfect solution, Mrs Webster,' I said. 'Why don't you drop into the *Gazette* with a photograph of your wedding day and I'll make sure it gets into the Saturday edition.'

'There,' said Ruth. 'Problem solved.'

'I'd better be going,' Amelia said. 'I'm meeting Jack at This-and-That Emporium this afternoon. We're going to buy presents for each other.'

'Presents for each other?' said Ruth with scorn. 'Since when could Jack afford to buy *you* a present?'

Amelia visibly recoiled. Even I was stung by Ruth's harsh comment and I struggled to fill *another* awkward silence. 'I hear that Elaine Tully is back in Gipping-on-Plym.'

Amelia gave a cry of surprise. 'I thought she married an airline pilot.'

Ruth snapped her fingers, 'I remember her now.

She went off to be an air hostess. She was always one for the high life.'

'Well, apparently she just lost her fifth husband.'

'*Fifth!*' they chorused.

'I never liked her,' said Amelia.

'It was decades ago,' Ruth said. 'Don't worry. I'm sure Jack's not up to his old tricks again. Let's be honest, dear, Jack's no oil painting these days.'

Amelia gave a little gasp of dismay. 'I really must go. You need to put a carpet down in that back corridor, Ruth. That hardwood floor is dangerous.'

Amelia retreated under the archway, gingerly navigating the new floor. There was a faint cry and a thump, but then the back door slammed, so she'd clearly exited in one piece.

'Poor Amelia,' said Ruth. 'Jack is such a brute. Every year she buys him a gift and every year he forgets their wedding anniversary.'

'But not this year.' I pointed to the large shell Ruth still held in her hand. 'Is that your secret worm-charming weapon?'

'It's an ocarina. I got the idea from that film, *The Lord of the Rings.*' Ruth fell silent for a moment. 'I couldn't stand it for Amelia, you see.'

'Sorry?'

'If Jack was ... well... Jack's not like my lovely John,' she said wistfully.

'Let's talk about your ocarina, shall we?'

'What the bloody hell happened?' boomed the deep voice of Ruth's lovely John. 'My God, woman! How stupid can you get?'

John Reeves strode towards us, his walrus moustache fairly bristling with fury. 'Didn't you realize you had a puncture?'

'Take off your shoes!' Ruth shouted gaily. 'Mind the floors.'

'To hell with the floors!' John shouted back.

'Say hello to Vicky, John,' she trilled. 'I'll open another bottle of Bolly.'

'No I don't want any damn champagne, I want to know what the hell happened?'

Ruth turned to me and whispered, 'He's had a hard day.' Then she called out, 'What are you talking about, darling?'

'You've got two flat tyres. Where were you? I thought you went to the hairdressers.'

'I did go to the hairdressers,' Ruth retorted. 'Are you calling me a liar?'

'Yes, I am calling you a liar.'

I looked at Ruth's hair again. It was hard to tell if she had or hadn't.

What had happened to the perfect couple?

I got to my feet. 'Shall I come back later?' But neither of them seemed to hear; they were too busy hurling insults at each other.

As I returned to my car I wondered what was wrong with everyone today. Jack Webster and his Asti Spumante, all apologetic and mild and picking blackberries for Amelia – a sure sign he was having an affair. John and Ruth Reeves, the apparently perfect couple, who 'had it all' but were arguing like the proverbial cat and dog. And then there was my admirer Steve Burrows who could always be counted on to make a girl feel special, but who had decided to give me the cold shoulder. Even Dave Randall's surprise confession of undying love didn't thrill me as much as it should have done.

Perhaps there was something going on with the planets?

Still, at least I had Mr and Mrs Evans to go home to. Living with them was the closest things I'd ever had to a normal life. They may be boring and predictable, but I always knew what to expect.

Chapter Six

'Of course, Ruth won't let me near her fancy new abode,' said Mrs Evans with a sniff. 'Isn't that right, Lenny?'

The three of us were sitting in the kitchen having finished a disgusting meal of liver and onions. Mrs Evans said she'd got the days mixed up – a further sign that perhaps I was right about the planets being misaligned.

Just a few weeks ago, Annabel had made it four at the table, but with the upcoming production of *Les Miserables* by the Gipping Bards, Mrs Evans had wanted her sewing room back and had told Annabel she had to leave.

Naturally. Annabel had suggested that she and I could share a room, but Mrs Evans sprang to my rescue. She'd been getting increasingly fed up with her Lenny and Annabel flirting openly over the kitchen table or spending too long in the garden shed, where Mr Evans kept his prize-winning snails in a terrarium.

With Annabel out of the way Mr Evans had become really friendly and Mrs Evans was treating me like the daughter she did have but couldn't bring home thanks to her Sadie's profession as a pole dancer at the Banana Club in Plymouth Hoe.

To be honest, I quite liked the new arrangement. Sometimes I pretended they were my real mum and dad. They weren't ideal and they bickered a lot, but then, didn't everyone's parents?

Most mornings, Mrs Evans would ask what I'd fancy to eat for dinner, although judging by tonight's menu, she seemed to have forgotten my aversion for liver. She'd even started doing my laundry, and when I offered to give her an extra three pounds a week for the chore, she'd said, 'Don't be silly. You're family.' Not family enough to refuse my weekly rent altogether, but I was working on it.

'Don't be daft, Millie,' said Mr Evans indulgently. 'Ruth will never hire the likes of you. You're too nosey.'

That didn't surprise me. Mrs Evans was my main source of gossip given that her cleaning company, Doing it Daily – a name I later learned was a horrible private joke between the married pair – had at one time or another been privy to every householder's secret in Gipping-on-Plym.

'How did they come into all that money anyway?' Mr Evans said. 'Robbed a bank?'

'Some relative or other.' Mrs Evans paused for a moment. 'I heard that someone slashed the tyres on her brand-new Mercedes.' I'd been thinking about those wheels. Getting a flat tyre was one thing, but two? '*And* her sunflowers were cut down.'

'Someone left a squashed worm on her doorstep, too,' I went on. 'You know everything, Mrs E. Any idea who would have it in for poor Ruth?'

'Could be anyone. We're all fed up with her winning the Trewallyn Chalice year after year, and now she's got all that money, she's gone all la-di-da.'

Noting that Mrs Evans's hair assumed the rigid look of the newly coiffed I said,

'You were at the hairdresser's today, weren't you?'

'I'm glad you noticed.'

Mrs Evans glowered at her husband, who rolled his eyes and muttered, 'It always looks the same.'

'I wondered if you saw Ruth's car parked outside?'

'No.' Mrs Evans shook her head. 'No. I didn't see her, but unlike some people who don't need to work, I have to squeeze it into my lunch hour.'

'Would Amelia Webster know, perhaps?'

Mrs Evans's warning look came too late. *You idiot, Vicky!* I had stupidly forgotten the upset between her husband and Jack Webster over the gypsy situation last summer, but it was too late.

With a look of outrage, Mr Evans drew himself up to his full height and slammed both hands down onto the kitchen table, causing the cutlery to leap and jangle. 'Never use the name Webster in this household!'

'Now, please don't upset yourself, Lenny – not tonight.' Mrs Evans glanced over at the kitchen clock. 'Not tonight of all nights.'

'I *am* upset!' he shouted. 'And don't tell me how I feel.'

'I'm really sorry,' I mumbled.

Mrs Evans reached over to give her husband's hand a comforting squeeze, and the cutlery attached itself to her magnetic bracelet – she suffered horribly with arthritis – with a clatter.

He brushed her away. 'Get off me! Why do you wear that stupid old-woman contraption?'

'Oh!' Mrs Evans tried hard to shake the utensils off. 'Blast!' She stood up and hurried to the kitchen sink, tearing the bracelet off and tossing it into the basin with a crash.

I felt terrible. This was my fault. I wracked my brains for a distraction. Spying last Saturday's edition of the *Gipping Gazette* I snatched it up and said, 'Ah, here's the paper!' and turned to page five. 'You owe me a pound!'

Ever since Barbara had launched her weekly agony-aunt column 'No-Frills Babs' Mrs Evans and I had tried to guess the author of the anonymous letters.

'Listen to this one,' I said. '"Dear Babs, I'm in love with someone else but I have manly needs—"'

Mrs Evans didn't appear to be listening. 'Let's not argue, Lenny,' she said desperately. 'Not tonight.'

'You're right, Millie,' Mr Evans cut in. 'What time's she coming?'

'Ssh!' Mrs Evans hissed.

There was a deadly silence.

I put the newspaper down and regarded my surrogate parents with a growing sense of unease. 'What's going on?'

'You didn't tell her, did you?' Mr Evans declared.

My heart began to thump in the most disconcerting manner. 'What's happening?'

'Sadie's coming home,' blurted out Mrs Evans, 'and she wants her bedroom back.'

There was another deadly silence.

Sadie was coming home. I felt as if the bottom had fallen out of my world. 'But ... I thought she was banned from Factory Terrace,' I stammered. 'And ... and ... Mr Evans doesn't like her.'

'Not like my Sadie!' shouted Mr Evans. 'Where did you get that idea from?' He swung round to face Mrs Evans. 'What's she talking about?'

'Don't upset yourself, Lenny,' said Mrs Evans quickly. 'I have no idea where you got that from, Victoria. Really. What a troublemaker you are!'

I was devastated. Utterly devastated. Hadn't I been the go-between for mother and daughter and kept their communications a secret? Hadn't I been the courier of care parcels to The Banana Club in Plymouth Hoe? Hadn't I comforted Mrs Evans and wiped away her tears on many a winter's evening whilst her Lenny was out cavorting with Annabel Lake?

'Sadie wants to come home and you can't be a stranger to your own kin,' said Mr Evans gruffly.

Blood certainly is thicker than water.

'You're right,' I said miserably. 'I don't know where I got that idea from.'

'There was a raid down at the club,' said Mrs Evans. 'It's been shut down.'

My landlady reached over and squeezed my shoulder. 'You must have known that Sadie would come home one day.'

To my dismay, I felt my eyes watering. Suddenly I felt terribly alone.

'Surely those aren't tears, Victoria?'

'Tears of happiness, Mrs E,' I said, muffling a sob. 'Tears of *absolute* happiness.'

'She's got a job at This-and-That Emporium,' Mrs Evans went on proudly. 'Working in jewellery and accessories.'

'We're going to dig up the vegetable garden,' said Mr Evans.

'The what?' I exclaimed. 'I mean ... did you say ... the vegetable garden? When?'

'This weekend, most likely,' said Mr Evans. 'Sadie and I are going to build a new terrarium for the snails.'

'Wait? You mean, Sadie is moving in this weekend?'

'Sadie is my life.' Mrs Evans's own eyes began to water. 'We're going to be a family again.'

I could hardly take it all in. I'd even grown to love the red walls, the crimson voile curtains and black satin sheets I'd inherited from Sadie Sparkles (to use her stage name). The only thing I'd replaced were Sadie's posters of Lady Gaga with one of my heroine, Christiane Amanpour.

Mr Evans pushed back from the table and stood up. 'I'd best go and smarten myself up.'

'I ironed that nice polo shirt,' said Mrs Evans. 'Sadie likes you in blue.'

The moment Mr Evans left the kitchen I said, 'I'm sure I'll be OK in the sewing room.'

Mrs Evans refused to look me in the eye. 'Maybe just for a day or two.'

'You mean, you're asking me to leave?' I could hardly believe my ears. *'Permanently?'*

'I think Olive Larch – I just can't call her Binns

– might rent you a room for a little while.'

'You're suggesting I stay with Ronnie Binns!' I couldn't think of anything more horrifying.

Mrs Evans's reply – had there been one – was drowned out by the sound of Westminster chimes drifting into the kitchen.

'That's her!' she gasped and jumped to her feet. 'That's my Sadie! Oh! She's here!'

'You said she was coming this weekend!'

'She's just bringing over a few things.' Mrs Evans removed her pink floral housecoat to reveal a smart navy dress and pearls that I'd only seen her wear at funerals.

This may as well as be my own funeral, I thought bitterly.

'Answer the door, Vicky,' said Mrs Evans, retrieving her lipstick and comb from a kitchen drawer. 'Hurry. Don't keep Sadie waiting. Lenny!' she screamed. 'Sadie's here! She's *here!*'

'Be right down!' I heard him shout back, followed by the sound of heavy footsteps overhead.

'Well? What are you waiting for?' Mrs Evans was practically expiring with excitement.

The doorbell rang again. And again. It was as if my feet were made of lead. I couldn't move.

'Vicky?' Mrs Evans shrieked. 'Hurry. Don't keep her waiting!'

I trudged to the front door and tried to arrange my features into a welcoming smile.

But Mrs Evans was wrong. It wasn't Sadie standing on the doorstep. It was Steve! Good old Steve!

Steve would understand, Steve cared about me. No, Steve didn't just care *about* me, he was in love with me. For one wild moment I even considered asking if I could sleep on his sofa in Flat 4, Badger Drive.

'Oh, Steve!' I exclaimed. 'I'm so happy to see you.'

Chapter Seven

'Whoa!' said Steve and jumped back like a scalded cat. 'Steady on!'

He was dressed in neat jeans and a leather jacket with a white T-shirt underneath that said, 'The louder you scream, the faster we drive'.

'I'm sorry we didn't have a chance to talk today,' I enthused. 'You look *great*. Have you lost weight?'

'Ssh!' Steve hissed and stole a look over his shoulder to where his Volkswagen Jetta 2.0 TDA was parked behind Mr Evans's bottle-green Austin Rover Metro. The Jetta's hatchback was open and a familiar-looking woman with blond hair swept into a high ponytail was digging around in the back.

It was Sadie.

'What the hell are you doing, Steve?' Sadie shouted from the car. 'I haven't got all day.'

'Steve will be right there, doll.' He shot me an agonized look, and then it hit me in a blinding flash.

I was shocked.

'You and Sadie are back together again,' I said in a voice I didn't recognize as my own.

Two betrayals in less than an hour! It was more than I could stand.

'Don't do this to me, doll – I mean, Vicky.' Steve ran his fingers through his short-cropped hair before adding hopefully, 'Are you jealous?'

'Why would I be jealous?' I exclaimed and I wasn't. Or was I? It was hard to say. I'd become so used to being the apple of Steve's eye that jealousy had never been an issue.

Steve looked miserable. 'Steve's just a man with manly desires,' he said in that annoying way he has of addressing himself in the third person. 'What am I supposed to do? Do you want me to die alone of a broken heart?'

'Steve!' Sadie yelled. 'Get over here!'

'You're killing me, doll – I mean, Vicky.' He turned away but looked over his shoulder, mouthing the words, 'It could have been you.'

Sadie shoved three black dustbin liners into Steve's arms and sauntered up the garden path. Her flinty eyes were lined with black kohl and she'd slathered on lipstick in pillar-box red. Tonight she was wearing a thin denim jacket, black boob tube and black leggings, while carrying a voluminous tote bag over her shoulder. Steve trotted along obediently behind, narrowly avoiding knocking over Dopey, one of Mrs Evans's garden gnomes.

I took in my landlady's front garden, which I'd always regarded with scorn. There was her beloved woodland collection of gnomes, deer, badgers and hedgehogs – most of which I had bought her over the past year that I'd been living at 21 Factory Terrace.

Suddenly I loved all those little creatures. This had been my home. I would miss it, and them, deeply.

With a heavy heart, I trailed after the lovebirds into the hall.

Despite carrying three plastic dustbin liners Steve still managed to throw one arm possessively around Sadie's shoulders as they ascended the stairs – with extreme difficulty, I was pleased to note.

'Get off me!' I heard Sadie say and then, 'Just dump those bags on my bed.'

'I don't think so!' I shouted. 'I still live here, you know.'

But Sadie ignored me and strolled into my bedroom.

Thankfully, Steve put the bags down on the landing next to Mrs Evans's plastic laundry basket containing newly ironed garments. I saw my jeans lying on top of one of Mrs Evans's floral housecoats and felt another arrow pierce my wounded heart.

In my bedroom, Sadie was inspecting the contents with a proprietary air. Even Steve scanned my bookshelves and drew out a well-thumbed volume of *Undercover Tips: Your Guide to Being Invisible.*

Sadie pointed to my favourite poster of Christiane Amanpour standing outside a mosque in Beirut. 'And I want that rubbish off my walls. Where's Lady Gaga? You better not have tossed her out!'

'I'll replace your posters this weekend,' I said coldly. 'Your mother only told me you were moving back about twenty minutes ago.'

It was hard to believe that twenty minutes ago my life had been almost perfect.

'Yeah well, I only decided this morning,' said Sadie.

'She's given up pole dancing,' Steve chipped in.

'I thought the club was closed because of a drugs raid,' I said.

Sadie looked startled. 'Yeah well. I was framed.'

Framed! A favourite word of the guilty.

'I'm surprised you two aren't moving in together.'

Sadie gave an unattractive snort. 'Not until Steve's proved himself and stopped all his womanizing.'

'It's only ever been you, doll,' Steve said in earnest and blew her a kiss.

I stifled a groan.

'Yeah well, we'll see,' said Sadie. 'A leopard doesn't change his spots.'

And I had to agree with Sadie on that score. I had witnessed those very same spots only moments earlier.

Sadie paused, arms akimbo, before pointing an accusatory finger. 'And I know about *you* and my Steve, Vicky Hill, so don't even try to deny it.'

'I will deny it,' I said. 'Steve and I are just friends.'

'Told you, doll,' said Steve. 'She means nothing to me. *Nothing.* I swear to God.'

'There. You see? I mean absolutely *nothing* to him.' How fickle men could be!

'Maybe you mean nothing to him, but I know he means something to *you*. He's told me about

67

you pestering him all the time.' Sadie opened her handbag and pulled out a framed photograph of her and Steve arm in arm, leaning over the iron railings on Plymouth Hoe, and promptly stuck it on my kidney-shaped dressing table. 'In case you forget.'

I snatched it up and handed it back to her. 'This may well be your room in the future. But for now, I've paid for it and it's still mine.'

Sadie scowled. 'I'll tell my dad.'

'Go ahead,' I said. 'Be my guest.'

'Vicky's right, doll,' said Steve smoothly. 'This bedroom will be yours again soon enough, though hopefully not for long.'

'Yeah well. Believe me, it's not exactly my choice.' Sadie popped a piece of gum. 'I wouldn't be moving into this dump unless I had to.'

'Sadie!' Mrs Evans called out from the top of the stairs. 'Come into the kitchen and have some dandelion wine and Victoria sponge.'

'I don't want to drink that muck,' Sadie shouted back. 'Don't you have any Cinzano?'

Steve shot me another beaten puppy-dog look, took Sadie's arm and steered her out onto the landing. I kicked the door shut behind them.

Much as I hated to admit it, I was really upset. *Get a grip, Vicky.*

I had never really wanted Steve and, frankly, life with the Evans's had become more difficult since Annabel had fled the proverbial nest. Far from being free to come and go as I pleased, Mrs Evans had become very possessive, demanding to know what time I'd be home and insisting I sit with her and watch the telly whenever her

68

'Lenny' was down at Plym Valley Social Club – which was practically every night.

If I was being honest, I envied Annabel's new-found freedom and having a place of her own. Of course, I hadn't seen it yet, but I'd heard enough about her luxury hand-held shower and the joys of cooking on an electric plate.

I would do the same.

There was still the problem of the Spat urns. Counting tonight, I had exactly three days to move them ... *and* find somewhere to live! A wave of panic swept over me.

Stop it, Vicky! This was no time to feel sorry for myself. It was time to take action!

I'd head back up to Ponsford Cross right this minute and get a message to Chuffy McSnatch, and to hell with the rules! Operation George was in danger of being exposed. Literally.

Besides, I didn't think I could stand to listen to the gales of laughter erupting from the happily reunited family downstairs, without a single thought for me – although I took some comfort in the knowledge that Mrs Evans's Victoria sponge had sunk in the middle and that her dandelion wine wasn't her best batch.

As my dad would say, 'When the going gets tough, the tough get going,' and that was exactly what I planned to do.

Chapter Eight

Twenty minutes later I had made my call to Chuffy McSnatch's pager and demanded he ring me back at eight thirty on the dot. This was an emergency.

Then, with an hour to kill, I fell into a pit of despair. What if I couldn't find anywhere to live? How dare Mrs Evans suggest I ask Ronnie and Olive Binns for a room! It was bad enough hearing my landlady and her husband swinging from the chandeliers every Friday and Saturday night – my bedroom was next to theirs – let alone a newly married couple. I'd overheard Barbara tell Phyllis Fairweather that Ronnie and Olive were 'at it like rabbits'!

Annabel had managed to rent her own place and yet we both earned the same salary. She claimed she'd given up finding a sugar daddy until her hair grew back – it had been a casualty of 'Man Stay', the magical hair-loss potion Mrs Evans had slipped into Annabel's fancy shampoo after Lenny returned to her bed – so she had to be managing financially somehow.

My thoughts turned to Ruth and her pink Mercedes. Was it too late to visit Reeves Roost right now? They could always turn me away and I *had* mentioned that I'd be back later. This wasn't America, where later means any time this century. This was England, so why not later today?

I set off, and had only driven five minutes along Honeysuckle Lane when a pair of headlights swept round a hairpin bend and came barrelling towards me. Fortunately, I'd just gone by a passing place, so I reversed deftly into it to allow the oncoming car to go by.

I caught a glimpse of Elaine Tully talking animatedly on her phone as she sailed past in her Audi TT Quattro without so much as a thank you. Since Honeysuckle Lane dead-ended in Reeves Roost and Brooke Farm I could only assume she'd visited the Webster's abode after all.

All was quiet when I drove into the courtyard at Reeves Roost. Not even a dog barked following old Rover's demise three months earlier at the grand old age of twelve.

A half-moon emerged through a cloud-scudded sky, throwing a silvery light over the Reeves's luxury toys. I parked behind Ruth's Mercedes and got out.

Retrieving my Mini-Maglite from my pocket, I switched it on and took a closer look at the tyres on her Mercedes. The front and rear wheels on the passenger side would need to be replaced – hubcaps and all. The aluminum rims were bent and, with very little tyre tread left, it was difficult to tell if there had been a puncture or something more sinister.

Most people would have known they'd had a flat tyre – not just because their smooth ride would have felt lop-sided, but because the noise would have been awful. Yet Ruth had been listening to 'old rubber lips', as my landlady called Mick Jagger, and most likely hadn't heard a thing.

I headed over to the farmhouse and knocked smartly on the front door. After several moments, the porch light flared and the door flew open.

'Back again so soon?' John Reeves's chuckle changed to one of disappointment. 'Vicky? Oh. It's you. What are you doing here?'

Prior to that afternoon, I'd always had a soft spot for John, and in particular his walrus moustache – he reminded me of a jolly Father Christmas – but today I'd seen a side of him, and his wife, that confirmed Mum's constant refrain that nobody knew what went on behind closed doors.

'Hello!' I said cheerfully. Upon noticing a few stray crumbs on his moustache I added, 'I hope I'm not interrupting your supper.'

'You are,' he said, 'And the Ukrainian Sheep-dog trials are about to start in nine minutes. Did you forget something?'

'Is Ruth going to watch the Ukrainian Sheep-dog trials?' I said slyly.

'No, why?'

'Good. Because while you're watching that, Ruth and I can finish up our interview.' I didn't mention that we hadn't actually started it. 'She was telling me about her ocarina.'

'Ruth's not up to it tonight. Sorry. Now, if you don't mind, I want to catch the opening cere-mony.' John went to close the door, but I was too quick and stuck my foot in the doorjamb. After all, nine minutes was nine minutes.

'I'm sure she's still upset about the tyres,' I said sympathetically. 'Do you think they were vandalized? Should we alert Eunice Pratt and her Citizens' Patrol?'

John gave a grim smile. 'I'm thinking about it.'

'I heard about the slashed sunflowers, the squashed worm and the bicycle.' John frowned. 'What bicycle?'

'Ruth told me her bicycle was stolen.'

John's frowned deepened. 'Ruth doesn't have a bicycle.'

'But...' I recalled how angry Ruth had got when both Amelia and I had asked about it. 'Are you positive? I heard it was stolen from the pannier market.'

'I can assure you, Ruth doesn't even know how to ride a bicycle.'

'Amelia said–'

'You don't want to pay too much attention to what Amelia says. I know that sounds unkind but...' John seemed pained. 'The truth is, we're disappointed by people's reactions to our good fortune – even people close to us. People we thought were our friends.'

Like the Websters, I wanted to say, but didn't.

'You wouldn't believe the number of begging letters we've had from neighbours wanting this and that.' John went on. 'That's why I'm taking Ruthie away for a little while.'

'That's sounds like a lovely idea,' I commented. 'When?'

'Sunday. After the worm festival, when Ruth will be announcing her retirement.'

'I'm sure people will be disappointed–'

'Or relieved. Give someone else a chance.' John cracked a smile. 'We're off to Miami – first class – and staying in a suite at the luxury hotel called Eden Roc right on the beach. A limousine is picking us up from here on Sunday evening.'

'Sounds lovely,' I said and felt a pang of jealousy. First-class airline tickets! A five-star luxury hotel! A limousine that I *bet* was one of those long stretch things with a telly inside.

'Now, if you'll excuse me, young Vicky.' John gestured to my foot, which I still had planted firmly in the doorjamb.

'Of course. Please tell Ruth it won't take more than half an hour.'

'As I said, Ruth's not up to it tonight. She's already gone to bed – feeling under the weather. Come back tomorrow afternoon.'

Thanking him, I returned to my Fiat and headed back to Ponsford Cross to wait for Chuffy McSnatch. I was nervous. And nerves made me desperate to go to the loo, but I daren't risk missing his call.

It was just as well I didn't, as at eight twenty-three, the phone rang – seven minutes early. I picked up the receiver, counted to five and said, 'How much did you pay for those shoes because I paid sixty pounds for mine.'

There was a long silence on the other end of the line and then, 'What the hell do you think you're playing at?' Chuffy McSnatch barked. 'Do you think this is some kind of joke? Do you think this is funny?'

'I'm really sorry about earlier,' I said. 'Someone beat me to the phone–'

'Who?'

'Nobody. Just a passer-by,' I said quickly.

'Your dad is angry, Vicky, I'd be lying if I told you otherwise.'

74

'It's an emergency,' I said. 'I've got to move out of Factory Terrace and the urns are buried in the vegetable garden, which they're planning to dig up.'

'Don't try to change the subject,' Chuffy Mc-Snatch said coldly. 'If you're dealing on the black market, you go through me. Do you understand?'

'Black market?' I said. 'Why would I do that? I'm not going to sell the urns on the black market!'

'You can't fool Chuffy.'

'But ... I've been waiting for you to contact me,' I stammered. 'I've been waiting for a whole week!'

'But you *didn't* wait, did you?'

'I don't understand what you mean. The urns are still buried in the garden.' A peculiar sick feeling swept over me. Were they? When had I last checked?

'Not the urns, you stupid girl,' Chuffy Mc-Snatch snarled. 'I'm talking about that nice little sideline you're running.'

'Honestly, Mr McSnatch–' I was practically in tears. 'I swear I don't know what you're talking about.'

There was a snort of disbelief on the other end of the line. 'Yeah, right. You don't know anything about a silver punchbowl, a few pillboxes and a couple of candlesticks?'

'Wait a moment. *Punchbowl?*' I said sharply. 'Was it stolen from Brooke Farm?'

'I never reveal my sources. That's classified information.'

'I swear this has nothing to do with me,' I said.

'Prove it.'

'I will,' I said, and I intended to. 'But what

about the urns? I can't keep them–'

'Bury them somewhere else and–' The rest of Chuffy's reply was drowned out by a wailing siren. An ambulance with its blue and white light flashing flew past and disappeared down Honeysuckle Lane.

By the time the noise had died down the line had gone dead. 'Hello? Chuffy? Mr McSnatch? *Hello?*' Damn and blast it! I rang his pager and tapped in a message to call me back immediately.

Seconds turned to minutes. I waited twenty more, growing even more desperate about wanting to pee. After ten minutes I realized he wasn't going to call me back so I darted into the neighbouring field and went behind a hedge.

Just as I was rearranging my clothing, I heard the ambulance siren again and managed to race to the gate just in time to see Steve speed by. He'd obviously been on call tonight.

I wondered who was in the back. It could only have come from one of the three homes along Honeysuckle Lane: the Websters, the Reeves and, of course, Eunice Pratt and her sister-in-law Mary Berry in Dairy Cottage. The absence of a police car meant this was not a life-or-death moment, despite the use of the siren. Steve put that on all the time, regardless of the condition of the patient on the gurney in the rear.

I hit speed dial.

'Steve?' I said. 'It's Vicky. Hello?' There was an odd crackling noise and then a recorded voice.

'Leave a message and your phone number and it will be Steve's greatest pleasure to call you back.'

'Steve. Vicky here. I've just seen the ambulance

at Ponsford Cross. Call me back and give me the scoop. Thanks!'

But he didn't. I tried once more but got his voicemail again.

As I turned for home, my thoughts turned to Chuffy McSnatch. I was confident that the Spat urns were still safely hidden in the garden. Mr Evans hadn't touched his potato patch all summer. In fact, the last time I'd looked the ground had been choked with weeds. Still, I'd better give it a quick look. It was Chuffy McSnatch's other comment that had seemed weird. Why accuse me of dealing on the black market? If the recent rash of thefts had nothing to do with my dad, then who was the culprit?

Were the Swamp Dogs – Gipping-on-Plym's resident gang of four – up to their old tricks? Perhaps it had something to do with the return of the glamorous Elaine Tully?

Either way, I owed it to Dad's reputation – and mine – to find out.

Chapter Nine

'You've lost your touch,' said Annabel as I strolled into reception on Thursday morning.

'If you mean, have I remembered Barbara's birthday...' I promptly put a sparkly gift bag on the counter that divided her domain from the waiting area. Gesturing to the cluster of hydrogen-inflated balloons bobbing behind the counter and silver bunting festooned around the walls I added, 'How could I forget?'

We both laughed, but Annabel's grin went on far longer than necessary. 'That's not what I'm talking about.'

'Where is the birthday girl?'

'In the loo.' Annabel looked fit to bursting. 'You'll *never* guess what's happened.' I felt the usual sense of panic that gripped me whenever Annabel wore her cat-got-the-canary look. I couldn't stand it.

'Haven't you worn that skirt before?' I'd seen the outfit – a tight candy-striped pencil skirt and frilly V-neck jumper with plunging neckline – at least four times. 'And what happened to your lovely designer Mulberry bag?' I recognized a cheap knock-off when I saw one.

It worked. Annabel scowled. 'I'm surprised you noticed, given your own fashion sense.'

It was true. I dressed for the field and didn't even bother about make-up, but frankly I didn't care. Annabel, however, did. She had always been obsessed with clothes and used to wear a different outfit every day. Not any more, though. I also detected a small smattering of brown creeping along the parting of her Nice 'n Easy natural copper red rinse.

Clearly life without a sugar daddy – though I still couldn't bring myself to put Mr Evans in that category – wasn't as easy as Annabel had made out. Welcome to the real world.

'As I was saying,' said Annabel. 'Oh–'

Barbara entered reception wearing a birthday-girl tiara of fake diamonds. She wore her long hair down and had donned a rather risque mid-calf red dress with trumpet sleeves. Without meaning to sound unkind, it looked very '60s and nothing like Barbara's usual attire of neat Crimplene frock under a hand-knitted cardigan.

'Happy birthday!' I said.

'Vicky didn't know,' Annabel declared.

'Know what?' My stomach gave a lurch. 'Will someone tell me what's going on?'

'Ruth Reeves has been murdered,' said Annabel gleefully.

'What!' I exclaimed. 'When? How?'

'Take no notice of Annabel,' said Barbara quickly. 'I don't know why you keep saying she was murdered. What a wicked thing to say.'

'What happened?'

'Nobody knows,' said Barbara. 'She just died.'

'You weren't there, Barbara,' said Annabel.

'Were *you?*' I was still trying to take in these shocking details. Obviously that was the reason for the ambulance I'd seen whizzing along Honeysuckle Lane late last night. I'd committed another journalistic SNAFU – I'd assumed that with no police presence there was no foul play and besides, Steve would have called me back. Barbara was right. Annabel was just making trouble.

'I got a call at six this morning,' said Annabel.

'What?' I said again. 'You got a call? From whom?'

'Steve, of course.' Annabel smirked. 'He thought I'd like to know.'

I had to grab the back of the leatherette chair to stop myself from falling over. *Steve!* What a traitor!

Annabel gave a nasty laugh. 'Looks like you're

no longer Steve's flavour of the month.'

'I told you that one day he'd tire of pursuing you, Vicky dear.' Barbara made a tut-tutting noise. 'Men won't wait for ever. Especially virile men with lusty appetites like Steve. He's obviously met someone else.'

'Steve and Sadie Evans are back together and I'm happy for them.' I turned to Annabel. 'And why do you think Ruth was murdered? What did Steve say exactly?'

'Seriously? I'm afraid I can't tell you.' Annabel gave a heavy sigh. 'Because I promised Steve. Sorry.' She gave a silly laugh. 'But I'll give you a clue... Steve told me Ruth said something very, very interesting before she died.'

'Steve was actually *with* her when she died?' Damn and blast! Ruth must have been alive when I saw Steve's ambulance sailing by, hence the absence of any police cars.

'Stop all this wicked nonsense!' Barbara scolded. 'Murder? What a notion. Who would want to murder our Ruth?'

'I bet her husband did it for the money,' said Annabel.

'It was John Reeves who inherited the money in the first place,' I pointed out.

'And now he doesn't have to share it, does he?' Annabel shot me another infuriating smile and strolled towards the door that led to the reporter room upstairs. 'Come along. Page-one meeting in ten minutes. You know how Pete hates to be kept waiting.'

'Not today,' Barbara chipped in. 'He called in. He's going to be late.'

Pete was never late for the weekly page-one update. It was always on a Thursday morning at nine sharp.

'That's weird,' Annabel frowned. 'I tried to call his mobile earlier but it said the number was no longer in service.'

'He has a new phone,' said Barbara.

'Is he all right?' Annabel asked.

'Yes, dear, he had an appointment.'

'What kind of appointment?' Annabel demanded.

'Don't repeat this but...' Barbara lowered her voice. 'Marriage counselling.'

Annabel turned red. Everyone knew that she and Pete had an on-again-off-again flirtation. 'Well, I need to get my notes together for this front-page scoop,' she muttered and darted out of reception.

So Pete may not have heard about Ruth's demise – yet. 'I think I'll wait here,' I said to Barbara.

'You let Annabel do that to you every time, dear,' said Barbara. 'She knows exactly how to wind you up.'

'Do *you* think Ruth was murdered?' I asked.

'Of course not.' Barbara picked up the gift bag. 'Is this for me? Shall I open it now or later?'

'Well, whilst you make up your mind, I'm just going to make a quick call.' I moved over to the star-spangled curtains that framed the nook for some privacy. Ducking inside, I pulled out my iPhone and hit speed dial.

'Yo! Wassup?' came Steve's voice on the other end of the line.

'Steve! Thank heavens. Hello?' There was a

click. I was stunned. Steve had actually hung up on me. I immediately redialled and it went straight to voicemail!

'He hung up on you, didn't he?' said Barbara from the other side of the curtain.

'Yes he did,' I exclaimed. 'I just ... I just don't believe it.'

'I know the feeling,' Barbara declared. 'Wilf still won't speak to me either.'

'I'm sorry,' I said, and I was. I knew she was still upset about the end of their engagement following her scandalous – albeit brief – affair with an old flame who unexpectedly turned up out of the blue.

For weeks Barbara had been listless, and she'd lost weight. Even the success of her agony column – 'No-Frills Babs' – had done little to brighten her mood, but she was determined to win Wilf back.

'Did you get anything nice for your birthday?' I said, changing the subject.

'I got something from Olive.'

'Where is Olive today?' I still couldn't get over the fact that heiress and snail-racer Olive Larch had actually married the extremely pungent chief garbologist Ronnie Binns.

'Where do you think? Doing the rounds with her husband.' Barbara handed me a slim book from under the counter. 'It's called *The Rules*. She said she thought it might help.'

'Help with what?'

'Winning back your man,' said Barbara. 'The book says you have to be happy and busy all the time. A man doesn't want to see someone with a long face. I'm going to use some tips for my column. You should try it with Steve. You sound too needy.'

'I'm not interested in Steve romantically.'

'And he knows it,' said Barbara. 'He knows you're just using him.'

'That's not true!' I said hotly, knowing full well it was.

I flipped open the book and laughed. 'Listen to this, "If you have a bad nose, get a nose job. Grow your hair long – men prefer long hair; it's something to play with and caress."'

'I told you!' Barbara declared. 'I told you men love long hair. Look at poor Annabel now that she's lost all her hair. No one wants her any more.'

'I think it's more a case of her reputation going before her.'

I opened the book to the title page. 'Speak of the devil. Look.'

'This book belongs to Annabel Lake' had been written on the inside cover, along with two Hello Kitty stickers.

'Oh!' Barbara scowled. 'How *typical* of Olive! I bet she found it at the tip.' She lifted the book and sniffed. 'It smells of cabbage.'

'Well, it's the thought that counts,' I said. 'I'd best get upstairs.'

'Just help me with one quick thing, dear.' Barbara threw open the wooden shutters of the casement window fronting the High Street. 'Fetch me that role of black crêpe and give me a leg up. With two pairs of hands it will only take me a minute.'

'What are you doing?'

'Out of respect for poor Ruth,' said Barbara. Inside the cramped space I took in a strange set

83

of implements ranging from garden forks to a six-octave xylophone and a double bass. Barbara's standard mannequin from the Gipping Bards storage unit was posed over a mound of earth with some plastic worms on loan from the toy department at This-and-That Emporium. He was dressed in protective clothing and wore a jaunty cap emblazoned with the word 'Charmerer'. In one hand he held a four-tine fork and in the other a hand bell.

A three-panelled board carried photographs of former champions dating back to the beginning of the newspaper, and there was one of Ruth holding the gold rampant worm trophy and her ocarina above a placard that said, 'Overall champion 2006-2014'.

On the wall behind was a large poster explaining the rules.

WORM CHARMING RULES!
TEAMS HAVE 3 MEMBERS –
CHARMERER, PICKERER
AND COUNTERER
APPOINTED GILLIE
(COMPETITOR WHO DOES NOT
WANT TO HANDLE WORMS) – OK
NO DIGGING – GARDEN FORKS MUST
BE MANUALLY TWANGED
MUSICAL INSTRUMENTS –
OK WOOD, SMOOTH OR
NOTCHED TO STRIKE FORK HANDLE
I.E. 'FIDDLE' – OK
NO WATER – THIS IS CONSIDERED
A STIMULANT

TEAMS ALLOWED 5 MINUTES
WORMING UP AND 15 MINUTES
WORM CHARMING
THERE WILL BE A CHARM-OFF
IN THE CASE OF A TIE
CHARMED WORMS TO BE RELEASED
AFTER THE BIRDS HAVE
GONE TO ROOST
THE INTERNATIONAL JUDGE'S
DECISION IS FINAL
CURRENT RECORD: RUTH REEVES 550
WORMS FROM A 3-YARD PLOT

'She won't be defending her title now, will she?'
I said. 'What do you think happened?'

'Natural causes, apparently,' said Barbara firmly.
'Now, take this.' Barbara passed me one end of the
black crêpe. 'I'm going to line the window. Hold
the tape dispenser, dear, won't you?'

'Don't you think the festival should be cancelled?'

'It wasn't cancelled during both world wars so
it won't be cancelled now.'

'I wonder what John Reeves is going to do?' I
said, thinking of their aborted holiday to Miami,
the luxury villa in Majorca and all his fancy toys.

'Men never stay single for long,' said Barbara
darkly. 'And especially not someone like John.'

'What do you mean, *someone* like John?'

'Nothing,' said Barbara quickly. 'Do we *have* to
talk about them on my birthday?'

I regarded Barbara with surprise. It was so
unlike her not to speculate. We finished taping
the black crêpe around the picture window in

85

silence, and Barbara draped the final piece around the mannequin's shoulders.

'Well, I hope you like your present,' I said. 'I can assure you that I didn't find it at the tip. I even kept the receipt from This-and-That Emporium in case you want to change it for something else.'

'I'm going to save it to unwrap tonight.' Barbara brightened. 'Amelia is going to make me a little birthday dinner.'

'A birthday dinner?'

'Life goes on.'

'You should ask Jack Webster if he ever found those blackberries,' I said.

'Blackberries?'

'For Amelia.'

'Oh Jack won't there,' said Barbara airily. 'He's got an important business meeting.'

An important business meeting – or a romantic rendezvous?

'I didn't know you were such good friends with the Websters.'

'Oh yes, Amelia's my best friend.'

'I thought Olive was your best friend?'

'She's annoying,' said Barbara. 'Ever since she married *him*.' Barbara pulled a face. 'All Olive talks about is Ronnie this and Ronnie that. Doesn't she realize my heart is ... broken?'

'Oh Barbara!' I couldn't help myself and gave Barbara a hug. 'It will work out, just you see. Wilf will come to his senses, especially now that you've got a copy of *The Rules*.'

The doorbell jangled and Pete Chambers strolled in wearing his usual attire of jeans, trainers and tattered tweed jacket. My eye was instantly

86

drawn to the heart-shaped badge on his lapel that said, 'I luv my wife'.

'I told Annabel that married men never leave their wives,' Barbara muttered.

'Vicky! Why the hell aren't you upstairs?' Pete pointed to his watch. 'You're late!'

'I was waiting for you.' I scurried after him.

As he took the flight of stairs, I told him what I knew – and what I'd heard from the rumour-mill – about Ruth Reeves's demise.

Pete stopped dead. 'What do you mean she might have been murdered?'

'That's what I'm trying to find out.'

'Was there an autopsy?'

'I'm looking into it.'

'What about your chubby friend? Isn't he your informer?'

'Steve Burrows. Um.' I hesitated. 'I haven't reached him yet.'

'So why does Annabel think Ruth Reeves was murdered?' Pete demanded. 'She must have her reasons?'

'I'm sure she does, but I really think this story should belong to me because...' I pointed to the 'I luv my wife' badge, 'Don't you think it might be easier for you if I handled it?'

Pete turned scarlet. 'Maybe.'

'And ... I'm almost certain that I was one of the last people who saw Ruth alive.'

Chapter Ten

I hated our chief reporter's office. It was cramped, stuffy and cluttered with ancient typewriters and piles of old newspapers. It also stank of stale cigarettes, despite the fact that Pete had given up smoking.

I took my usual spot on the cushion crack of the two-seater tartan sofa, sandwiched between Annabel and our sports reporter. Tony Perkins.

Pete went straight to his desk and flopped down in the wooden swivel chair. 'Where the bloody bollocks is Edward?' he demanded.

'Taking a slash,' said Tony. 'You're late.'

Pete shrugged and reached into his jacket pocket. He pulled out an electronic nicotine inhaler.

With a squeak, Annabel jumped up and darted over to Pete's desk. Seeing my chance, I scooted into her place.

'Naughty boy,' she said, snatching the inhaler from his lips. 'Those fake ciggies are bad for you. They're made in China.'

'Don't do that.' Pete grabbed her wrist and prised the cigarette from her fingers. 'Sit down, Annabel.'

'Who's a grumpy–' Annabel's jaw dropped and her face reddened. I guessed she'd spotted Pete's heart-shaped 'I luv my wife' badge, and for a moment I even felt sorry for her.

'Annabel,' I hissed. 'Come and sit down.'

Annabel slunk back to the sofa, sitting between Tony and me without so much as a grumble at having to straddle the crack in the cushions.

Tony gave her nudge with his elbow and said in a low voice, 'Does this mean you're back on the market?'

'Shut up,' she whispered.

Fortunately Edward Lyle – the *Gazette's* court reporter and a walking encyclopedia – chose that moment to return. Pointing to an identical badge that he was sporting on his yellow polo shirt he said, 'Hey! How did it go, Pete? Cheaper than a divorce, eh?'

'Come on, let's get started,' Pete snarled, neatly avoiding the question. 'We've already wasted half the bloody morning.'

Edward grinned and took his place on the hard wooden chair in front of the filing cabinet. 'What have I missed?'

'Ruth Reeves has been murdered,' Annabel declared.

'You're kidding? I don't believe it!' Edward seemed horrified. 'Nice lady. She showed me how to charm my very first worm.'

'Yeah, well, that's the rumour,' said Pete. 'But unless Annabel has facts, photos and evidence, Vicky's handling it.'

Annabel gasped in dismay. 'But Pete! I'm the one–'

'And Vicky saw her last,' said Pete.

Annabel turned to me, eyes blazing. 'You liar!'

'I didn't actually see–'

'Vicky, tell us what you know,' said Pete.

'Um well ... since the police weren't involved–'

'How do you know they weren't involved?' Annabel demanded. 'Were you at Reeves Roost when the ambulance came?'

'As a matter of fact, yes,' I said – well, I'd been close enough. 'I was there last night and, according to her husband John, she wasn't feeling very well. And then the ambulance came.'

'But did you *see* her?' Annabel persisted.

'No. She was resting, he said.'

'So you *didn't* see her,' Annabel gave Pete a knowing nod. 'She could already have been dead! And you know what they say, suspicion always falls on the spouse.'

'Don't be ridiculous,' I said, trying to squash the remote possibility that Ruth could have been dead – or at the very least close to it – when I was chatting to John Reeves on his doorstep. I thought back to John's anger about Ruth's new Mercedes and, frankly, Annabel had a point. But instead I said, 'They were devoted to each other. Everyone knows that. John seemed perfectly friendly and normal to me. In fact, he was about to watch the Ukrainian sheepdog trials.'

'That doesn't mean anything,' Annabel declared. 'John Reeves had inherited a lot of money, and we all know that money changes people. He might have wanted it all for himself.'

'Why would John get rid of his wife when the money was already his?' Edward pondered.

'Exactly!' I agreed.

Annabel thought for what seemed like for ever, then suddenly screamed with excitement. 'I know! I know! Maybe John was having an affair and he wanted Ruth out of the way, but he didn't want to give her half his fortune!'

'An affair with whom?' I said, thinking instantly of Elaine Tully. In fact, John Reeves had even mistaken me for Elaine when I'd showed up. 'Seems unlikely. Pete? What do you think?'

'Yes, *Pete*. What *do* you think?' said Annabel pointedly. 'Was John Reeves having an affair? I know some men have affairs, and then just discard their mistresses like a pair of old shoes.'

Pete coloured slightly. 'It's not my job to think!' he exclaimed. 'It's my job to present the facts. Do I need to remind you that this is a page-one meeting and so far we don't have a page-one lead this coming Saturday.'

'The murder is page one!' Annabel was practically hyperventilating. 'We can tie it in with the worm festival. Wait! Let me think.' She frowned. 'Got it. How about WORM DAY GOES AHEAD UNDER CLOUD OF FEAR?'

Tony groaned. 'If John did Ruth in, he'd hardly present a threat to the community, Annabel. It would be a domestic dispute. Right, Edward?'

Edward nodded. 'But so far the police haven't been involved, so really this is all circumspection.'

'Exactly,' I said again. 'Thank you, Edward.'

'But what about those death threats you told me about on the stairs, Vicky?' Pete asked.

'They weren't exactly death threats–'

'*Death* threats!' Annabel's eyes bulged.

'Someone stole Ruth's bicycle, slashed her car tyres and battered her prize-winning mush-rooms–'

'They were sunflowers,' I corrected. 'And we're

91

not sure about the tyres.'

Annabel turned on me angrily, 'Why didn't you tell me?'

'I haven't had a chance to get a word in edge-ways,' I said. 'I'll be getting in touch with the police–'

'No need,' said Annabel smoothly. 'I've already put in a phone call to Colin.'

'Colin? Who the hell is Colin?' Pete snapped.

'Detective Inspector Probes,' said Annabel. 'Such a poppet. He's going to call me back.'

I couldn't believe it! Not only did Annabel have Steve in her proverbial pocket, she was now after 'my' Colin.

'Fine,' said Pete. 'Vicky, when you hear from that fat bloke–'

'Steve and I are already in touch,' said Annabel.

'You've already spoken to him?' Pete exclaimed. 'I thought he was Vicky's informer.'

'Not any more,' said Annabel smugly. 'And I'd like to point out that Steve mentioned he'd some more information for me, but on one condition...'

'Go on,' said Pete.

'That it's just *me* who's handling the case.'

'That's not fair!' I exclaimed.

Pete chewed on the end of his electronic cigarette. 'Right. Well. Looks like he's got our balls in a vice.'

Annabel and I exchanged looks of revulsion at Pete's pet phrase, and for a moment we were friends, until Pete said, 'Right. This is what we'll do. You girls are going to work together–'

'Steve doesn't want Vicky on the case,' Annabel whined. 'Why are you being so mean? I'm the one with the contacts. I'm the one talking to the police–'

'Cut it out!' Pete shouted. 'Vicky's the one who interviewed Ruth yesterday for the "Day in the Life" feature. Regardless of whether we're dealing with a murder inquiry, we can use that for Ruth's obituary. Where's the copy, Vicky?'

With a sickening jolt I realized I didn't have any copy to give Pete – nor would I ever have. I'd spent those precious moments with Ruth talking about Amelia, but I hadn't got round to asking Ruth any questions because John Reeves had turned up, furious. When I'd returned later ... well ... it had been too late.

'I left it at home,' I lied. 'I got caught up in the Dave Randall–Jack Webster fight.'

'Not again,' groaned Edward. 'Détente is over.'

'Over where?' Annabel asked.

'Détente? The Cold War?' said Edward. 'You know, throughout the summer months the cutters and jumpers agree not to touch the hedges because of all the nesting birds and wildlife, but come September it's each to his own.'

'Thanks for the history lesson,' Pete grumbled.

'Did you know that worm charming is a real skill?' Edward went on. 'It's all about fooling the worms into believing it's raining. Studies have shown that the vibrations created by the best charmers uncannily replicate those produced by moles. Moles are a worm's worst nightmare as the shovel-footed beasts are able to eat their weight in worms every day.'

'Wow!' gushed Annabel. 'That's so fascinating, Edward.'

'At least Webster will go to gaol this time,' said Tony, changing the subject. 'I couldn't believe he only got community service after that fiasco last summer.'

If you asked me, helping Gipping's chief garbologist, the pungent Ronnie Binns, to do his rounds and sift through tons of recycling rubbish was a sentence worse than prison.

'Actually,' I said. 'Dave Randall hit Jack Webster first and, believe it or not, Jack didn't want to press charges.'

'Speaking of going to gaol,' Annabel said, shooting me a look. 'Pete, as you know, I've been working on a story that's very dear to my heart – in my own time, naturally.'

'Well? What is it?' said Pete.

'One of the ten most wanted criminals in the world.' She gave an expectant pause. 'The Fog.'

'Not him again,' Tony grumbled.

'He's active and he's *here* in Gipping-on-Plym,' said Annabel. 'As you may or may not know, there's been a spate of thefts in Honeysuckle Lane.'

'You're obviously talking about Amelia Webster,' I said. 'I'm sure the stuff she has is hardly up to The Fog's high standards.'

'And you should know,' said Annabel. 'But *au contraire!* A silver punchbowl, some pillboxes and a few candlesticks have been reported missing – that's what a representative from the Citizens' Patrol told me.'

'You mean Eunice Pratt told you,' I said.

'It was verified by Colin – sorry, I mean DI Probes.'

'We'll put that into "Citizens' Patrol Round-Up",' said Pete grudgingly. 'But does this mean there's still no sign of those bloody urns?'

'I'm afraid so,' said Annabel. 'Her ladyship is very upset and is threatening to do something *frightful* – that's the word she used: "frightful". She wants to do a house-to-house search. She's convinced they're in the area.'

'Can we go back to the Jack Webster–Dave Randall scrap please?' Edward flipped to a new page on his notepad. 'What was the name of the arresting officer, Vicky?'

'No arrest was made,' I said. 'In fact, their scrap can't go in the newspaper.' All eyes turned towards me in utter disbelief.

'I promised. Seriously. I'll tell you everything after next Wednesday.'

'*Randall!*' Tony spat. As an active member of Greenpeace, it was no secret that he disliked Dave Randall intensely. 'I heard he's building a secret course somewhere.'

'Eunice Pratt called the cops and the paper.' said Pete. 'That goes on record.'

'I know,' I said, 'but the incident happened on Grange land, so it wasn't in a public place and neither party wants to press charges.'

Edward nodded. 'But Webster was trespassing.'

'Not according to Eunice Pratt,' I said. 'She said her ladyship had invited people to pick black-berries and that Jack was picking them for Amelia.'

'Bloody hell,' said Pete. 'Webster picking black-berries.'

'Yeah. Paige and I are going blackberry picking down by Gipping canal tonight,' said Edward.

'Dr Jenn feels it promotes intimacy.'

'She told me that, too,' said Pete, 'but you won't get me picking bloody blackberries.'

Maybe the Websters were in marriage counselling as well. It seemed like everyone else was.

'Wait, though,' Edward paused. 'Randall and Webster both had restraining orders – neither could trespass on the other's property.'

Annabel tapped her front tooth with a pencil that had a silly pink pompom on the end. 'I'll double check with her ladyship and find out if she gave Webster permission to pick blackberries. She's a personal friend of mine.'

I stifled a groan.

'Good work, Annabel.' Pete touched his 'I luv my wife' badge as if it could ward off temptation.

'So, am I right in assuming that Vicky didn't get anything on the Randall–Webster scrap *or* the Reeves interview?' said Annabel. 'What on earth have you been doing with yourself?'

Pete sniggered. 'Our Vicky's been having a lunchtime rendezvous.'

'What?' Annabel exclaimed. 'You've got a *boyfriend? Who?* Who is it?'

'It's none of your business,' I retorted.

'What car does he drive?' Annabel demanded. 'I *bet* he's married!'

'Leave her alone.' Edward leaned over and whispered, 'Don't tell them anything.'

'Speaking of marriage,' I said. 'I take it you forgot about the Webster's ruby wedding anniversary this coming Saturday, Annabel?'

'Oh *that*,' said Annabel. 'I've been far too busy to bother with "Wedding Anniversary Round-

Up", and anyway, Jack Webster told me he didn't believe in any of that rubbish.'

'Well, he must have changed his mind,' I said. 'Amelia told me they were going shopping for anniversary presents yesterday afternoon.'

'Why don't *you* interview Amelia?' said Annabel. 'I've got too much on my plate.'

For a moment, I was going to protest, but then I realized that talking to Amelia might be a very good idea. If anyone knew the truth behind Ruth's demise it would be her best friend.

'You're right. You *do* have far too much to do,' I said. 'I'm happy to help.'

'Thanks.' Annabel thrust her boobs in Pete's direction. 'Pete, I really need to talk to you in private.'

Out of the corner of my eye I caught Edward shaking his head vehemently and mouthing the words, 'Don't do it!'

Pete was saved a reply when the door flew open and Wilf Veysey, our illustrious editor, strolled in.

We all jumped to our feet.

'Morning, morning,' he said, scanning the room with his one good eye. 'As you were. Sit.'

I narrowly missed landing on Annabel's lap. In the brief moment that Wilf had entered the room, she'd scooted over and taken back her spot on the sofa.

Wilf withdrew his Dunhill pipe from his corduroy jacket. 'What's our lead story?'

'Working on an angle following Ruth Reeves's death, sir,' said Pete.

'She was murdered!' blurted Annabel.

Wilf's good eye bugged out. 'Where did you hear that?'

'We're looking into it,' said Pete, glaring at Annabel. 'We need to be sure of our facts first. Ruth Reeves was very popular, as you know.'

'Motive?' Wilf barked.

'Either her husband did her in to keep all the money he'd inherited, sir,' said Annabel, 'or it could be someone who's fed up with her winning the Trewallyn Chalice nine years running.'

'As I say, sir,' said Pete, giving Annabel another frosty look, 'we're looking into it. For now, we're going to run Vicky's interview with Ruth on page one. It'll make a nice intro into Sunday's worm charming festival at Fairweather Farm.'

'I'm confident I'll have proof that she's been murdered, sir,' said Annabel. 'I'm waiting for calls from the police station, and I have a meeting with my informer.'

Wilf nodded again. 'You seem to be on top of things, Anita.'

'It's Annabel, sir,' she said. 'And yes, I am.'

'On top of who, is the question,' Tony muttered.

'There's something else, sir.' Annabel gave Pete an anguished look and mouthed the words, 'Sorry.'

'Go on, Anita.'

'I'm very close to getting a break on the Spat urns.'

'When you've got one, we'll discuss it,' Pete said coldly. 'Hearsay is the curse of the amateur journalist.'

'Pete's right,' Wilf declared. 'We only deal in cold hard facts at the *Gipping Gazette*. I am surprised you didn't know that, Anita.'

'Yes, sir.' Annabel looked down at her lap. For a

very brief moment I felt sorry for her for a second time that morning.

There was a knock and Barbara loomed in the doorway, still wearing her birthday tiara. We all mumbled happy birthday.

Barbara beamed, 'How nice of you all to remember.' She threw Wilf a dazzling, cartoonish smile that looked as though she'd been practising it in front of the mirror for quite some time.

'I'm sorry to interrupt, but Elaine Tully is downstairs. She insisted I tell you.'

'Ah yes, Elaine.' Wilf nodded. 'Good.'

A faint flush appeared on Barbara's face. 'You mean you remember her, sir?'

'Oh yes,' said Wilf. 'I remember Elaine Tully all right.'

'What does she want, Barbara?' said Pete. 'We're in a meeting.'

'She says she doesn't need a reporter at today's Women's Institute meeting and that she's got it covered but–'

'I'm covering the Women's Institute today, sir,' I said.

'Yes. That's what I told her.' Barbara hesitated, miraculously maintaining her smile. 'I thought it highly irregular and ... well ... I wanted to check with you first, sir. I wouldn't have interrupted such an important meeting, otherwise.'

'You could have rung from downstairs,' Wilf snapped.

'Oh!' said Barbara. 'But I could hardly tell you this in front of her, sir, and besides, the exercise does me good.'

'Who's manning reception?'

99

'I ... I ... me, sir.'

'But you're up here,' he said. 'Just tell Elaine I'll be down in a bit. Make her a cuppa.'

Barbara's jaw dropped. 'Make her a ... *cuppa?*'

Barbara's unnatural smile faltered for a moment, but she rallied with another one and, after giving us all a gay wave, withdrew from sight.

Wilf left the office shortly afterwards and we all heaved a sigh of relief.

'Old Wilf's still got it in for Barbara,' said Tony with a chuckle.

'She's making such a fool of herself,' Annabel declared. 'Throwing herself at him like that. Who is Elaine Tully anyway?'

'Apparently she used to live around here about forty years ago,' I said.

'Before my time,' said Pete.

'And mine,' chorused Tony and Edward.

Pete's phone rang. Annabel darted over and snatched up the receiver. 'Chief reporter's office,' she said in a breathy voice, then turned pale. 'Um. No, Mrs Chambers, this is... Vicky speaking.' Thrusting the phone at Pete, Annabel mumbled, 'It's for you.'

'Hello Ems, my luv,' said Pete softly and turned away to take the call out of earshot.

Tony gave me a nudge and a knowing wink. Not only did Pete rarely mention his wife at work, the shortened term of endearment from Emily to Ems made it clear that – in their case – marriage counselling was working.

'Excuse me. Must go. Busy.' Annabel dashed out of the room.

I found her in the ladies loo, staring in the

100

mirror over the washbasin. 'Are you OK?'

'No,' she whispered. 'She never calls him at work.'

'I thought you and Pete were history.'

Tears welled up in Annabel's eyes but she tried to blink them back. 'He said he couldn't afford to divorce her so they were trying again for the sake of the children.'

How original.

'Maybe you should write to "No-Frills Babs" for advice?' I suggested.

'I hardly think Barbara is an expert. Look at her sad life,' said Annabel. 'Do you think he got a new mobile number because of me?'

'Don't be silly.' But I suspected she was right. 'Never mind. Wilf thinks you're a good reporter. Even though he keeps calling you Anita.' I gave her, a playful punch on the arm. 'Come on. What are you doing with all these old farts anyway?'

Annabel nodded. 'Yes, yes, they're all so old!'

'I mean seriously? Mayor Rawlings? Dr Frost? Lenny Evans–'

'He dumped me when my hair fell out,' she said sadly.

'But look at you now! You're still gorgeous.'

'Yes! Look at me now! I'm gorgeous!' Annabel smiled at herself in the mirror. 'I'm young, I have my own place – and you don't.'

'There you are then,' I said. 'And speaking of having your own place, don't you have the plumber coming?'

Annabel checked her watch and gasped. 'Oh yes!' She gave me a quick hug. 'Thank you, Vicky. You're such a good friend. You really are.'

'We're a great *team*,' I said firmly. 'So why don't you tell me what Steve said to you about Ruth Reeves?'

'Oh Vicky,' she said with mock dismay. 'I'm so sorry but I just can't. And to be honest, I'm sick of you getting all the front-page scoops when I do all the work.'

'You're kidding, right?'

'No I'm not,' said Annabel coldly. 'And what's more, you think I don't know who you really are. Do you think I'm stupid?' She gave a nasty laugh. 'You're not an orphan, and nor were your parents eaten by lions on safari – I checked!'

'Then your sources are wrong,' I cried. 'Why would I make up such a horrible story?'

'Because you're *weird*,' said Annabel.

'Prove it!'

'Oh, I intend to. You see, I'm on to you, Victoria *Ada* Hill.' Annabel tossed her head. 'I can't wait to be famous and get out of this dump.'

'You're making a mistake,' I said, though truthfully I was scared.

'I'm *going* to be famous!'

Annabel swept out of the bathroom, leaving me shaken to the core, but I knew she was bluffing. I *always* covered my tracks and I *only* dealt in cash. It was only the Spat urns – were they to be discovered – that might link me with Dad.

I had never allowed Annabel to get the better of me, and I wasn't about to start now. I'd have to act fast.

Chapter Eleven

I hurried downstairs and strode into reception, where I found Barbara, Annabel – who had clearly let the plumber wait – and Elaine Tully embroiled in an intense debate about hair.

'So I thought, why not cut it off,' I heard Annabel say. 'So that's what I did.'

'I'm telling you,' said Barbara firmly. 'Men love long hair. If you don't believe me–' She withdrew her copy of *The Rules* and opened it up to a dog-eared page. 'See? It says so right *there*.'

'Oh heavens, Barbara,' scoffed Annabel. 'Where on earth did you get that? It's a load of rubbish. I threw my copy out. Men want you to be available twenty-four seven. They want to hear how much you love them, don't you agree, Elaine?'

'You remind me so much of myself in my younger days,' said Elaine wistfully.

'And that's no compliment,' Barbara declared. 'You were a *trollop*, Elaine!'

Elaine laughed. 'Talk about the pot calling the kettle black.'

Barbara dismissed that comment with a wave of her hand. 'I'm just saying that short hair can be so *manly*.'

'You have to have the right cheekbones to get away with short hair,' said Elaine.

'Have I got high cheekbones?' Annabel said desperately.

Elaine stepped back and gave Annabel the once over. 'Very high.'

Annabel shot Barbara a triumphant look.

'Vicky!' Barbara saw me at last. 'What do you think?'

'I'm not sure what you're all talking about,' I lied.

'Allow me to introduce you to our junior reporter, Elaine,' said Annabel. 'Elaine Tully, this is Vicky Hill.'

'We've already met,' I said.

'Oh!' Annabel seemed taken aback.

'Vicky and I bumped into each other yesterday afternoon while she was waiting for a call at Ponsford Cross.' Elaine gave me a wink.

Barbara's eyes widened. 'You mean ... the *old* telephone box?'

'That's right,' said Elaine. 'Those were the days, weren't they, Babs? No caller ID, untraceable calls...'

Annabel narrowed her eyes with suspicion. 'Why can't you use your iPhone?'

'Oh dear, I am sorry,' said Elaine. 'Did I put my foot in it?'

Annabel's jaw dropped. 'Was it about your ... your ... *boyfriend?*'

I was about to deny anything and everything but thought again. 'It's complicated.'

'It always is, isn't that right, Babs?' said Elaine.

'You're the expert.' Barbara cocked her head. 'So, what were *you* doing up at Ponsford Cross, Elaine?'

'If you must know, I was talking to John Reeves about this Saturday's service for Ruth.'

'*This* Saturday?' Annabel and I chorused.

'She's being buried *already?*' said Annabel.

I was equally shocked.

'Yes,' said Elaine. 'I'm helping John organize a celebration of life service – so much nicer than a dreary funeral.'

'But you can't,' Annabel cried. 'There has to be an autopsy. She was murdered!'

Elaine looked startled. 'That's the first I've heard of it.'

'I told you she wasn't murdered,' Barbara chipped in. 'I *told* you it was all stuff and nonsense.'

Annabel bit her lip. 'But Steve told me–'

'Steve must have given you the wrong information,' I said, and felt glad, although it did seem strange.

'Yes but … no.' Annabel frowned. 'He was very clear about her last words as she lay gasping for breath.'

'It was heart failure, apparently,' said Elaine. 'I heard Herman–'

'Herman?' Barbara chipped in. 'Who is Herman?'

'Sorry. I meant the Reverend Whittler.' Elaine smiled. 'I met him on a trip for <u>solitary singles</u> in Florida and had no idea he was a man of the cloth until he told me at the top of Splash Mountain in Disney World.' She gave a low chuckle at the memory. 'I was screaming, "God help me!" and he said, 'Look no further, child.' After that, we became firm friends. *Platonic*, friends, I might add. Paul, my fourth husband, was a vicar – I met him on a flight to Rome – and I'd never marry one again. You can never take a Sunday off, you know.'

'But doesn't there have to be an inquest?' Annabel persisted.

'Herman talked to Coroner Cripps and apparently hubby John wanted to rush it along because he's going on holiday and, of course, the coroner left for his annual boys-only fishing trip to Canada this morning.'

'Something isn't right,' said Annabel and I had to agree with her. 'Steve knows what he's talking about. He used to be Vicky's informer and now he's mine, and I trust him.'

Say what you like about Steve, but if he thought Ruth's death was suspicious, then suspicious it was.

'I'm going to talk to Steve again,' Annabel went on. 'In fact, I'm going over to Gipping Hospital right now!'

'What about the plumber?' I said.

'Damn! I nearly forgot.' Annabel gave a heavy sigh. 'That's the problem when you have your own place. Maintenance! Repairs!'

'Here, take this.' Elaine withdrew a business card and handed it to Annabel. 'Call me tonight. We should talk.'

I saw Annabel's eyes widen, and the surprised expression on her face filled me with dismay.

Annabel grinned broadly. 'Thank you,' she gushed. 'I will,' and scurried out of reception.

Did Elaine know something about Ruth Reeves's demise that she would only share with Annabel? And what about Elaine? I'd seen her lurking around the neighbourhood not once, but twice. And I knew for a fact that she'd visited John Reeves on the night that Ruth died. Maybe she was earmarking John as husband number six?

'Which brings me to why I'm here,' said Elaine, breaking into my thoughts. 'I'll be doing a presentation at Gipping's Women's Institute later this afternoon, so I thought I'd save you a trip, Vicky.'

'I usually cover the WI,' I said.

'No need, dear. Can we...?' Elaine gestured discreetly at Barbara, who was regarding her with obvious disdain.

'We could go into the nook,' I suggested.

'The nook is full of worm-charming paraphernalia,' Barbara declared.

Elaine clapped her hands with delight. 'Worm charming! I loved worm charming in my teens,' she said. 'I thought your window display looked a little wormy. Am I too late to register?'

'Talk to Phyllis Fairweather,' said Barbara.

'She's still married to Errol?' Elaine said. 'I am surprised.'

I pointed to the brown leatherette chairs. 'Take a seat.'

We both sat down and Elaine leaned over and whispered, 'Babs has never liked me.'

'Let's talk about the meeting this afternoon at the Women's Institute.' I said. 'I don't recall there being a presentation this month. Everyone was told to bring a childhood memento to share.'

'Oh no, that's a dreadful idea,' said Elaine. 'I spoke to Herman and he talked to – who is the secretary?'

'Olive Larch,' said Barbara, who had crept up behind us.

'God! Not Olive.' Elaine swivelled round. 'Seriously? We really need someone dynamic to be the secretary. I'm willing to step in. I ran the Women's Institute on the Isle of Man and I know what I'm doing.'

'Don't you have enough to do, what with meddling in everyone's business?' said Barbara.

'What's the presentation about?' I said quickly.

'Green burials,' Elaine declared.

'Green what?' Barbara said.

'Green burials. Eco-friendly coffins,' said Elaine. 'You know, co-existing with nature.'

Barbara laughed. 'You've been away too long, dear. That will never happen here.'

'I'll tell you what I told Herman, you're running out of space.'

'Space for what,' said Barbara.

'Bodies, Babs,' said Elaine. 'The cemetery at St Peter's the Martyr is absolutely jam-packed. We need alternatives.' Elaine produced a transparent plastic folder from her tote bag and put it on the small table between us. I glanced down at the package. The information was neatly typed out in double spacing and featured scenic vistas of woodland and green meadows covered with wild flowers and bubbling brooks, while the letterhead was bordered with fluffy white clouds intertwined with cherubs playing miniature harps.

'What about Ripley and Ravish?' said Barbara.

It was a good question. Dust to Dust With Dignity had had the funeral market cornered since time began.

'Oh, we're not in competition at all, Babs,' said Elaine smoothly. 'Our services are highly specialized.'

'A lot of people prefer to be cremated these days

108

anyway,' Barbara said doggedly. 'So there won't be any need to make space in the churchyard at St Peter's.'

'Ah, but that's where you're wrong, Babs,' said Elaine. 'We like to suggest an ash scattering ceremony across the meadows at sunset. People often bring champagne and a picnic, rather like they do for the opera season at Glyndebourne. We have access to musicians – a string quartet is always a favourite. And then we have a simply *gorgeous* sideline.' She touched one of her long, dangly earrings. 'Can you guess what it is?'

'No,' said Barbara. 'And I don't want to.'

'Cremation jewellery,' Elaine said. 'We have quite a lot of styles to choose from. In fact, we're looking for a sales representative, so if you know of someone who would like to earn a bit of money on the side, send them our way. Perhaps you'd be interested?'

'Me?' Barbara pulled a face. 'Why would you think I'd... Oh, good morning again, sir.'

The inner hall door opened and Wilf strolled in, smoking his pipe.

'Hmm. What's that divine smell?' said Elaine. 'I know! It's Sir Walter Raleigh, isn't it? It smokes as good as it smells.'

Wilf's ears turned pink. 'You are correct.'

'Professor Calloway – he was my third husband – he used to smoke a pipe,' said Elaine. 'He was a botanist and I met him on a flight to Zurich.'

Barbara stalked back to the counter and opened the flap, dropping it with an earsplitting crash.

Wilf jumped. 'I hope our receptionist made you a cuppa.'

Receptionist? Not even, Barbara?

'Not yet,' said Elaine.

'We've run out of teabags,' Barbara lied, making a monumental effort to smile with her lips turned up, which gave her the unfortunate look of a rabid dog about to attack.

'Then allow me to invite you to my office,' said Wilf. 'I've a small private stash of Yorkshire Gold.'

'Very tempting – but I'm rather busy today,' Elaine said coyly. 'Perhaps we could continue our conversation this weekend. I'm told I'm an excellent cook. You could come over after Ruth Reeves's celebration of life on Saturday evening.'

'Ruth's *what?*' Wilf seemed horrified. 'What are you talking about?'

'The coroner released the body, sir,' I said.

'But ... that's highly irregular,' said Wilf. 'Why weren't we informed?'

'John called me an hour ago,' said Elaine.

'So what was all this foul-play nonsense Anita was talking about?' Wilf sounded annoyed.

'I told everyone it was just malicious gossip, sir,' Barbara shouted from the sidelines.

Wilf turned to Elaine. 'So what can I do for you?'

Elaine thrust her folder into Wilf's hands. 'This is what I'll be presenting this afternoon at the Women's Institute meeting. I think you'll find it won't need any editing.'

'What's all this about?' he said.

'Green burials,' said Elaine. 'Carlos DiCaprio – my fifth husband–'

'Which plane did you meet him on?' Barbara called out, but Elaine pretended not to hear.

'As I was saying,' she went on. 'Carlos and I

110

started this business together.'

Wilf, puffing furiously on his pipe, flipped through the pages. 'Interesting.'

'If you know of any farmers anxious to come in at the ground level, so to speak, we're looking to buy plots. I offer a very competitive price and, naturally, there's a hefty discount should the investor wish to purchase a plot for their personal use. Let's face it the grim – or in our case, *green* – reaper comes for us all.'

Wilf nodded. 'I'll take a look.' He offered Elaine his arm. 'Can I escort you to your car?'

'No need.' Elaine pointed to the Audi TT Quattro visible through the glass front door, parked illegally on the double-yellow lines outside. 'That's me.' She gave him a bright smile. 'And do let me know about Saturday night. I cook a mean curry.'

Wilf gave a chivalrous bow and, without giving either Barbara or me a second glance, exited reception.

'You were lucky your car wasn't towed,' said Barbara.

'I kept Paul's placard, "Vicar on Call",' Elaine said, suddenly adding, 'Is Wilf married?'

'Our editor is spoken for,' I said hastily. Judging by the way Barbara was holding the office stapler I sensed she was ready to attack.

Elaine shrugged. 'I'd best be off. See you later, Vicky.'

The moment Elaine left, Barbara slumped over the counter. Her face was etched in misery. 'Why was Wilf so unkind? Did you hear him call me 'the receptionist"?'

'He's probably still finding it hard to accept that

you loved someone else before he came along.'

'It didn't seem to bother him that Elaine's been married five times.'

Here we go again.

'He's not in love with her. He's in love with you.'

'And he's never once offered to escort me to my car.'

'Barbara, you don't have a car,' I said wearily. 'You have a bicycle, which reminds me, did you know that Ruth's bicycle was stolen?'

'Her Raleigh was *stolen?*' Barbara cried. 'I warned her! I told her to be careful.'

'So she definitely, *definitely* had her own bicycle?' I said.

'What?'

'Bicycle?'

'Yes, yes she did. She asked my advice on what model to buy – you can't get bicycles like mine any more. I've had it since nineteen forty–'

'One,' I said. 'I know.'

'Ruth wanted a wicker basket.' Barbara frowned. 'And there's something else...'

'You know who stole it?'

'Wilf didn't even wish me a happy birthday.'

Clearly I was wasting my time trying to get anything out of Barbara, who was acting like a lovesick teenager. 'Well, at least you have something to look forward to this evening,' I said briskly. 'A birthday dinner.'

'Amelia's a terrible cook.'

'And speaking of Amelia,' I said. 'I've been assigned the ruby anniversary story. I think I'll head over to Brooke Farm now. I've got bags of time before the WI meeting.'

And with that I bid Barbara adieu and left the office, feeling very uneasy – and hungry.

My tummy grumbled – a stark reminder that today Mrs Evans hadn't made me a packed lunch. I suppose I was as good as gone from her life now that her precious Sadie was moving back home. I couldn't even pick up a sandwich from the Copper Kettle café across the street as it had been months since Topaz Potter had opened her doors for business. I suspected they'd never open again, seeing as Topaz had wholeheartedly embraced her birthright as Lady Ethel Turberville-Spat of The Grange. I felt a pang of nostalgia for the good old days.

I couldn't shake off the sense that, regardless of the claim that Ruth's death was through natural causes, something didn't feel right. It wasn't just about the lack of an autopsy or inquest; seeing Jack Webster picking blackberries for his wife or the return of Elaine Tully after forty years in the cold – no, I was convinced that something else was going on. I just had to find a way to get back into Steve's good books.

The Warming Pan was at the wrong end of the High Street so that only left This-and-That Emporium's Grab-and-Go. Since they just had a limited selection, I was anxious to miss the lunchtime rush and set off at a trot.

Chapter Twelve

Established in 1865 by the Triggs dynasty, This-and-That Emporium sold everything you could think of, from Christmas tree lights to haemorrhoid cream. The superstore was a row of three-storey Edwardian houses, which had been converted into a higgledy-piggledy rabbit warren of narrow corridors and crooked staircases. It was always a challenge to find the exit, which made it something of a fire hazard, but no one ever seemed to do anything about it.

Fortunately, the Grab-and-Go sandwich stand was close to one of the three entrances and there – to my delight – was Steve! Not only that, he was alone!

Dressed in his white medical coat, he was holding a wire basket filled with sandwiches and crisps, staring at a variety of bottled fizzy drinks that were on special offer – two for the price of one.

I tapped Steve gently on the shoulder, but when he spun round, his ready smile collapsed and, far from being pleased to see me, he looked terrified.

'Not here, doll – I mean, Vicky,' he hissed and steered me behind a plastic palm tree – Grab-and-Go bordered the beachwear and bucket-and-spade department.

'Why aren't you returning my calls?' I whispered.

'You've got to stop this,' he whispered back, eyes

scanning the area. 'You've *got* to stop following me.'

'I'm not following you,' I said. 'I have to ask you something.'

'Yeah, sure you do.' He groaned. 'Oh why, *why* do you do this to me?'

'It's work-related, Steve, and it's vitally important,' I said. 'Tell me about Ruth Reeves.'

Steve clapped his hand over his mouth and mumbled, 'Don't tell her Steve. Be strong.'

'Did *you* know her body has been released for burial?'

Steve dropped his hand and gawked.

'I thought so! Steve,' I continued urgently. 'You have an instinct, a *brilliant* instinct for knowing when there's something fishy going on. Just tell me exactly what Ruth said to you before she died.'

'I can't.'

'Is this about the promise you made to Annabel, because if it is, she's already been dropped from the story.' This was a blatant lie. 'We've always been a team, haven't we? Come on, Steve. Doesn't Ruth deserve justice?'

'Yes, but ... Sadie...'

'If you don't tell me what happened last night, I will tell Sadie about...' I wracked my brains. 'About the time I came over to your flat and we practically slept together.'

'You wouldn't!' Steve was aghast. 'And we didn't.'

'Ah-ha,' I said. 'But who would Sadie believe? You? Or me?'

'Jesus, Vicky. You're killing me.' Steve looked distraught, and for a moment I suffered a pang of guilt. Fortunately it didn't last long.

'I know you're only using me,' he said quietly.

'Oh. Steve, I've never used you,' I lied again. 'We had something special – you and I both know that – but it's all about timing. That's all.'

He studied my face with such devotion in his puppy-dog eyes that I had to look away. 'And it's obvious you love Sadie, anyway.'

'Yeah but, she's not you, is she?' He reached out as if to touch me, but then slapped his hand away. 'Sorry. You're just too tempting but...' He gave a heavy sigh. 'Ruth was a nice lady and, well ... it was horrible, doll. Really horrible.'

'Go on.' I could hardly keep the excitement out of my voice. 'What did she say? *Quickly!*'

'And it wasn't just what she said,' Steve said. 'Her face went such a funny colour.'

'Right. Yep. But what did she *say*,' I repeated. *'Hurry!'*

'Let me get this right.' He closed his eyes for a moment. 'She said "Tell John it's–"'

'What the hell is going on?' Sadie thrust her head through the plastic palm fronds. Dressed in a green-and-white striped nylon tunic with matching ballet slippers, she wore a name badge, saying, 'Just ask Sadie' above the word 'Jewellery'.

'Nothing!' Steve and I chorused.

'We were just talking, doll,' said Steve. 'Honest to God.'

'Get out.' Sadie shoved me roughly aside. I fell against the plastic palm tree, which toppled over backwards, sending a pyramid of upturned plastic buckets flying, and ended up in the kiddy sandbox.

I was furious! I'd been so close to getting Steve to talk and Sadie had ruined it all.

Dad always said that attack is the best form of defence, so I yelled, 'What is *wrong* with you?'

'What's wrong with *me?*' Sadie poked her finger into my shoulder. 'Do you think I was born yesterday?'

'It's not what you think, doll. It's not. I swear,' Steve cried.

'I warned you, Steve–'

'You know Steve loves you, doll!' said Steve.

'And don't talk to me as if you're not Steve!' Sadie shouted.

'But I am Steve!'

'I think Sadie means she doesn't like you talking in the third person,' I pointed out. 'Look, let's all calm down and move away from the beach.'

Steve tried to put his arm around Sadie, but she shrugged him off. I herded them into a corridor that opened into Kitchenware, making sure Sadie was nowhere near the knives.

'This is my fault,' I said. 'I wanted to talk to Steve about Ruth Reeves.'

'Why? What's *she* got to do with Steve?'

'She died,' I said quickly, 'and there's going to be a celebration of her life on Saturday at St Peter's the Martyr. You should both come.'

'I thought we should go,' said Steve desperately. 'You know, make a day out.'

'To a funeral?'

'It's a celebration of life,' I said. 'Quite different.'

'And I suppose if I don't go, you'll be going anyway, Steve, and she–' Sadie poked her finger into my shoulder again – 'will be there.'

'I really want you to come, doll,' said Steve.

'I'm not going if *she's* going.'

'Oh for heavens sakes!' I exclaimed. 'I have no interest in coming between you and Steve. I give you my word, cross my heart and hope to die, that I have absolutely no designs or intentions on breaking up your relationship.'

Steve grabbed Sadie's hand and they stared at me open-mouthed.

It was rare for me to lose my temper, but this was getting silly. 'In fact,' I went on. 'I hope you'll get married and have a hundred children. Nothing would make my life more complete than to have to write about your fortieth wedding anniversary in the *Gipping Gazette*.' What a terrible thought! Would I really still be living in Gipping-on-Plym in forty years' time?

'You really mean that?' said Sadie.

'Yes, I do.'

'What kind of jewellery do you get when you've been married forty years, then?' asked Sadie.

'Ruby, doll.' Steve beamed. 'And do you know what the ruby symbolizes?'

'Tell me, my luvver.' Sadie gazed into Steve's eyes.

'It symbolizes an eternal inner flame that's said to mark lasting passion in a marriage.'

I caught a glimpse of unbridled lust pass between them and wanted to gag. Steve blew Sadie a kiss.

'All right,' said Sadie. 'Have it your way. I'll come to this funeral, then.' She frowned. 'Funny how one moment you're alive and the next you're not.'

Hilarious, I thought.

'I only saw Ruth Reeves yesterday,' Sadie went on.

'You did?' I said sharply. 'Where?'

'On the train. She's got a fancy car but she takes the train.'

'On the *train?*' I said. 'Which train?'

'Plymouth to Gipping-on-Plym,' said Sadie. 'Remember, Steve?'

'Yeah. She got off Sadie's train at Gipping station,' said Steve. 'Her Mercedes was parked in the station car park.'

'What time was this?' I asked, pulling out my notebook.

'About two-ish.'

Ruth had claimed she'd had a hair appointment. Perhaps her new stylist was in Plymouth? Plymouth was an hour away, but even so, wouldn't it have been more convenient to drive?

'Did you notice anything odd about her Mercedes?' I said. 'A flat tyre or two, perhaps?'

They looked at each other and shook their heads. 'Only that it was parked by the dumpsters,' said Sadie. 'I thought it was a funny place to leave such an expensive car.'

It would seem that my enthusiasm for their relationship to last forty years had changed Sadie's opinion of me and she was being quite civil.

'I thought to myself,' Sadie paused, 'I'd be pissed off if Ronnie Binns and his dustcart came by and hit it.'

'Thanks,' I said. 'This is really helpful.'

'So you really think we'll make it to ruby, Vicky?' Sadie said suddenly. 'Don't suppose there are many couples in this town that make it to their ruby wedding anniversary.'

'John and Ruth Reeves did,' I said. 'And Jack and Amelia Webster are about to. As a matter of fact, I'm just off to interview Amelia for this week's "Wedding Anniversary Round-Up"!'

'You're kidding? That old fart,' said Sadie. 'I can't imagine being married to him for more than a day, let alone forty years. Wait a minute,' Sadie brightened. 'You mean, you're going to Brooke Farm?'

'Yes.'

'Good. Then you can do me a favour,' said Sadie.

'It depends on what it is,' I said cautiously.

'Personally I can't stand Jack, though who'd have thought he'd be such a softie,' she went on. 'He's had a ring custom-made for Amelia. It's ready for collection, though he needs to pay for it. I'd call him myself but their phone's out of order.'

'A custom-made ring?' First the blackberry picking and now a custom-made ring for Amelia.

'There's no way I'm asking him for money,' I said.

'My boss will handle that. Says he's going to send over his heavies and 'persuade' him. But, well, forty years is a long time and I've got nothing against Amelia. She's always been nice to me.'

'All right,' I said, thinking that Sadie wasn't so bad, after all.

'Come with me, then,' said Sadie, adding, 'I'm not leaving you two alone. You're not out of the woods yet, Steve.'

Sadie grabbed Steve's hand and dragged him behind her through the claustrophobic maze of the emporium. I wished I'd brought a loaf of bread so I could leave a trail of crumbs. Every so often Steve flung a look over his shoulders and mouthed the word, 'Sorry!'

We broke into the jewellery area, where I was astonished to find glass showcases filled with a variety of jewellery from costume to real gems.

'Thought you'd gone to lunch!' called out a stout woman with bad teeth who I recognized as Lily Kirby. She raced snails and charmed worms with her husband Bernard.

'Trying to,' said Sadie.

'That's not...' Lily gave Sadie a look that I recognized as one exchanged by the duped wives of Annabel's conquests.

'Hi Lily,' I said. 'You'll be in with a chance now that Ruth's out of the championship this week-end.'

'Yeah, finally,' said Lily, but she wasn't really paying attention and whispered something to Sadie that sounded very much like, 'Let me scratch her eyes out.'

The mark of a true friend, I thought. Would any-one ever scratch someone's eyes out on my behalf?

Sadie retrieved a small gift-wrapped package adorned with ribbons from a locked drawer.

'Thanks,' she said and, almost as an after-thought, added, 'Oh, and look, I'm sorry about you having to move out.'

After twenty-five minutes and three accidental forays into the fly-fishing department, I finally emerged into watery sunshine clutching a cream cheese and celery sandwich and curry-flavoured crisps. Not my favourites, but it was just as I had

121

initially feared: by the time I got back to the Grab-and-Go, the selection was almost non-existent.

Still, things were definitely on the up. True, I didn't get Ruth's entire confession from Steve, but I was confident I would eventually. Meanwhile, I had a very exciting lead that called for a quick detour via Gipping Railway Station.

I found Paul Carew, Gipping's stationmaster, wandering along Platform One. It just so happened that Paul was one of Dave Randall's hedge-jumping cronies. He was whippet thin with long, spindly legs. It was said that his Fosbury Flop had to be seen to be believed, and since I hadn't, I decided to take Dave's word for it.

'How's the hedge-jumping practice coming along?' I asked.

'Vicky!' Paul beamed, then swiftly steered me behind the vending machine. Eyes darting left and right, he lowered his voice and said, 'Glad you can keep a secret. I heard what you did for Dave at Boggins Leap.'

'Fingers crossed Dave gets selected,' I said.

'He's been having nightmares about old Webster cutting down the course. He told me the old bugger's been hanging around a lot.'

'Boggins Leap still stands,' I said. 'Dave showed it to me this morning. Very impressive.'

Paul nodded. 'Yeah. Well. We owe you big time for keeping quiet about it. If there's anything we can do...'

'As a matter of fact there is,' I said. 'Do you know if Ruth Reeves bought a round-trip ticket to Plymouth yesterday?'

'Sure I remember,' said Paul. 'She goes to visit

her ninety-year-old aunt every Wednesday in Dawlish.'

'*Every* Wednesday in Dawlish?' So Ruth hadn't been at the hairdresser's after all, and what's more, she'd lied to her husband. Who was this ninety-year-old aunt living up the line in Dawlish? Maybe it was someone John Reeves disapproved of. I knew Mum often lied about visiting a friend or relative that Dad didn't like, just to keep the peace.

'Nice lady, Ruth,' Paul said. 'Heard she died.'

'What did you hear exactly?'

Paul shrugged. 'My mate Tom works with Steve Burrows, and they were called out last night to Reeves Roost. She wasn't feeling too well. Gippy tummy and too much champagne.'

'Did Tom say anything else? Did he think it suspicious?'

Paul shrugged again. 'Not really.'

'I heard she got two flat tyres in the station car park yesterday,' I said. 'There's been some vandalism. Have you had any trouble here?'

'Not since we installed our CCTV cameras,' said Paul. 'We've got twenty-four-hour surveillance and I check the tape every morning. Now there's a funny thing...' He scratched his head. 'I heard John bought her a pink Mercedes, but she parks it over by the dumpsters.'

Which was exactly what Sadie had said.

Rich folks are funny, aren't they?' Paul went on. 'Spend their money on fancy cars but quibble about paying eight pounds for parking.'

All further questions were drowned out by a deafening station announcement that the next train arriving on Platform One was from Paddington en route to Penzance. Paul bade me a hurried goodbye and brandished his whistle.

I headed back to the car park in search of the dumpsters.

I found them, along with a bottle bank, beyond the car-park boundary under a bank of trees well out of view of any CCTV cameras and the £8 parking jurisdiction.

What an odd place to park. Even if her tyres had been vandalized, without the CCTV footage I'd never find out who was responsible.

Then I saw the broken bottles. Scattered on the ground were shards of glass. Ruth must have run over them.

My vandalism theory was wrong. But there was still the puzzle of her stolen bicycle, and I was determined to solve that one at my very next stop. If anyone had known what Ruth was up to, it would be her best friend, Amelia.

Chapter Thirteen

Brooke Farm, the Webster's smallholding, was tucked away down a stony drive flanked by the usual hedge-banks and unruly barbed-wire fencing. A quadrangle of farm buildings was set around a courtyard and a cobbled passage led to the dairy, behind which I could hear the faint hum of milking machines awaiting the arrival of the Webster's prize-winning Red Ruby cows for the afternoon's milking.

Jack Webster's green Land Rover was parked inside a lean-to along with Amelia's white Hillman Imp, which was up on cinder blocks.

The yard was littered with the usual farming paraphernalia – bits of old tractor, an assortment of rusting harrows and a broken rotator. I was instantly struck by the neatness of Reeves Roost compared to the Webster's yard, which rather resembled Gipping County Council's rubbish tip.

The farmhouse – a traditional Devon longhouse – had been built in the seventeenth century and was accessed by a short flight of steps and a picket gate. As was usual in old farms, the vegetable garden was in front, with a few chickens scavenging for scraps. The garden had long been abandoned and was now a sea of weeds, ragwort and stinging nettles.

With a faded red front door and a roof in dire need of re-thatching, Brooke Farm was rather depressing.

Slipping Amelia's anniversary gift into my safari jacket pocket. I picked my way around the side of the house to the rear door.

To my dismay, I heard loud, angry shouts coming from inside. For a moment, I faltered. The last thing I wanted was to walk in on an argument. There was the sound of crashing china, a cry of indignation and then – silence.

I counted to twenty before knocking smartly on the back door.

'Hello? Anyone home?' I cried cheerfully. 'Vicky Hill! *Gipping Gazette!*'

At first there was no reply, then a loud click that sounded like a key turning in the back door lock.

I had a horrible thought. Since the argument had seemed violent, what if Amelia had been hurt?

I tiptoed over to the window and peered inside.

To my astonishment, Amelia was crouched under the oak trestle table with her eyes trained on the back door.

I let a few moments pass and, sure enough, Amelia began to crawl.

I rapped on the window. 'Amelia!'

She screamed and reared up, hitting the back of her head on the table. 'Sorry!' I mouthed and pointed to the back door. 'Can I come in?'

Amelia seemed annoyed. As she brushed down her tweed skirt and straightened her sweater, I wondered if she'd been avoiding me.

Moments later, the back door opened a crack. 'Yes?'

I searched her face for signs of bruising but she seemed perfectly all right to me. 'I thought I'd save you a journey.'

'For what?'

'Your wedding photograph?' I ventured. 'For this Saturday's "Wedding Anniversary Round-Up"!'

'Oh.' Amelia sighed.

I stepped over a broken cup on the floor by the door.

'Is everything all right?' I asked.

She followed my gaze. 'I dropped it.'

To say the atmosphere was frosty was putting it mildly. 'I've actually got something rather special for you.'

'For me?'

'But I know that Jack would want to give it to you personally. Is he around?'

'He's upstairs resting,' said Amelia. 'What is it?'

'A surprise.'

'A *surprise?*' Amelia's eyes widened. 'Jack has a surprise for me?'

'Why don't we have a little chat and then, hopefully, he may come downstairs?'

'Yes. Yes. Let's do that. Please, sit down.'

I walked over to the trestle table, taking in the plethora of black and white and colour photographs strewn across the surface. I pulled out a chair.

'Oh! Not there!' Amelia cried as a pile of unopened bills tumbled onto the floor. 'Oh, I'm so sorry!'

She darted forward and, with surprising agility, fell to her knees to scoop them up.

'Let me help.'

'No. I've got them!'

I got a glimpse of large red letters saying 'Final Notice' on at least four of them – one being from British Telecom, which probably explained why the Webster's phone was out of order.

Amelia opened a drawer in the oak dresser and shoved them inside.

We sat at the table. There was an awkward silence.

'I'm so very sorry about Ruth,' I said. 'I know you were close.'

'I can't believe she's gone.' Amelia looked haunted. 'I should have been there for her, but I didn't know! The phone...' She trailed off and gave a little shrug of despair.

'Tell me about these photographs,' I said brightly.

'John brought them over this morning,' said Amelia. 'He's organizing a ... what's it called? It's American. Celebration something.'

'Celebration of life,' I said.

'He wants me to read Ruth's favourite poem.'

'What poem is that?'

'"The Owl and the Pussycat".'

'That's a lovely poem.'

Amelia nodded. 'And he wanted me to pick out some photographs for the slide show.' She shook her head and made a peculiar gulping sound. 'I just can't believe she's gone. She was my best friend.'

'Amelia,' I said gently, 'do you think someone was trying to hurt Ruth?'

'No,' Amelia shook her head. 'Everyone loved Ruth.'

'Did John mention anything about her death to you – anything strange?'

Amelia frowned. 'Just that she had a gippy tummy. I don't think the champagne helped but Coroner Cripps said it was natural causes.'

'And John seemed satisfied with that explanation?' I asked.

'He was too upset to say much. The same thing happened to Violet Covey last year. She died suddenly and no one knew why.'

'Violet Covey was ninety-eight,' I pointed out, 'and very frail.' I thought of Ruth driving into the yard in her pink Mercedes, listening to Mick Jagger; she'd seemed anything but frail.

'Can you tell me a little bit about Ruth's stolen bicycle?'

Amelia looked startled. 'I made a mistake. She

128

didn't have a bicycle.'

'What about the squashed worm? The sun-flowers?'

At this, Amelia's expression hardened and her eyes flashed with anger. 'Dave Randall had something to do with *that*.'

I decided not to pursue that line of questioning as it would be a complete waste of energy.

'Have you ever met Ruth's aunt in Dawlish?'

'Aunt? No. Poor John.'

I waited for Amelia to go on but she just sat there staring into space.

'How *is* John doing?' I asked. 'I know you are close.'

'He's *very* unhappy about the location of the grave.'

'Oh?'

'Apparently St Peter's is packed, and the only available spot is next to the Carews.'

'And the Carews are ...'

'Why, they're *jumpers!*'

How could I forget? I had just spoken with Paul Carew at the railway station. I knew that the feud between the cutters and jumpers was volatile at the best of times, but I didn't know it extended beyond the grave.

'Of course, Jack and I have a plot in Albert Square.'

'Albert Square?' This was surprising. Albert Square was a private enclosure situated in the sheltered southwest corner of St Peter's and it was home to the great families of Devon.

'Oh yes,' Amelia went on. 'My family has a vault, you know. The Brooke-Luscombes?'

'I didn't realize you were one of the Brooke-Luscombes.'

'My family is listed in the Domesday Book,' Amelia declared. 'Jack can't even trace his back more than one hundred and fifty years. Father gave me Brooke Farm and the Ruby Reds as a wedding present.'

I took in my surroundings with fresh eyes. The kitchen, although shabby and in need of a coat of paint, contained good-quality furniture and was clean and tidy. Even the recycling bins were lined up in a neat row against the rear wall. A seventeenth-century oak dresser contained china plates, tureens and jugs, mostly with colourful chicken-themes.

Above the Aga hung a spectacular billhook with a carved wooden handle.

It occurred to me that perhaps Amelia had married 'down' when she met Jack. At one time the Brooke-Luscombes owned Luscombe Coal, supplying coal and fuel to most of the West Country. Following the closure of the coalmines in the '80s and '90s the company had gone the same way as most of England's coal industry – out of business – and Luscombe Hall, situated on the outskirts of Exmoor, was now a ruined shell.

'Oh yes,' Amelia went on. 'My mother was Pandora Luscombe. She and Lady Clarissa Trewallyn – not that funny little niece, the fat one with the wig – were great friends. But it's different now.' Amelia fell silent, seemingly lost in some distant memory.

'You've got quite a job sorting out all these photographs. I wouldn't know where to start.' I

130

picked up a black and white snap labelled 'Gipping High School 1968', showing a group of twenty teenage girls dressed in uniform. 'Which one is Ruth?'

'Can't you tell?' Amelia pointed a finger to a figure in the back row that stood a head taller than everyone else. 'There she is.'

I could see the young Ruth – the displaced Alice band, the dishevelled hair; even the uniform didn't fit quite right.

'And where are you?'

'Oh, I didn't go to the local school,' said Amelia. 'I went to Cheltenham Ladies' College in Gloucestershire.'

'You went to boarding school?'

'I met up with them in the school holidays at the Young Farmers' Club. I was an only child and my parents thought it would help me make friends.'

'I know what it's like to be an only child,' I said. 'Lonely.'

'Yes. Yes it was.'

I brought out my notebook and iPhone. 'Mind if I record this?' When Amelia didn't protest, I said. 'So let's talk about you. When did you first meet Jack?'

Amelia brightened. 'At a Young Farmers' barn dance. Jack was such a bad boy.' She sifted through the photographs and picked up one of Jack sitting astride a Harley-Davidson. I recognized John Reeves and Ruth standing in the background, dressed in 1960s regalia.

'Jack was always up to no good.' A wistful smile spread across Amelia's face. 'My parents were furious. They forbade us to walk out, you know.

131

Father wanted me to marry someone of my own class, not a farm boy.'

My mother had said much the same about her parents' view when she took Dad home one Christmas while he was on parole.

'There's something very attractive about a bad boy,' I said, thinking back to my brief fling with the gypsy last summer and the romantic evening we spent together in his bow-topped caravan.

Amelia passed me a handful of photographs. A montage of life in the swinging '60s – motorbikes on the sand, snail racing, Morris dancing, worm-charming contests, tar-barrel racing on bonfire night and, of course, hedge-cutting competitions, where the ladies looked on as the men – stripped to the waists – brandished their loppers. 'We had so much fun together.'

'Who is this?' I pointed to a voluptuous woman in hot pants and huge sunglasses, sitting with one cheek on Jack Webster's knee and the other on John Reeves'.

'That's Elaine Tully.'

'Goodness, she's so glamorous.' I pointed to another – a woman with curly, waist-length hair dressed in overalls that accentuated a trim figure. She was holding a silver trophy and a billhook that I recognized as the same one hanging over the Aga. 'Is this you?'

'Yes,' said Amelia. 'I won the 1972 Grand Prix.'

'I didn't know you were a cutter.'

'Oh yes,' said Amelia. 'Jack got me started but...' She shrugged. 'I gave up competing. It was more important that Jack do it than me.' She gave a brave smile and fell quiet again.

'Where is that trophy now?' I said. 'I'd love a photo for the newspaper.'

'It was stolen by that chappy – the killer thief. The Fog.'

I let that one go. I knew for a fact that Dad would never steal a trophy.

'Let's take a look at your wedding photos,' I said, swiftly changing the subject.

'I'll get the album.' Amelia got up and retrieved a white leather-bound book from the oak dresser.

I leafed through it, recognizing many of my regular mourners, who looked so young with their whole lives in front of them. I felt instantly depressed. Life passed by so quickly.

'Can we use this one?' Amelia gestured to a photo of the bride and groom framed in the church doorway.

'It's perfect,' I said.

Amelia wore an empire-line white satin dress with her hair swept up in a beehive, a la Dusty Springfield, and a tiny crown on top. A narrow veil cascaded down her back. Jack wore a tuxedo and looked very handsome, with his thick, black hair framing his face. In fact, he resembled a young Marlon Brando – one of Mrs Evans's favourite film stars. I studied the wedding photograph again.

'Isn't that Ruth?' Dressed in pale blue, a splash of what looked like chocolate stained the bodice of her dress.

'Ruth was my matron of honour.' Amelia gave a wistful sigh. 'It was such a lovely day. We all went on motorbikes to Slapton Sands afterwards. That was the last time Daddy ever spoke to me.'

133

'Oh, I am sorry.' I knew what it felt like to be excommunicated from your family. And here was Amelia, forty years later and married to a brute. I wondered if she thought it had been worth it.

'Of course I was supposed to finish university,' said Amelia.

'Really?' This was a surprise. Very few of my female mourners had gone to university.

'Oh yes. Cambridge,' said Amelia. 'I completed my first year and then, well...'

'You dropped out?'

'I've never regretted it. Not once.'

'And children?' I said.

'Robert emigrated to Australia when he was eighteen,' said Amelia. 'He's got a farm in Humpty Doo.'

'Humpty what?' I said.

'It's in the Northern Territory,' said Amelia. 'I'm hoping we'll go and see him for Christmas. It's so hard to get away, though, because of the farm.'

'How old is Robert now?' I asked.

'Why?' Amelia said sharply.

'I'm sure our readers will want to know,' I said, 'especially those who went to school with Robert.'

'I'd rather not say.'

I took a second look at the wedding photograph and guessed the reason. There was a definite bulge beneath Amelia's handheld bouquet.

'What about grandchildren?'

'Daisy and Cameron,' Amelia beamed. 'I'm so looking forward to seeing them again. We haven't been to Australia for five whole years as the flights are so expensive these days.'

134

Ten minutes later I had the required answers to the standard wedding-anniversary questions. I had to admit that the man Amelia was talking about seemed a very different Jack to the one I knew.

'I know he can be difficult,' said Amelia. 'But he drinks too much, that's all. Stress.'

'What's your tip for a happy marriage?'

'Never going to bed angry.'

'Never?'

'Oh. I know what you're thinking,' said Amelia. 'Jack and I have a very volatile relationship, but he's a passionate man. Very passionate.'

'Where will you be celebrating your wedding anniversary?' I asked.

'Well, we might wait a little now because of...' Amelia's eyes teared up. 'Because of Ruth – it wouldn't seem right.'

'Of course,' I said. 'Do you think we can persuade Jack to come down for a photograph now?'

'Oh, I don't think so.'

'Maybe if you tell him that I have something of vital importance from This-and-That Emporium, he might be tempted?'

'My *surprise?*' Amelia hesitated. 'I'll go and ask him.'

The moment Amelia left the room I skimmed the photographs scattered on the table. Many of them were of just John, Jack and Ruth, with Ruth in the middle, laughing and playing the fool. Presumably, Amelia had been the one with the camera. There were snaps of Blackpool Pier; a ferry trip to Boulogne, and one with the four of them posing outside – *good grief* – Gipping Nudist Colony. Fortunately, they were holding clumps of vegetation in the pertinent places, but that was more than enough for me, and I hastily shoved it to the bottom of the pile.

Amelia returned to the kitchen with Jack, who looked bleary-eyed and grumpy. I noted that the gash on his forehead had been covered with a large Band-Aid.

'What's all this nonsense about This-and-That Emporium,' he demanded.

I retrieved the gift-wrapped package from my safari jacket pocket. 'I thought it'd save you a trip.'

'What's this?' said Jack.

'Oh Jack, thank you.' Amelia squealed with delight, and before he could make a move, she'd snatched the package out of my hands and was tearing at the paper.

Jack's jaw dropped. For a moment he seemed confused, and then he smiled. 'I hope you like it, my luvver. Happy anniversary.'

It was the first time I'd heard a term of endearment directed at Amelia. It was rather sweet.

She opened the box with a gasp. 'Oh, Jack!' she cried again. 'Look, Vicky!' She turned the box around. Inside was a diamond eternity ring.

'It's beautiful,' I said.

Jack really was full of surprises today. The stone should have been a ruby, but then again, not all men were anniversary-gemstone savvy Steve.

'I love it,' Amelia gushed and slipped it on her wedding ring finger. It was far too large, but she didn't seem to care. She tiptoed over to Jack and kissed him on the cheek. 'Oh, but can we afford it?'

'For you. Yes,' said Jack.

'It's a little big but–'

'If that's all the thanks I get,' Jack snarled, 'I'll take it back.'

Amelia childishly hugged her hand to her chest. 'No, it's *mine!* I want to keep it.'

'Mind if I take a photo of this wonderful moment?'

'I don't want my picture taken,' Jack cried.

'Sorry.'

'It's OK, Jack.' Amelia stroked his arm and gazed adoringly into his eyes. 'I'm giving Vicky that lovely framed one of the two of us in the church at St Peter's.'

'I'll make sure to return it,' I said. 'Are you coming to the Women's Institute meeting this afternoon?'

'Oh yes,' said Amelia. 'We've got to bring a favourite memento and I just can't decide.'

'Don't worry,' I said. 'Elaine Tully has changed the programme.'

'Elaine Tully,' said Jack sharply. 'What's she got to do with it?'

'Apparently, she's doing a presentation on green burials,' I said.

'Amelia's not going and that's final,' Jack declared.

'Oh, but I have to,' Amelia faltered. 'I always help with the tea and with Ruth… Please, Jack, please. It's only for a few hours.'

'Doesn't our ruby wedding anniversary mean anything to you?' said Jack. 'Let's go for a nice walk around the field.'

'Oh Jack, *yes!* I'd love to.'

'Good. That's settled. Go and put your boots

137

on. I'll meet you by the barn.' And with that, Jack stomped out of the back door.

Amelia turned to me, eyes shining. 'Vicky, would you mind telling them I can't come. But I did make a cake. Will you take it with you?'

I waited while Amelia made a meal of wrapping up a lop-sided Victoria sponge – containing very little jam – in parchment paper and slowly lowering it into a circular Quality Street tin.

I left her putting on her outdoor coat and galoshes and headed back to my car. I felt depressed *again*.

Why were relationships so complicated? If it weren't for the fact that I felt I was missing out on the more physical aspects of life, I couldn't imagine the point of having one.

I thought of Annabel and her string of broken love affairs, always conducted with unavailable men, and Barbara, whose heart belonged to a man in her past, but who was still in torment at losing our one-eyed editor (who wasn't much of a catch, frankly). Then there was Jack and Amelia's uneasy marriage, kept together – one assumed – by passion. Rather like Steve and Sadie. Even my landlady and Mr Evans's steady marriage had been rocked by Lenny's mid-life-crisis flirtation with Annabel Lake. The only truly happy couple I could think of was John and Ruth Reeves, and she'd just died. Seriously, was it all worth it?

As I left Honeysuckle Lane and headed to the Plym Valley Social Club I had to wonder. What kind of man would want to be with the daughter of a criminal anyway?

Looking on the bright side, though, being single

was a good thing. I never needed to ask permission to go a WI meeting or feel tormented by the possibility that my boyfriend – or husband – was having an affair. And when the chance came for me to fulfil my dream and become the next Christiane Amanpour, I could just say, 'Yes please!' Having no ties or loyalties to anything or anyone was just brilliant.

Talking of loyalties, I couldn't help thinking that Amelia was hiding something. She had lied about Ruth having a bicycle, and she also seemed vague about the aunt in Dawlish – and I knew for a fact that Ruth had claimed to have an appointment at the hairdresser's on the day she'd *been* to Dawlish, because I'd heard her say so. Maybe Amelia was protecting her old friend, but from whom and why?

I was determined to find out, and as luck would have it, the Gipping Women's Institute was a great place to start.

Chapter Fourteen

Plym Valley Farmers' Social Club in Bridge Street was the monthly venue for Gipping Women's Institute.

Built in the late 1800s, the three-storey building housed solicitors – J. R. Trickey & Associates – on the ground floor, with the social club taking up the first and second floors. It used to be a private home, and access to the upper floors was through a blue side door.

This afternoon the door stood open, and out on the pavement was a freestanding sandwich board announcing WI SPECIAL GUEST: THE GREEN REAPER. Some joker had crossed out the word *green* and written *grim* in black marker pen – not very original, I thought.

Having found a space to park in a neighbouring street, I climbed the narrow stairs to the first floor, which had been converted into an open-plan meeting area. Wooden tables and chairs were set up in rows facing a podium to the side of a red velvet curtain, which screened a games area behind, consisting of a small pool table, darts, dominoes, chess and the ever popular shove ha'penny.

The room was abuzz with my readers making small talk, and just as I'd hoped, it was all about Ruth. I heard 'too much champagne', 'high cholesterol', 'Sunday's festival should be cancelled' and 'John's on the market'.

Perhaps Ruth *had* died of natural causes, after all. She'd certainly been very popular. It wasn't just her skills as the reigning worm champion for nine years straight, or her efficient running of the WI refreshment counter, nor her tireless involvement with the Gipping Bards, where she was in charge of props; Ruth had been loved by all and would be missed by many.

Would I ever be remembered so fondly? I wondered.

I headed over to the long bar-cum-counter that hugged one side of the room. There sat three bottles of Phyllis Fairweather's dandelion wine, a vast industrial-sized tea urn and all the china and cutlery paraphernalia, but no food. For once, Amelia's Victoria sponge would be welcomed.

Olive Binns née Larch emerged from the adjoining kitchenette carrying an empty platter adorned with a paper doily. Dressed in a 1970s pale blue trouser suit with a matching pale blue barrette clipped into her sleek grey bob.

'Vicky!' said Olive sharply. 'Have *you* seen Amelia? It's not like her to be late.'

'She's not coming.'

'Not *coming?*' Olive looked horrified. 'But she's supposed to bring a cake.'

'I've brought the cake.' I handed Olive the Quality Street tin.

'She's never missed a meeting.' Olive lowered her voice. 'Is it ... did Jack do ... is she ... you know ... unwell?'

'Not at all,' I said. 'In fact, they're spending some time together.'

'Spending some time *together?*'

'It's their ruby wedding anniversary on Saturday and they're celebrating early.' I didn't add that this involved walking around a field.

'Their ruby *wedding* anniversary?' Olive repeated in that annoying way she had. '*Jack* and Amelia are celebrating their ruby wedding anniversary?' Olive leaned in closer. I got a whiff of Elizabeth Arden's Blue Grass. 'Did he buy her a present?'

'Yes and I saw it. It's a beautiful diamond ring – an eternity ring to be exact.' I knew I was gossiping, but I just couldn't seem to help myself. For some reason, I derived great satisfaction from Olive's shocked reactions.

'A *diamond* ring!' Olive's eyes were as wide as

141

saucers. 'But ... but how can they afford it? Amelia told me they were strapped. They were even talking about selling the herd.'

'Maybe Jack has been saving up his pocket money,' I joked.

'Pam!' Olive shrieked as she spotted the director of the Gipping Bards walk into the room. 'Pam! Pam! Over here! You'll never guess what!'

Pam Green needed no persuasion and scurried over.

'*What?*' she demanded. 'What will I never guess?'

Olive quickly repeated our conversation.

'Amelia told me they were strapped for cash,' said Pam. 'Don't you think it rather callous? You know, the pair of them out celebrating and buying expensive jewellery when their best friend isn't yet cold?'

'I think the ring was ordered months ago.' Why I felt compelled to come to Jack's defence was a mystery to me.

'Whose best friend?' Barbara thrust the front wheel of her beloved pink bicycle into our little group, which had now swollen to five. How Barbara had managed to manhandle it up the narrow staircase was anyone's guess.

'You can't bring that thing in here.' Olive pointed to a circular sign with a drawing of a bicycle struck through. 'No bicycles. It's the law.'

'I don't care,' said Barbara. 'I'm not leaving it outside. Not after Ruth's was stolen.'

Ruth's bicycle again! I made a mental note to get to the bottom of *that* mystery.

'Poor Ruth,' whispered Olive. 'We're going to

142

miss her.'

'I'm sure Ruth's aunt is going to miss her, too.' I said slyly. 'I hope that John – in all his grief– has thought to inform her.'

Olive, Pam and Phyllis Fairweather, who had drifted over to join in the gossip, seemed confused.

'Aunt?' said Pam.

'The one in Dawlish,' I said.

'But didn't that aunt die?' said Pam with a frown. 'What was her name? Stella something? Had a stroke.'

'She made a full recovery,' said Barbara quickly.

'Perhaps John can go and pick her up?' Olive suggested.

'Let's not bother poor John about that,' said Barbara. 'He's got enough on his plate with the funeral.'

'You mean, celebration of life,' said Pam. 'That's what it's called. Apparently.'

'Where's all the food?' Barbara deftly changed the subject.

'Ruth was in charge of that,' said Olive. 'Poor Ruth.'

'What happened to the phone tree?' Pam asked.

'Phone tree?' said Olive.

'You're the secretary. You're supposed to organize a phone tree if there's a problem,' said Barbara. 'Sometimes I wonder if you're all there.'

'Where?' Olive said.

Barbara rolled her eyes. 'Oh, never mind.'

I set down the Quality Street tin. 'At least we've got Amelia's Victoria sponge.'

'No one's going to eat that,' said Barbara. 'You

143

may as well throw it out unless you want diarrhoea.'

'I love sponge,' Olive protested.

I felt exhausted by all their bickering and went to find somewhere to sit right at the back so I could beat a hasty exit. On my chair was a fluorescent pink flyer. In fact, the flyers had been placed on every chair and there, hovering by the door, stood Eunice Pratt, holding a stack of them in her arms. Her sister-in-law, Mary Berry – dressed in grease-stained orange overalls – was with her, clutching a copy of *Automotive Weekly*.

I picked up the flyer and, given its creator, wasn't remotely surprised by the message.

DEAD BONES ON OUR LAND?
SAY NO TO 'GRIM' BURIALS!

In the corner of the flyer was a stock photograph of a skeletal hand rising from the earth – an idea I knew Eunice must have got from the Gipping Film Club's recent screening of the horror film *Carrie*.

As if sensing my eyes upon her, Eunice gestured that she wanted to talk to me afterwards. I nodded, but fully intended to give her the slip.

'Seats please, ladies! Seats!' Acting chairwoman, the statuesque Gillian Briggs, took the podium wearing an elaborate livery collar of rabbit fur and a silver chain draped around her navy suit.

As a former cook in the WRNS, or Womens' Royal Navy, Gillian knew how to handle a crowd.

'Atten-*shun!*' she boomed and, just as I'd expected, the room immediately settled down.

'Good evening, hello and welcome,' said Gillian. 'I'm sure that by now you have all heard about poor Ruth.' Murmurs of sympathy and cries of 'poor Ruth' were spoiled by some bright spark shouting, 'No wonder there are no sandwiches!'

'So let's begin with a minute's silence in memory of our dear sister's departure.' Gillian retrieved a kitchen timer from the cubbyhole under the podium and deftly tapped out sixty chirps. Setting it next to the microphone – which she didn't need to use – Gillian held up her hand, paused and then shouted, 'Go!'

A minute's silence is a long time, although it wasn't as silent as Gillian had hoped, being peppered with sniffles, coughs, much scraping of chairs and, infuriatingly, a mobile phone's Morris dancing ringtone that took too long to silence.

Finally, the timer went off and everyone relaxed.

Gillian held the gadget aloft. 'And don't forget, these kitchen timers are still available at a special price of five pounds ninety-nine. They can be found over on the merchandise table. Olive! How many do we have left?'

'I'll count them,' Olive shouted.

We waited for at least another minute. I could hear Barbara mumble, 'She's so slow.'

'Four!' Olive shouted again. 'No. Three. Wait. No. It's four.'

I jotted down, 'Four kitchen timers still available for purchase,' on my pad.

Gillian scanned the room anxiously. 'Has anyone seen our guest speaker?'

'Not a good sign, if you ask me,' Eunice said loudly.

145

'Well, we've got a lot to get through this afternoon,' said Gillian. 'So we'll have to start without her. Pam, take it away.'

Throats were cleared and there was more scraping of chairs as the ladies got to their feet. Pam Green sat at the piano and straightened her sheet music. 'And a one, two and three!'

The opening bars of Britain's most loved hymn number 294 from *Hymns Ancient & Modern New Standard* and the Albert Hall's *Last Night of the Proms* favourite, 'Jerusalem', filled the room and the ladies began to sing.

And did those feet, in ancient time,
Walk upon England's mountains green?
And was the holy Lamb of God
On England's pleasant pastures seen?
And did the countenance divine,
Shine forth upon our clouded hills?
And was Jerusalem builded here,
Among those dark satanic mills?

Then came my favourite bit. The tempo changed abruptly, sending my feet tapping and body swaying to the gospel-style beat. The ladies belted out a verse from the racy song, 'It's Raining Men', before switching back into the sombre second and final part of 'Jerusalem'.

'...In England's, green and pleasant land,' I sang.

Everyone clapped and sat down as Gillian Briggs beamed at her flock. 'We'll be singing this at the Sunny Meadows Retirement Home for the Elderly next Tuesday afternoon. Olive? Do you have the sign-up sheet?'

'Yes. No. I...' Olive sifted through a stack of papers on the table before brandishing a clipboard. 'Yes! It's here.'

Gillian ran swiftly through the minutes of the last meeting with the usual topics – a Parish Boundary Walk, the upcoming auditions for the Gipping Bards production of *Les Miserables* and the non-existent progress of the WI Facebook fan page.

'I thought Barry Fir was doing it?' Pam called out.

'Hogmeat Harris and the Wonderguts are touring,' said Naomi Fir, Barry's wife. 'He can't do everything.'

There were grumblings of disappointment.

'Barry wasn't even getting paid,' Naomi cried. 'It was causing him too much stress.'

I jotted down, 'Barry. Stressed out. Still no Facebook page.'

'Thank you, Naomi,' said Gillian. 'Which brings me to Any Other Business.'

Eunice raised her hand.

'Ah yes, thank you,' said Gillian. 'If you haven't already done so, please sign Eunice's petition to stop the development of a wind farm being built on Seven Stars Heath.'

'They want to build fifteen turbines!' Eunice called out. 'We must stop them!'

There was a rumbling of agreement and I had to admit – much as I was supposed to be impartial – they really were ugly things.

'Settle down, *please!*' Gillian boomed. 'I wanted to save this announcement till last.' She gave an expectant pause. 'I'm thrilled to report that John

147

Reeves has founded the Ruth Reeves Memorial Cup for this Sunday's worm festival.'

'What category?' Phyllis Fairweather, who was the organizer, demanded.

'The heaviest worm,' said Gillian.

I jotted down, 'Ruth Memorial, heaviest worm.'

'Good afternoon, ladies!'

'And – oh!' said Gillian. 'Here you are at last.'

Elaine strolled in, looking sophisticated and professional in a black suit and black heels. She was pulling a small suitcase on wheels plastered with The Green Reaper's logo, which looked very similar to the Starbucks logo, except that the wavy green spokes were replaced by scythes and the siren had been transformed into the hooded head of the grim reaper.

'May I introduce Elaine Tully. Welcome home, Elaine!' Gillian led the applause, and as it gradually died down I heard, 'Air Hostess', 'Isle of Man', 'married five times' and 'lock up your husbands'.

'Thank you, everyone,' said Elaine. 'I hope you don't mind but I took the liberty of ordering pizza.'

'I do mind and–' but Gillian's protests were drowned out by ragged cheers, followed by, 'always liked Elaine,' and 'always so generous'.

I jotted down, 'Pizza. Surprise.'

'Order! Order!' Gillian banged a wooden rolling pin on top of the podium.

'I knew that Ruth was usually in charge of refreshments,' Elaine went on, oblivious to Gillian's acute disapproval, 'so I thought you might all be starving.'

She placed her suitcase on the counter, opened it and withdrew white and green paper plates, matching serviettes and plastic cutlery – all stamped with The Green Reaper logo.

Elaine zeroed in on Pam. 'Pam, be a dear and help me set this up.'

'It's not time for refreshments!' Gillian exclaimed. 'Not for another ten minutes!'

'It's your decision, of course, Gilly,' said Elaine. 'But who wants to eat cold pizza?'

Pam hurried over to the counter and the two women hugged.

I jotted down, 'Ruffled feathers. Court Martial.'

Mary Berry stood up. 'Where *is* the pizza anyway? I can't see any?'

The door opened again to reveal a man carrying a tower of pizza boxes, accompanied by a delicious smell.

'Here we are,' said Elaine. 'Put the boxes on the counter, Keith.'

'Hawaiian, BBQ, vegetarian, pepperoni,' Keith shouted out as chairs fell to the ground and bunions were trampled on as the members surged over to the counter, with Mary Berry leading the way shouting, 'Pizza!'

I perked up. So this was the Keith that Elaine claimed was one of my biggest fans. I tried to see what he looked like but he was shielded by a gaggle of hungry women.

'It's pizza from that new place in Chagford,' shouted Pam Green excitedly.

'You can thank Keith,' cried Elaine. 'He drove over to pick them up. Special order.'

Gillian Briggs looked on with a face as black as

149

thunder, and when Phyllis brought her a slice, she shook her head with disdain.

Suddenly I felt a tap on my shoulder and there, holding a plate of Hawaiian pizza, was one of the oddest-looking men I'd ever seen.

Dressed in black trousers with a black T-shirt sporting The Green Reaper logo, he oozed sophistication and ... something I couldn't quite put my finger on. I took in his wispy blond hair with its receding hairline and skin so white it was practically translucent. Dark shadows bloomed beneath his steel-grey eyes.

I was currently reading *New Moon*, the second in Stephenie Meyer's Twilight series, and had been feeling an affinity with the virginal Bella Swan. Keith reminded me of Edward Cullen, the vampire.

'You look hungry,' said Keith, offering me a plate of pizza.

'I'm starving,' I replied 'Thanks.'

'You're Vicky Hill.' He smiled and I noticed his upper eyeteeth were actually pointed. 'I'm Keith. I'm your biggest fan.'

'Why, thank you,' I said bashfully.

'"On the Cemetery Circuit with Vicky",' he said. 'I love that column, and something tells me we're going to be seeing a lot of each other.'

'We are?'

'Do you fancy a drink after this?'

I felt a rush of nerves and immediately lost my appetite. Maybe he was attractive after all – in an unusual way.

But before I could answer, the door flew open *again* and a woman burst in. She was partially hidden by a large cardboard box, from which protruded a collapsible projector screen and a trailing line of power cords. With a shriek, she tripped and pitched forward, upending the box's contents all over the floor.

Someone began to laugh and there was a chorus of laughter at the poor newcomer's misfortune.

'Order! Order!' shouted Gillian Briggs, whacking the rolling pin on the podium again.

The woman lay sprawled on her face.

'Excuse me,' said Keith. 'I'd better go and help the damsel in distress, but don't go away. I'll be right back.'

Gallant and thoughtful, too! Which was more than I could say for the circle of ladies who'd surrounded said fallen damsel.

'Ah!' said Elaine. 'Allow me to introduce the newest member of my street team. Please say hello to Annabel Lake.'

Chapter Fifteen

I hardly recognized her at first. Annabel was wearing black trousers, a black T-shirt with The Green Reaper logo and trainers with the laces undone – clearly the cause of her tumble.

I jotted down, 'Annabel moonlighting! Trainers. Tripped.'

Keith helped Annabel pick up the equipment – which didn't appear to be broken – and carried it gallantly over to the counter as the ladies continued to polish off the pizza. Elaine handed Keith her laptop and the trio set up the equipment.

My initial feelings of jealousy as the pair worked closely together soon vanished as Keith repeatedly looked over and winked at me.

Finally. Annabel sought me out. 'It's not what you think.'

'Don't tell me, you and Keith are just good friends,' I said drily.

'What? *Him?* Good God no. He's seriously *weird.*' She lowered her voice. 'I'm talking about Elaine. About all of this.'

'What do you mean?'

'I'm just helping out.' Annabel seemed anxious. 'Please don't tell Wilf or Pete.'

'I won't.'

'Don't I look awful?' She pointed to her feet and pretended to gag. 'Awful.'

'Well, I've never seen you wearing ... *trainers.*'

'They're Elaine's.' Annabel pulled a face. 'She said all her street team wore uniforms, but...' she shuddered. 'This is disgusting. This T-shirt hangs like a sack. I think it's a man's.'

I had to admit that it did nothing for Annabel's voluptuous figure.

'I have a darling one in black with a V-neck, but Elaine made me take it off.' I was struck by one of my brilliant ideas. 'I'd love to take your photo.'

'Vicky! No!' Annabel shrieked as I pulled out my iPhone and took a quick snap.

'Omigod! You've got to delete it! Please delete it!'

I slipped the iPhone back into my pocket. 'I will delete it, on the condition that you tell me exactly what Steve told *you* about Ruth's dying words.'

152

'Oh, *those*,' said Annabel dismissively. 'It hardly matters *now*, does it? I mean, she's being buried on Saturday anyway.'

'I'd still like to know.'

'Why? Barbara called me to say that Wilf wanted me to drop it.'

'I still want to know.'

Annabel regarded me with suspicion. 'Why?'

'I don't think you're in a position to make conditions,' I said. 'Do you?'

'Fine. OK. But it wasn't anything. Really.' Annabel closed her eyes and thought hard. 'It was in the hospital. Steve and Ruth were alone; John Reeves had gone to the loo. Steve said, 'Ruth, is there anything I can do for you, doll–'

He called Ruth *doll?*'

'And then he said–'

'Annabel!' shouted Elaine. 'Over here!'

'Coming...'

I grabbed Annabel's wrist. 'You come right back here afterwards,' I said, 'otherwise you'll be in this Saturday's newspaper wearing your trainers.'

As Annabel walked away, I discreetly took a few more photographs of her. It was great news that she was no longer pursuing the Ruth Reeves murder angle, but it didn't hurt to have some leverage.

After a few minutes the room had settled down again.

'Well, it looks like our guest speaker is finally ready,' said Gillian drily. 'Let me present Elaine Tully from The Green Reaper.'

There was a smatter of polite applause.

'Thank you, Gilly.' Elaine took the podium and rewarded everyone with a broad smile. 'First of

153

all, let me say I'm thrilled to be back. I was just twenty-five when I joined BOAC, or British Airways as it's known today–'

'Get on with it!' shouted Mary Berry. 'No one wants to hear about all your husbands.'

Elaine reddened. 'Of course.' She cleared her throat. 'Um. Thank you for giving me such a warm welcome.'

'Only because you brought pizza!' Mary Berry called out, to which there was a chorus of assent.

'And I'm glad you enjoyed the pizza The Green Reaper provided for you all as a gesture of good will,' said Elaine. 'Keith, the lights please.'

Keith dimmed the lights and then moved over to his laptop, which was sat atop a portable table on wheels.

The room fell quiet as a series of sterile and grim images of overcrowded church cemeteries filled the white pull-down screen.

'As you can see,' Elaine used a laser pen to make her point. 'Overcrowding has been a problem for a long time, despite the increasing use of double-decker graves.'

'Which church is this supposed to be?' Eunice Pratt cried. 'That cemetery doesn't look anything like St Peter's the Martyr.'

There was a buzz of agreement.

'Eunice is correct,' said Elaine. 'But these sobering slides are a clear illustration of what to expect by the end of the year in a cemetery near you.'

Another series of slides showed headstones and memorial stones that had been moved – one particularly shocking image showed broken-up head-stones and bore the caption 'Hard-Core Landfill'.

'As survivors, don't we want to think of our ancestors' graves being there for ever?' Elaine looked pained. 'Our research has shown that unless family members are visiting their loved ones on a regular basis, some cemeteries have decided they can reuse the plots.'

There was a universal cry of horror.

'At first, the idea of D–I–G or *"Dig"*, which we in the trade call 'direct-in-ground' burial may sound disturbing,' said Elaine. 'As you know, the body is decomposed primarily by living organisms and moisture, as seen here.' More slides of worms, ants and maggots flashed across the screen, and the room fell so quiet you could hear a pin drop. 'We all know that the deceased has no physical presence on earth any more, which is why survivors are often comforted by the idea of an environmentally friendly memorial–'

Suddenly the darkened room exploded with light.

'Unless you have a family vault,' came a familiar voice from behind me.

Everyone swivelled around and there were cries of 'It's her ladyship!'

Topaz – aka Lady Ethel Turberville-Spat – was standing in the doorway with her hand on the light switch. Dressed in her lady-of-the-manor attire of tight-fitted and heavily padded jodhpurs, a cream polo-neck sweater and a green tweed jacket, today Topaz had switched her 1960s Jackie O-style wig with a 1950s-style finger wave.

A couple of iPhones were whipped out by the younger members, anxious to take a photograph of the celebrity in our midst. Even Elaine and

155

Keith seemed temporarily thrown by the intrusion.

'I'm afraid I have some very bad news,' she declared. 'You're all going to be frightfully disappointed.'

Chapter Sixteen

Gillian Briggs, looking uncharacteristically flustered, hurried to greet Topaz. 'If I'd known you were coming, your ladyship, we would have saved you a seat. Phyllis!' she shrieked. 'Get off that chair.'

'I have an important announcement to make about this Sunday's worm festival.' Topaz strode to the podium and thrust Elaine aside, who promptly whispered something into Annabel's ear.

'I say! *You!*' shouted Topaz. 'It's rude to whisper. If you have something you'd like to share – whoever you are – we'd like to hear it.'

There was a stunned silence. Elaine coloured and actually seemed embarrassed.

Topaz pointed to the frozen image on the screen of a particularly voracious worm that was tucking into what looked like a limb.

'How apt!' she said coldly. 'As you all know, it's traditional to hold the post-worm festival reception in the ballroom at The Grange...' she paused to scan the rows of people who seemed transfixed by her presence. 'But with the theft of the *priceless* Spat urns, which are still missing, and the spate of

156

burglaries that have taken place at the Webster's farm, I have decided to cancel this event.'

As the members erupted with cries of disappointment I jotted down, 'Urns. Reception cancelled. World coming to an end.'

'Quiet please!' shouted Gillian Briggs. 'Her ladyship is speaking.' The unhappy women gradually settled down once more.

'I'd also like to point out,' Topaz went on, 'that Grange land is private property and trespassers *will* be prosecuted.' Topaz paused again to scan the audience. 'And we know who we are, don't we? Will Ruth Reeves please stand up?'

There was a horrified silence and whispers of, 'her ladyship doesn't know' and 'no one told her', until Mary Berry called out cheerfully, 'She's dead!'

'Since when?' Topaz demanded.

'Yesterday,' Mary Berry replied.

'Oh.' Topaz shrugged before turning to Elaine and saying, 'Do carry on.' Then she swept to the back of the room and slid into the seat next to me. 'I think I put my foot in it,' she whispered.

I had a sudden thought and, keeping my voice low, said, 'If you don't want anyone trespassing on Grange land – and I saw all the no-trespassing signs – why are you inviting any old Tom, Dick or Harry to pick blackberries?'

'Are you mad?' she hissed. '*Nobody* is allowed to pick the Spat blackberries! Where did you hear that?'

I pointed to where Eunice Pratt was seated – she was easy to spot with her lavender-coloured perm – and repeated our conversation.

'She's a liar, liar, pants on fire!' Topaz whispered back. 'I'd never invite that oaf onto Grange land. Dave is my gamekeeper, and any enemy of Dave's is an enemy of mine.'

It looked like Dave Randall had been right about Jack Webster spying on him, and for some reason Eunice Pratt had decided to cover for him. Interesting.

'As her ladyship said earlier,' Elaine boomed. 'For those unfortunate enough *not* to have a family vault, let's look at what options you have in these dangerous times – and at what cost? Who do you trust to take care of the graves in your absence? Certainly not the British government.'

'Hear! Hear!' said Eunice Pratt. 'They don't care about us. They just want to build more turbines.'

'What about cremation!' Pam called out. 'That would save space.'

'Thank you Pam. I'm happy you asked.' Elaine smiled again. 'Keith?'

The slideshow began again with a Disney World Haunted House soundtrack accompanying a series of coffins entering the flames of an incinerator.

'Ladies,' Keith took up the cause. 'On average there are around four hundred thousand cremations a year. It takes one to one and a half hours to burn a coffin in a crematorium – or three to four hours if it's a wooden casket.'

Everyone was either too shocked to comment or horrified into silence by the images that now marched across the screen.

Keith pointed the laser pen at a skull. 'See these teeth? Mercury fillings or implants emit poisonous gases into the atmosphere.'

'Just as well I've got dentures!' shouted Mrs Evans.

Annabel nervously raised her hand. 'What about fake ... fake ... boobies?'

All eyes turned to Annabel. She shrugged. 'I'm not asking for myself, I'm asking for ... for a friend.'

'Fake boobies? An excellent question,' said Keith. 'And an easy answer. Any non-degradable material will not disintegrate.'

Mary Berry got to her feet. 'What about foot and mouth?'

'We're not talking about cattle, Mary,' said Elaine quickly.

'We farmers all know that an infectious disease can survive death by as much as five years,' Mary Berry declared. 'This means that both the soil and groundwater can suffer from contamination.'

'Good to know, but as I was saying,' Keith went on, 'each cremation uses as much fuel as driving a family car to London and back. But on the up side ... Annabel, over to you?'

'Thank you, Keith.' As Annabel stepped up to the podium, he handed her the clicker and laser pen. 'Let's talk about ... cremation jewellery.'

There were cries of excitement. I jotted down, 'Cremation jewellery. Seriously?'

Annabel aimed the red dot at the next selection of slides – pendants, earrings and bracelets – which were all tastefully photographed against a backdrop of fluffy white clouds.

'As you would expect,' she went on, 'everything is an original one-of-a-kind. There are no copies

159

or fakes. How often can you say that in this day and age?' Annabel tossed her head, drawing attention to her dangly earrings. 'I'm wearing a pair of those earrings right now.' She gave a little twirl. 'You like?'

'Whose ashes are those?' someone shouted.

'One of her cast-offs, I reckon,' came another voice. 'She wears those old men out.'

There was a chorus of laughter – made louder by Topaz's joining in with her distinctive bray.

Annabel looked mortified. 'No ... um ... oh ... I borrowed these.'

'Yes! Like you borrow our husbands,' shouted Mrs Evans. There was another ripple of laughter.

'Thank you, Annabel.' Elaine swiftly took Annabel's place at the podium. 'If you buy the luxury package, all jewellery is twenty-five per cent off. And speaking of packages, we hope you enjoy this short film. Keith, music please.'

Suddenly, the opening bars of the soundtrack from *Out of Africa* exploded in quadraphonic sound via four speakers that had been strategically placed around the room.

The Green Reaper Starbucks logo slowly formed, followed by the title card, 'The Green Reaper: Moving on to Pastures New.'

After the initial murmurs of appreciation and comments about Robert Redford in his prime, the audience seemed transfixed by a series of idyllic, pastoral scenes. There were fields of wild orchids, red poppies and buttercups, where picnic tables showed happy families eating sausage rolls and drinking champagne. Always tucked somewhere in the background was a string quartet playing,

160

though of course we couldn't tell what they were playing – or if they were playing at all – thanks to the soundtrack and Elaine's voice-over narration.

'As Celine Dion would say, "the heart lives on,"' she said. The camera zoomed in on a tender sapling encased in deer-proof wire.

'So why not plant a tree – a tree for every member of your family who crosses to the other world?' A montage of different species of trees eventually morphed into a large clump.

'Convert those precious nutrients from your loved ones' remains to create woodlands that will provide food, shelter and give a safe haven for wildlife.' Lambs frolicked, deer grazed, birds nested and baby rabbits played in the long grass.

'Know that you can be part of your grand-children, great-grandchildren and great-great grandchildren's education.' We see little children studying nature under the watchful eyes of their schoolteacher. One picks up a bird's nest; another peers through a magnifying glass at a large beetle.

'Ask yourself this,' said Elaine, 'do you really want to reuse old claustrophobic graves when you can own a personal burial plot measuring fifteen feet by fifteen – that's far bigger than the average grave plot in your churchyard.' The screen split to show a packed cemetery on the left and an open meadow on the right, with plots marked out with green balloons.

'Our cremation plots measure seven feet by seven – far larger than a typical columbarium of three foot square.' The screen split again showing the coldness of a stone wall covered in plaques versus a field of flowers.

161

By now, everyone was mesmerized, including me.

The screen dissolved into the word 'Locations'. An aerial shot showed the English countryside before dividing into three with title cards – 'Heavenly Meadows: Isle of Man'; 'Celestial Comforts: Somerset' and 'Angel's Rise: Gipping-on-Plym', showing a spectacular view of the Isle of Man coastline – 'Who wants to be buried on the Isle of Man?' someone shouted – a breathtaking view of Exmoor National Park and a beautiful meadow running down to a river with five huge turbines on the horizon.

It was the exact photograph that Elaine had shown me yesterday afternoon at Ponsford Cross.

'Turbines!' shouted Eunice. 'A disastrous blight on our land!'

The short film came to a close with the reminder:

YOUR GREEN REAPER
REPRESENTATIVE IS ELAINE
07777 733000.
PLEASE LIKE US ON FACEBOOK

The soundtrack ended, the lights came up and, for a moment, no one moved, until Gillian Briggs remembered her manners. She hurried to the podium and led the audience in a round of energetic applause.

Annabel and Keith passed out glossy brochures, and I heard snatches of, looks expensive', and 'I've always wanted to be buried in my own orchard'.

I turned to Topaz, who sat there motionless.

She hadn't said a word throughout the entire presentation.

'What's wrong?' I said. 'Didn't you enjoy the show?'

'I'm not happy,' Topaz mumbled, 'but I don't know why.'

'Thank you, Elaine,' beamed Gillian. 'I'm sure our members will have lots of questions.'

'I do.' Mary Berry stood up. 'What about the badgers.'

Elaine looked startled for a moment, 'Badgers?'

'You know, badgers. Foxes. Digging up the bodies.'

Eunice joined her sister-in-law. 'And flooding. Our lands are susceptible to flooding. Won't the bodies just come up to the surface?'

'Thank you, Mary and Eunice,' Elaine said warmly. 'Both *very* good questions that Keith will be able to address. Keith?'

'Thanks, Elaine.' Keith joined his mother at the podium, holding the clicker, and the screen came to life once more.

'Biodegradable ecopods,' he said, pointing at a sausage-shaped coffin that looked as if it were made of rattan. 'We make these ourselves. You can choose from cardboard, bamboo, willow, banana leaf or papier-mâché.'

'Or, for those purists who prefer something less structured, how about a wrap in natural felt. Annabel?'

Annabel appeared – barefoot – from the kitchenette dressed in white fabric. Keith reeled off the available colours as she sashayed, hand on hip, across the room. Paused, for a moment, then

163

quickly did a runway turn and sashayed back to the kitchenette. Those who were within reaching distance leaned out to feel the fabric. Many seemed impressed.

'You'll find more details in the back of the brochure,' Elaine enthused. 'And although we don't take Visa and MasterCard, we do offer two options. Keith?'

'We have two payment plans. One, buy your plot right now. Today. And you'll get a fifty per cent discount,' said Keith. 'Two, take up our highly attractive payment plan and we'll pay the money into a savings account on your behalf.'

'Yes,' Elaine said. 'The beauty being that your funds will continue to make money for you until the day you die!'

'Sounds a bit fishy to me,' I whispered to Topaz, who continued to sit motionless beside me.

'Incidentally, we've been getting a lot of interest in our Devon plot from people up north who've always wanted to visit the British Riviera but could never afford to.'

'In fact,' Keith said, joining his mother at the podium again, 'we're on the lookout for new plots.'

'Where is Angel's Rise?' Topaz said suddenly.

'Right here in Gipping-on-Plym, your lady-ship,' said Elaine.

Pam stuck up her hand. 'Whose fields are we talking about? Which farmer? Is it one of us?'

'I'm afraid that's confidential at this time,' said Elaine smoothly.

'So ... let me get this straight,' said Mary Berry. 'You want to buy *our* land to bury *your* bodies. What's in it for us?'

'It's a franchise opportunity,' said Elaine.

'I could ask my Errol,' said Phyllis. 'We missed out on the dot.com business.'

'But what's the upside?' Mary Berry demanded, showing a savvy side to her nature that I'd never seen before.

'In addition to getting a share of the profits, you get a commission for every body buried,' said Elaine.

'Sounds like a lot of bodies are needed to make a profit,' Mary Berry declared. There was a ripple of agreement.

'Vicky?' Elaine said sharply. 'Tell them how many funerals you cover a week.'

All eyes swivelled to me.

'At least four or five,' I said. 'It depends on the time of year. If we get a cold snap, or that flu epidemic we had in March, I've sometimes covered six.'

'By my calculations, that would be at least two hundred a year,' said Elaine. 'Where are you going to put two hundred bodies in St Peter's cemetery? The Green Reaper *is* the way forward.'

'Wait!' Topaz stood up and her chair fell over with a crash. 'I must look at Angel's Rise again.'

'Excuse me?' said Elaine.

'Is everything OK, your ladyship?' Gillian Briggs cried.

'No, it's not,' said Topaz coldly. 'Angel's Rise. Immediately, please!'

'Quickly now! Her ladyship wants to see Angel's Rise immediately.'

Even Keith seemed unnerved by Topaz's demands. He hurried back to his laptop and quickly

165

scrolled through to the images of Heavenly Meadows, Celestial Comforts and Angel's Rise.

'There!' Topaz exclaimed. 'I knew it!'

There was a buzz of consternation as Topaz continued to glower at Elaine. 'What have you got to say for yourself?'

For the first time, Elaine seemed truly flustered. 'I can assure your ladyship that everything is above board—'

'That is for me to decide,' Topaz declared. 'Please come to The Grange tomorrow at nine thirty sharp so that we can discuss this *charade* further.'

And with that, Topaz swept out, throwing the room into chaos that not even Gillian Briggs's rolling pin could control.

I duly noted, 'Topaz upset. Charade.'

Topaz's exit had broken up the meeting prematurely and people began to leave. Annabel and Keith started to dismantle the equipment.

I went after Elaine and found her exiting the Ladies'. 'Great presentation,' I said. 'Wasn't Angel's Rise the photograph you showed me yesterday?'

Elaine seemed upset. 'No comment.'

'Is this something to do with Jack Webster?'

'No comment,' she said again, 'Please excuse me – oh! There's Phyllis. I must talk to her about the worm festival on Sunday. Phyllis! Phyllis!'

'Ah, there you are!' said Keith, stepping alongside. 'I've been looking for you.'

'Great presentation,' I said again. 'I was just talking to Elaine about Angel's Rise. Is this something to do with Jack Webster?'

'I honestly don't know,' he said, and I was inclined to believe him. 'But what I *do* know is that I want to take you away from here. Right now.'

I felt myself go hot at the thought. 'Well–'

'Keith! Keith!' Annabel hurried onto the landing. 'You're not *leaving* are you?'

Keith threw his arm around my shoulder. 'Vicky and I are off to the pub.'

'Yes, we are.' I couldn't help but feel smug. Keith had asked *me* out for a drink instead of her!

'But what about all the equipment?' she said.

'Is it packed up?'

'Everything is in the box. Elaine took the jewellery samples.'

'I'll go and get it. Thanks.' Keith turned to me. 'Stay right here, Vicky.'

Rather than the jealousy I was expecting from Annabel, she seemed highly amused. 'Please don't tell me that Keith's your secret lover.'

'No,' I said. 'This is just business.'

'Phew, that's a relief.'

I knew I shouldn't ask but I couldn't help myself. 'Why?'

'You'll find out soon enough.'

'It's just work,' I said. 'I'm covering the WI meeting.'

'I know.' Annabel smirked. 'Good luck!' She actually skipped down the stairs – there appeared to be certain advantages to wearing trainers – and it was only when I heard the outside door slam that I realized I'd forgotten to ask Annabel what Ruth's dying words had been.

Chapter Seventeen

'Your carriage awaits.' There was a beep as Keith pointed his key fob at a matte-black Tercel estate with tinted windows.

'Interesting colour,' I said.

'Gang members in the States call it "murdered-out".' Keith grinned, showing rather attractive dimples. 'Hop in.'

'Can you take me to my car and then I'll follow you.'

Keith regarded me with amusement. 'Why? Don't you trust my intentions?'

I laughed but felt a thrill that he had intentions. Not only that, he had intentions for *me*.

'I like to be independent,' I said, 'just in case a story breaks. You know a reporter never sleeps.'

My stomach filled with butterflies. I'd never come across a man who knew his own mind so quickly. He was a real man and I liked it! This wasn't Steve and his silly infatuation, Dave and his childish declarations of love, or me fighting with Eunice Pratt for a piece of her nautical nephew's heart. I was dealing with a grown man who knew his mind – a businessman with a murdered-out Tercel.

Keith gallantly opened the passenger door and I slipped inside. Behind me, the rear seats had been folded down to accommodate three long sausage shapes covered over with a black sheet.

'Are those bodies?' I joked.

'Ecopods,' said Keith. 'I wanted to bring them to the meeting but Mum thought it was too ghoulish.'

Keith started the car then reached over and took my hand. He kissed the inside of my wrist. Goose pimples raced up my arm and I snatched my hand away.

'Don't be so nervous,' he said, flashing me a brilliant white smile. 'I don't bite.'

Five minutes later I was in the safety of my Fiat and following his Tercel out of Gipping-on-Plym and into the open countryside. It had never occurred to me to ask him where we would be going, but as we turned off the main road and darted down a narrow lane I had a horrible feeling that we were going to the one place I didn't want to go: The Three Tuns. Even worse, Thursday was market day, and that meant the bar would be jam-packed with farmers.

The pub car park was nearly full, but I found a spot sandwiched in a row of identical Land Rovers. I noticed Steve's Jetta and felt a twinge of unease. Despite his reunion with Sadie, I wasn't sure how he'd react to seeing me with another man.

Keith parked his Tercel in front of the annex containing the skittle alley, which was often used for snail racing. The sign clearly said, 'No Parking and This Means You!' but he didn't seem to care. I like a man who bucks convention.

'I love this pub,' he said as we headed for the door to the public bar. 'The steak and kidney pie is always good.'

'The Nag and Bucket is better.' I ventured, hoping he would get the hint. In fact, in the two minutes that I'd been waiting for him to park, I had decided going here was a very bad idea. I wasn't in the mood for Arthur, the landlord's, boring jokes about my non-existent love life.

Keith stopped in his tracks. 'I'm sorry! I didn't think to ask what you wanted to do. Next time, you choose.'

There was going to be a next time! 'OK. I will.'

'Great. I've got a business meeting later and he's going to meet me here.'

Typical! Remember *The Rules*, Vicky. Be happy and busy! 'I've got to write up that WI report anyway.'

'Great. My business meeting won't take long,' said Keith. 'We'll still have the whole night ahead of us.'

The whole night? This was moving rather too fast for my liking. I'd only met him less than three hours ago.

'Don't worry.' He grinned. 'I always bring a Thermos and plenty of snacks.'

Keith took my hand and we entered the public bar, which was heaving with men in Barbour jackets and tweed flat caps. With its low-beamed ceilings and walls filled with horse brasses, paintings, gin traps and old keys. The Three Tuns felt claustrophobic at the best of times. It was also extremely hot, thanks to a roaring fire burning in the inglenook fireplace.

'Who is that?' Keith pointed to John Reeves holding court with his hedge-cutting cronies. They seemed to be enjoying a very funny joke

170

and John was slapping his thighs with laughter.

'That's John Reeves,' I said. 'Ruth's husband.'

Keith seemed shocked. 'Ruth as in Ruth Reeves, the lady we're burying on Saturday?'

Even though I'd learned that 'life went on' whatever happened when you lived in the country, even I thought it a bit sudden.

'To be honest, we're all a bit surprised that she's being buried so quickly,' I said slyly. 'There's a bit of a mystery surrounding her death.'

'Wasn't there an autopsy?' Keith asked.

'Apparently not.'

'I suppose this means he's single again,' said Keith tightly.

'Yes, I suppose he is. Why do you ask?'

'No reason.'

'He's very cut up about Ruth,' I protested. 'They were devoted to each other.'

'Of course they were,' said Keith. 'They always are.'

I regarded Keith with curiosity. 'You sound cynical.'

'I *am* cynical,' he said. 'And you would be too if your mother had been married five times.'

'Oh.'

'Grab that, will you?' Keith pointed to a small table that was next to Steve and Sadie, who were huddled together in deep conversation.

'You OK with a bottle of bubbly?'

Another bottle of bubbly! 'It's all I ever drink.'

Keith pushed his way to the bar as I edged mine over to the spare table that I now saw was right next to the open fire – little wonder that no one wanted to sit there.

171

Mere seconds later the bell sounded three times and the bar fell silent.

'There she is!' shouted Arthur. 'The lovely, the one-and-only heartbreaker in Gipping-on-Plym – let's give our Vicky a warm welcome.'

There was a ragged cheer and round of applause, and I found myself the centre of attention in the midst of small clearing. I could feel Steve's eyes boring into the back of my skull.

I did a modest bow and waved at Arthur. 'Thank you, thank you. I'll be signing autographs later.'

'Whose heart are you breaking tonight, my lovely?' Arthur called out.

'She's breaking mine!' Keith cried.

'What?!' I heard Steve gasp.

'Then you're a lucky man,' Arthur exclaimed. 'We all love our Vicky.'

Conversation started up again. Keith made his way back to my side and we both sat down.

'Arthur's bringing the bubbly over,' he said. 'Wow! You're one popular lady. Do you know everyone here?'

I scanned the room and nodded. 'Yes, I do.'

Arthur appeared with an ice bucket containing a bottle of Moët & Chandon – not Asti Spumante I was pleased to see – along with two champagne glasses.

'I'll do the honours,' said Keith and deftly opened the bottle with a resounding pop. Steve turned around and gave him a filthy look.

Keith poured out two glasses. 'Here's to new friends, long nights and beautiful sunrises.'

I shivered with anticipation. This was *it*. Keith was the one. He wasn't strange at all. Annabel

172

was wrong.

We clinked glasses and drank.

Out of the corner of my eye I saw Steve, who seemed to be hanging on my every word. He was leaning so far back in his seat that I feared it might tip over at any moment.

'Hey, you,' Keith suddenly said to Steve. 'Have you got a problem?'

'No. Have *you?*' Steve demanded.

'Just leave us alone, Vicky!' Sadie put in.

Keith raised an eyebrow. 'Ex-boyfriend?'

'Of course not,' I exclaimed.

'She's lying!' Sadie said. 'Go and sit somewhere else. Why do you have to sit near us? You won't make my Steve jealous, you know. He's with me now.'

'Wait!' Keith snapped his fingers. 'Don't I know you?'

Sadie looked startled. 'I don't think so.'

'The Banana Club! Plymouth Hoe,' Keith exclaimed. 'You're Sadie Sparkles!'

Steve's expression was thunderous. 'You *know* each other?'

'You had the cage in front of the piranha fish tank!' Keith said. 'I was there last week when they had that drug raid.'

'You were both there?' Steve and I chorused.

I felt a stab of disappointment. I hadn't expected Keith to frequent such low-class establishments.

As if reading my mind, Keith took my hand and gave it a squeeze. 'Don't worry. I was entertaining a client.'

'Yeah, I do remember you!' said Sadie. 'You were a big tipper.'

'I bet he was,' Steve muttered.

Sadie tried to take Steve's hand, but he snatched it away childishly.

'We only just managed to give the police the slip,' Keith continued with a chuckle. 'What happened to you?'

'I didn't get arrested.' Sadie went on. 'Trapdoor in the stage.' She gave a cheeky grin. 'They closed the place down and I lost my job.'

'She's working at This-and-That Emporium now,' Steve said coldly. 'Right, I've had enough of this. Let's go.'

Steve jumped to his feet, taking the tablecloth with him. Out of habit, I leapt up and managed to save the cutlery, plates and glasses from crashing to the floor – not that I got any thanks for it.

'And by the way, Vicky,' Sadie said, 'I'm moving in on Saturday morning, so make sure you've got all your stuff out of my bedroom.'

Steve grabbed her hand and the pair walked off.

'Well,' said Keith, 'there's someone who's still in love with you.'

'I told you, we're just friends.'

'Look, Vicky,' Keith went on, 'you and I have just met. I've got a past. You've got a past. I don't believe in secrets. It's no big deal. But what's this about you having to move out?'

Sadie's comment had brought me back down to earth with a bump.

I explained my domestic situation at Factory Terrace and how I was being evicted.

'What are you going to do?'

'Live in my car,' I joked. 'I'll be fine. Honestly.'

'I may just know of somewhere,' said Keith

slowly. 'Leave this to me.'

I regarded Keith with suspicion. There was no such thing as a free lunch. 'OK. What's the catch?'

'No catch,' said Keith. 'Relax, Vicky. Take a chance. You seem like a woman who doesn't trust easily. But you can trust me.' He filled up my glass again. 'Cheers! To new adventures.'

We clinked glasses again. Twenty minutes later we'd devoured our individual steak and kidney pies, drunk half a bottle of champagne and I was feeling in a very good mood.

Keith looked at his watch. 'He's late.'

'Who?'

'Jack Webster,' said Keith. 'I thought he'd be here by now.'

I knew I was right! 'Angel's Rise is Webster's land, isn't it?' I said. It certainly explained how Jack could afford a custom-made diamond eternity ring. 'Why didn't Elaine say so?'

'It's a bit more complicated than we thought.' Keith seemed worried. 'I'll tell you once we know what's going on. I just hope he shows up.'

'Did you have an arrangement?'

'No. But I asked around and apparently he's always here on a Thursday night. Market day in Taunton or something.'

'He should be,' I said. 'At least give me a clue as to what's going on.'

'All I can tell you is that Webster is not sticking to his end of the bargain.'

That didn't surprise me. 'In what way?'

'Strictly off the record – unless I say otherwise – and I mean it, Vicky.'

'Agreed.' We shook hands.

'He keeps avoiding us, making excuses about why he can't show us the location of Angel's Rise.' Keith seemed worried. 'I just hope Mum hasn't been ripped off.'

'Why would she be?'

'It happens,' he said. 'A lot. I have to keep an eye on her.'

'That's lovely,' I said, trying hard to shake off a feeling of déjà vu. Lieutenant Robin Berry had felt the need to protect his odious aunt, too.

'Someone has to. Mum was so sure she could persuade her old boyfriends to sell a field or two at the very least and invest in The Green Reaper.'

It certainly explained why Elaine had been hunting him down yesterday and what she was doing in Honeysuckle Lane last night. I felt disappointed. Maybe I'd got the wrong end of the stick after all.

'Well, I'd be careful around here,' I said tactfully. 'Many of the farmers haven't quite recovered from that foot-and-mouth epidemic a few years ago, and they're all struggling to make ends meet. People are very cautious about trying anything new.'

'We even paid Webster in cash because he wanted to buy a houseboat.'

'A *houseboat?*' I exclaimed. 'Why would he want a houseboat?' A diamond ring, possibly, but a houseboat? It made no sense at all. 'Are you *sure?*'

'That's what he told me. A surprise or something,' Keith waved a dismissive hand. 'Anyway, Mum told me we could trust him. You see, I promised Dad I'd always look out for her.'

'And your father was...?'

'Professor Clarence Calloway, the botanist,'

said Keith. 'Husband number three.'

'The one she met on a flight to Zurich?'

Keith gave a wry laugh. 'That's the one. Dad was pretty old and more like a grandfather to me. He died when I was ten.'

'And the two before that?'

'Pilots,' said Keith ruefully. 'She stopped flying when she married Uncle Paul; he was a vicar.'

'That was on a flight to Rome.'

'Yep. Mum gave up flying and got all religious for a bit, until he fell in love with the woman who arranged the church flowers. Then finally there was Uncle Carlos. He was in the funeral business. You could say he opened up a whole new world for me.'

For once I felt as if someone had had a worse upbringing than me. 'So it's just the two of you–'

There was a sudden commotion at the bar as Elaine strolled in and was greeted warmly by John Reeves and his cronies with cries of 'Can't believe you're back!' and 'Get the girl a drink.'

'Just the two of us – for now.' Keith rolled his eyes. 'But enough of me. Tell me about you. Why Gipping-on-Plym? I can tell from your accent you're not from around here– Hey! Steady on, mate.'

'Vicky!' Dave Randall, clearly inebriated, pulled out a chair and sat down heavily at our table.

'Dave!' I caught the acidic whiff of cider mixed with damp leaves. A few twigs were stuck in his navy Guernsey sweater. 'Can't this wait?'

'Thank God I found you–'

'Hey! Wait a moment,' said Keith sticking out his jaw. 'You're interrupting our evening, mate.'

177

'Who are you?' Dave barked.

'Keith – Dave; Dave – Keith.'

'Webster's been at it again,' Dave exclaimed. 'This time I'm going to kill him.'

Chapter Eighteen

Dave suddenly reared back. 'Is this ... is he ... is *this* the bloke you threw me over for?'

'Excuse me?' said Keith.

'It's not what you think,' I said, trotting out that tired old line again.

Keith grabbed my hand. 'It's everything you think, mate, so just clear off. Hang on...' Keith paused. 'Are you talking about Webster? Jack Webster?'

'Yeah,' said Dave. 'He was down at the byre again. I frightened him off, but I followed him here. His Land Rover's in the car park–'

'Wait a minute,' said Keith. 'You've had dealings with Webster?'

'He's a nasty piece of work,' Dave whined. 'Always in trouble with the police. Always trying to rip people off, the bastard.'

Keith turned on me. He seemed angry. 'Why didn't you tell me this?'

'What is there to tell?' I retorted. 'I don't know what you and Jack agreed.'

'Agreed?' said Dave with scorn. 'I'd rather poke both my eyes out with a burning stick than do business with Webster.'

'Great, that's just great.' Keith's expression hardened. He dropped my hand and stood up, scanning the packed bar. 'You say he's in here somewhere?'

'Got to be.'

'Whoa!' Dave's eyes widened. 'There he is! There!'

Jack Webster sauntered into the bar and, before anyone could stop him, Dave charged over and brought Jack down in a rugby tackle. The floor cleared, patrons formed a circle and the room erupted in cheers as the two men rolled around like schoolboys, punching and kicking out at random. There were cries of 'Fight! Fight! Fight!' Someone shouted out, 'Call the police!' Another yelled, 'Get Amelia!'

Keith turned to me in amazement. 'Is this what people do in the country?'

I saw Elaine catch Keith's eye. Both looked grim.

'I've got to rescue Dave,' I said and pushed my way through. Dave was straddling Jack, who seemed to be getting the worst of it, although Dave's punches were rather pathetic and more like little slaps. Everyone heard 'keep away from me' and 'kill you'.

Keith plunged into the fray, and between the two of us we managed to tear them apart – much to the dismay of the onlookers, who had started to place bets.

While Keith contained Jack, I held on tightly to Dave.

'Dave, you should leave,' I said urgently. 'The police–'

But it was too late.

There was a deathly hush as DI Probes and DC Bond strode into the bar. Keith and I let our hostages go.

Probes regarded us all with suspicion. 'Hello, hello, hello? What's going on here, then?' It was such a cliché that I couldn't help but snigger.

'A fight has been reported,' said Probes, coldly taking in the fact that Dave had slipped his arm around my waist.

'Not here, officer,' I said. 'Dave and I were just having a chat.'

'And poor Jack fell over, officer.' Elaine slipped alongside Jack, who was sporting a nasty swelling on his forehead, next to the gash he'd received the day before.

'I see.' Probes regarded Elaine and Keith with a look I couldn't quite fathom. 'Very well.'

Then he turned his attention back to me. 'And why am I not surprised to see you here, Ms Hill. Wherever there's trouble, somehow you always seem to be involved.'

'I don't see any trouble here tonight, officer,' I said. 'Just a slight misunderstanding.'

Probes scowled. 'I hope neither you, *Randall*, nor you, *Webster*, plan on driving tonight, because we will arrest you both for drunk and disorderly conduct if you do.'

'Amelia's on her way,' Arthur called out.

Dave was practically in tears. 'Please don't arrest me, officer.'

'How are you going to get home?' Probes demanded.

Dave pulled me closer and planted a kiss on my

cheek. 'Vicky is driving me tonight.'

'Ah. Of course she is,' Probes said grimly.

'I don't think so, mate,' said Keith.

'Please, Vicky, please!' Dave pleaded.

I looked at Dave, who I feared was about to collapse with despair, then said to Keith, 'Don't you have your meeting? I'll only be twenty minutes.'

Keith looked at Probes, then at Dave, then at me and laughed. 'Arthur's right, you're a real heartbreaker.'

'And you, Webster?'

'Jack's with us,' said Elaine quickly.

'Right then, move along now,' said Probes to the punters who had crowded around us. 'There's nothing here for anyone to see.'

Jack didn't utter a word. He just stood there, hands dangling by his side. I thought of the Asti Spumante and my earlier suspicions that he and Elaine had been indulging in an affair, but now I wasn't so sure. For the first time ever I mistrusted my instincts.

'Let's go,' said Dave happily.

Dave steered me out of the pub and into the car park just as Eunice Pratt's silver Fiesta pulled up with Amelia riding shotgun. I remembered seeing her Hillman Imp up on blocks and, of course, she didn't have a phone. Presumably Arthur had called Eunice to do the honours and help get Amelia's husband home. Poor Barbara's birthday dinner must have been cut short.

As Dave and I drove by, Eunice and Amelia were engaged in animated conversation given the amount of arm flapping going on. Dave wriggled close to me and put his hand on my leg, mumbling

181

something incoherent that sounded like 'bed' and 'give you one'.

'In your dreams, Dave, in your dreams.'

I had a feeling that tonight was going to be a long night.

Chapter Nineteen

As I drove Dave, who was now snoring loudly in the passenger seat, home to Cricket Lodge I wondered why I'd agreed to drive him. I should have stayed and eavesdropped on Elaine and Keith's meeting with Jack Webster.

In a funny kind of way, Dave and I had 'history', or whatever the Americans called it. Dave had been my very first serious crush when I'd moved to Gipping-on-Plym, and if he hadn't been such a wimp, so fond of his scrumpy or such an appalling kisser, perhaps we could have made a go of it. But now I had a new beau: Keith! I couldn't wait to dump Dave off and tear back to The Three Tuns.

I turned off the main road and into a lane signposted 'To the cricket pavilion'. The lane – often impassable in bad weather – led past the abandoned cricket pavilion and ended at Cricket Lodge – the name given to the gamekeeper's cottage where Dave lived.

Dave had been given the grace-and-favour lodge for the duration of his lifetime. I knew that Dave played around at being a gamekeeper; there were pheasants and he did a spot of logging, but other than his hedge-jumping hobby, he seemed to do very little.

I pulled up in front of Cricket Lodge, which was a miniature replica of The Grange, complete with gargoyles peering from beneath the gabled roof.

Dave stirred and gave an unattractive belch.

'Come on,' I said. 'Let's get you into bed.'

'You know I love you.' Dave threw the passenger door open and promptly fell out, face down into the mud.

'For God's sakes,' I said sternly. 'Get a grip. When is the Inter-Continental selection committee coming?'

'Wednesday. Wednesday. Wednesday.'

'That's less than a week away. Promise you'll lay off the scrumpy.'

'I can handle it.'

'If you don't,' I said, 'I'll tell Jack exactly where he can find Boggins Leap. In fact, I'll help him cut it down.'

'*Whaaaaat!*' Dave shrieked. 'Why would you do that?'

'Because I don't want you to mess this up. Promise me.'

'Promise.' Dave belched again. I couldn't imagine Keith being so vulgar.

With Dave leaning on me heavily, I managed to get to the front door, but found it was locked. 'Since when did you start locking your door?'

'Webster,' said Dave. 'Webster and his snooping. Trophies.'

'Where are the keys?'

Dave looked blank.

'Please don't tell me they're in your Land Rover.'

'They're in my Land Rover.' Dave grabbed me so tightly it hurt. 'Got to go back and get them. Have to. Webster. Steal my stuff. Land Rover.'

'Don't you have a spare set?'

Dave slapped his face, presumably in an attempt to sober up. 'Spare set. Yes. Woodshed.'

'OK,' I said, peering around in the dark. 'And where is that?'

Dave gestured to a path that skirted the lodge. 'Yonder. Flowerpot.'

How original. I couldn't be bothered to point out that under a flowerpot, under the front door mat and dangling on a piece of string through the letterbox were the first places a would-be burglar would check.

'Stay here.' I propped Dave against the door, but he slowly slithered to the ground, legs open, head lolling about like a bladder on a stick. Thank God we'd never been an item romantically.

I set off for the woodshed using my Mini-Maglite to light the way. As the only building behind the lodge, it was easy to spot. I dragged open the old door that was half off its hinges and stepped inside.

Sweeping the beam around the interior, my stomach did a peculiar flip.

There, leaning in the corner, was a ladies bicycle with a wicker pannier basket. The brand – Raleigh – was marked clearly on the crossbar. I distinctly remembered Barbara mentioning that Ruth had bought a Raleigh, and how she'd encouraged her to buy a wicker pannier basket, and yet this purchase had been denied not just by John, but by Amelia, too.

184

The bicycle had to belong to Ruth, I was sure of it, but what on earth was it doing in Dave's woodshed?

As the crow flies, Reeves Roost and Brooke Farm were directly across the valley from Cricket Lodge, but to get from there to here was a circuitous route via an ancient 'green lane' – one of hundreds of thoroughfares used in medieval England.

It made absolutely no sense.

Once again, I circled back to Ruth. Ruth who was to be buried on Saturday and whose death seemed suspicious only to Steve and I. Was the bicycle connected in some way?

Retrieving the key from under the flowerpot I rejoined Dave, who was slumped on the front door step, snoring loudly.

'Come on,' I said kicking him sharply. 'Wake up.'

The inside of Cricket Lodge was just as I remembered it, smelling of damp and wet socks. With a low ceiling and dirty leaded light windows, the place resembled a cave.

Dave switched on the lights – well, one light: two bulbs had burned out. I took in the worn brown sofa that was pushed up against one wall, a coffee table piled with magazines, including *Jumper Jamboree!* and *Azerbaijan Extreme Adventures* and a 1980s-era TV unit containing an old television set. On the mantelpiece above the Victorian fireplace stood Dave's hedge-jumping trophies. He staggered toward them and counted each one with exaggerated care.

'Are they all there?' I said.

'Yep!'

'You're getting paranoid.'

Dave turned back to me. 'Oh, Vicky,' he said. 'You're the best. You really are. Stay here tonight – after you've gone back to the pub and got my Land Rover.'

'You'll be lucky,' I said. 'I'll get your keys and bring them over in the morning.'

'So stay here now.' Dave lurched toward me. 'I'll give you a night to remember.'

'You already have,' I said drily. 'Actually, you can come and pick them up from Factory Terrace in the morning.'

'Like. How?'

'On your bicycle.'

Dave pulled a face. 'I don't have a bicycle.'

'There's one in the woodshed,' I said. 'Maybe it was your old girlfriend, Loretta Lovedale's.'

'Nah. She rode a moped.' Dave took three steps and pitched face first onto the sofa. Within seconds he was snoring again.

Minutes later I was zipping back along the main road when a car came zooming up behind me, flashing its headlights. My heart sank. I'd definitely drunk half a bottle of champagne and, for the first time ever, I'd forgotten all about the stringent drink-driving laws. Knowing my luck it would be DI Probes driving an unmarked police car.

With a feeling of dread, I pulled over into a lay-by and waited for the knock on the window.

Tap, tap, tap!

To my surprise, it was Steve, his face a picture of anguish.

'What's happened?' I said. 'Is everything all right?'

'I've got to talk to you,' he said miserably. 'But not in the car. I don't trust myself in an enclosed space.'

I got out.

'I can't stand it,' Steve went on. 'Seeing you with that reaper bloke and then you go back to Randall's place... I'm just... I'm in agony, doll.'

'Where's Sadie?'

'She's staying with Lily Kirby. I just dropped her off. We had a fight.'

'How did you know where to find me?'

'Arthur told me you went home with Randall.' He gave a heavy sigh. 'I just hate myself.'

'Why?'

'I've always been your informer.' Steve shook his head in despair. 'It was wrong of me to call Annabel.'

'Yes it was,' I said firmly.

'Will you ever forgive me?'

'It'll be hard,' I said.

'Ask me anything, doll. Anything at all.'

'Ruth Reeves,' I said. 'And don't try any funny business.'

'No funny business. Steve swears.' He stepped in closer. I became aware of the familiar tingle whenever he was near. It was like an energy that radiated from his body to mine, but I stood my ground.

'Go on.'

'Well, Cripps signed off on natural causes because he was going off to Canada on a fishing trip,' said Steve. 'But when we brought Ruth in, she looked really funny. She was complaining of stomach cramps and had the trots.'

'Go on,' I said again.

'She was severely dehydrated – she'd been drinking champagne all day and hadn't eaten much.'

'I know all this,' I said. 'What about her dying words?'

'Oh yeah! That's right. I forgot about those.' Steve frowned for a moment then said, 'Tell John it's done.'

'That's it?' I said again. 'What's done? Who's done what?'

'I don't know. But it seemed important.' Steve thought for a moment. 'She grabbed me, like this.' He fastened his hand on my arm. 'And she pulled me close, like this.' He pulled me close. 'And she said it three times. The last time she added, "Miami".'

I felt frustrated. I knew there was something in Steve's revelations but I couldn't see it. 'Why didn't Ruth tell John herself?'

'He wouldn't see her.'

'He wouldn't *see* her?'

'Said he couldn't handle it?'

'He couldn't *handle* it?' Was I was turning into Olive Larch the parrot, repeating everything people said?

'So what did John say when you told him it was done ... and Miami?'

'Nothing.'

'No reaction at all?' I exclaimed. 'Not even a question about what she meant?'

Steve shook his head.

'Did you ask him?'

'Course I did. But to be honest, I don't think he was listening. He was too upset. Never seen a

188

man so broken up,' Steve went on. 'And then I got to thinking, how would Steve feel if it was you in the hospital bed? And I got all upset, too.'

'That's very touching, Steve. Thank you. But luckily it wasn't me. I'm standing here right now.'

For some reason I kissed his cheek, and the next thing I remember is being blinded by the glare of oncoming headlights as I lay on the bonnet of my Fiat. My entire body was on fire, and I was no longer wearing my safari jacket or top.

'Oh God! Sorry!' Steve hurled himself off me. The buttons of his shirt were undone, exposing naked flesh, and he was distraught. 'Oh God! Don't tell Sadie.'

I was dazed and more than a little confused. As I readjusted my clothing, Steve retrieved my top and safari jacket from the ground and handed them to me. I pulled both on just as the car in question drove by very, very slowly.

How on earth had this happened? Who had made the first move? Surely it couldn't have been me?

'This never happened,' I said.

'Never happened,' said Steve gratefully. 'Sadie will kill me – but ... if...'

'Good night,' I said firmly and scrambled, shaking, into my car.

Steve returned to his vehicle, floored the engine and drove off at high speed. I headed back to The Three Tuns trying to push what had just transpired to the back of my mind. Get a grip, Vicky! Focus!

What had Ruth meant when she'd said, 'Tell John it's done. Miami.' Of course, I guessed

'Miami' was to do with their upcoming holiday. But what had Ruth done? Why was her bicycle in Dave's shed? And who had slashed her sun-flowers? I began to feel depressed. Maybe there was nothing fishy about Ruth's death, after all – although Steve's description of her ailments did seem to point to something sinister – but it was too late. Ruth was being buried on Saturday and that would be that.

I turned into the car park at The Three Tuns and my spirits sank even lower. Not only was there no sign of Keith's Tercel or Elaine's Audi TT Quattro, save for one solitary Land Rover, the pub was in complete darkness.

With horror, I realized my romp with Steve had caused me to lose track of time. Keith must have thought I'd decided to stay with Dave after all.

I pulled up beside Dave's Land Rover to re-trieve his keys, but found the vehicle was locked. It was then that I realized the driver's door didn't sport the Jump Azberjam 2016 logo. It wasn't Dave's vehicle.

One of Dave's many nightmares had come true: his Land Rover had been stolen.

Chapter Twenty

I spent a restless night dreaming of Steve corner-ing me in Dave's old woodshed watched by a yellow-faced Ruth Reeves sitting astride her bicycle. I was very glad when my alarm went off, saving me from what I could only assume was a tryst too horrifying to think about.

Today was Friday and promised to be a busy day. It was vital that Ruth's so-called 'celebration of life' was stopped and a full autopsy was ordered, but I didn't have the evidence no matter what Steve said.

There was no obvious foul play nor was there a motive. To be honest, I had more pressing matters to deal with. I had to find somewhere to live, and hopefully, Keith was still willing to help me despite the fact that I'd stood him up the night before. Then, there was the matter of the urns! Chuffy McSnatch said to bury them somewhere else – but where? And what about Dave's missing Land Rover? Maybe he'd taken the bicycle and cycled back to The Three Tuns to get it himself.

Suddenly I had a headache. When did my life get so complicated?

First, a hearty breakfast was in order – until I caught a glimpse of my reflection in the bathroom mirror. My face was covered in red blotches and I had an unattractive love-bite on my neck. I knew the lumps would go down by midmorning, but everyone at the *Gazette* would know what they meant, and I definitely couldn't face Sadie's mother downstairs.

Why oh why did Mother Nature play such a cruel trick: making me inexplicably attracted to a man I didn't fancy as well as making me allergic to his caresses?

I plastered foundation on my face from a sachet sample Annabel had given me because the colour was 'too orange' for her 'porcelain skin', but she thought it might suit me. It did even out my complexion a little, but it also made me look like a reality star from one of Mrs Evans's favourite shows, *The Only Way is Essex*. Donning a scarf around my neck, I set off for the *Gazette* on an empty stomach.

I was just about to make the turn out of Factory Terrace and onto the main road when I saw Dave pedalling towards me on a lady's bicycle. My heart sank. Dave had obviously not recovered his beloved vehicle.

I stopped alongside him and immediately saw he'd been crying. His eyes were like slits. I knew at once that it was because of his Land Rover. Why else would he be a) here and b) riding a woman's bicycle?

I felt a stab of irrational guilt, but then reminded myself that it was Dave's fault he'd left the keys in the ignition, and that he shouldn't have drunk so much.

'What's wrong with your face?' he said.

'I've developed an allergy to nuts,' I said. 'Why are you riding a bicycle?'

'It's over,' he wailed. 'My life is over.'

'Oh, for heaven's sakes,' I said crossly. 'I'm sure your Land Rover will turn up somewhere.'

'Eh?'

'I said I'm sure your Land Rover will turn up somewhere.'

Dave gave a cry of dismay. 'You mean ... you don't have it *here?*'

'Why would I?' I said, far more sharply than I'd intended.

'But...' Dave's face crumpled.

'No more tears, Dave,' I said. 'Let's go to back to The Three Tuns and ask Arthur. Someone obviously took your Land Rover by mistake. You know they all look the same.'

Dave started to sob uncontrollably.

With a sigh, I got out of the car and went to comfort him. He smelled terrible.

'Last night I had a nightmare,' Dave began. You're not the only one, I thought. 'In my nightmare, Webster had found Boggins Leap and ... and ... he cut it all down with a chainsaw.'

'It was a nightmare, Dave,' I said wearily.

'No ... no ... it wasn't. That's the thing. It was ... true.'

I looked at his face, wracked with grief, and realized he wasn't joking. 'You're serious, aren't you?'

'He's destroyed everything.'

'Get in,' I said. 'Leave the bike here. We'll get it later.'

Dave didn't need a second invitation. He threw the bike down and jumped into my car.

As we sped off to Boggins Leap, Dave's misery turned to a healthy anger. 'I want you to put it on the front page. How's this for a headline: WEBSTER DESTROYS ATHLETE'S DREAM – the bastard.'

'You've still got five days before the Inter-Continental selection committee come. Maybe you can find an alternative?'

'Have you any idea how long it took me to build it?' Dave exclaimed. 'And he's a bloody coward. I went to see him at Brooke Farm this morning and his missus tried to tell me he never came home last night. Does she think I'm stupid?'

193

I often thought Dave stupid, but in this instance he was right. I'd seen Amelia and Eunice arriving at The Three Tuns myself.

'Well, we'll give Webster something to cry about,' Dave gave a bitter laugh. 'Me and the lads are going to pay him a visit.'

'Well, before you do that, let's at least make sure that Webster is the guilty party.'

I reached for my iPhone and put on my headset.

'What are you doing?'

'Telling my boss. This is a big story. We go to press today.' Dave's headline was good, but mine was better – GIPPING CHAINSAW MASSACRE: A VICKY HILL EXCLUSIVE! I had to triple check the damage, though, as Dave was prone to exaggerate.

'*Gipping Gazette,* how can I help you?' came Barbara's voice on the other end of the line.

'Morning, Barbara.' I said. 'Is Pete there yet?'

'He's seeing his counsellor this morning,' said Barbara.

'Again?'

'They each go separately,' said Barbara. 'And then, twice a week, they go together. Pete's told me he will be driving straight to the printers in Plymouth.'

It seemed hard to believe that in this day and age the *Gipping Gazette* still went elsewhere to be printed, but Wilf was a stickler for tradition.

'Annabel said that if you called in, to tell you she's on her mobile,' said Barbara.

'Why would she tell you that?' I said, instantly suspicious. 'Isn't she always on her mobile?'

'I heard she's following a lead on that silver

thief chappy. The Mist.'

My stomach turned right over. 'What do you mean, a *lead?*'

'She's had a tip about the Spat urns.'

'A *tip?*' I was doing an Olive Larch again.

'She wouldn't elaborate, but Wilf is still here. Shall I get him for you?'

'No, no, it's OK. Thanks. I'll call back around eleven.'

'Remember the deadline is at noon.'

I disconnected the line. What lead did Annabel have on Dad? And what kind of tip did she have on the Spat urns? I was sick with worry.

'You didn't tell them about Boggins Leap,' said Dave. 'Why didn't–?'

'Shut up,' I said irritably. 'I told you I needed to be sure of my facts first.' I thought for a moment and rang Barbara back.

'It's me again,' I said. 'Have you spoken to Amelia this morning?'

'No. Why?'

'I thought perhaps you might have thanked her for dinner.'

'She doesn't have a phone.'

'Did Eunice come over?'

'Eunice? Why?'

'Because there was some trouble at The Three Tuns and Jack got into a fight. Eunice brought Amelia to the pub to pick him up.'

'I don't know anything about that,' said Barbara quickly. 'I went home on my bicycle quite early. I don't like cycling in the dark, especially on country roads. Why?'

'Apparently Jack didn't come home last night.'

Dave gave me the thumbs up.

'How do you know that?' said Barbara sharply.

'I wondered if you'd heard anything?'

'No. Why would I? I really must go. My other line is ringing.' Barbara hung up.

'What did she say?' Dave asked.

'She had to go.'

This was strange. For the first time ever, Barbara didn't seem interested in idle gossip.

Moments later we turned into The Three Tuns car park. The Land Rover from the night before was still there.

'That's Webster's Land Rover!' Dave exclaimed as we drew up alongside. There was a decal of a heart with 'Devon Cutters Rule!' in the windshield, which I hadn't noticed before. Eunice and Amelia must have driven Jack home after all.

'I knew his missus was lying! I knew it!' Dave exclaimed.

'But where's *your* Land Rover?'

'Webster stole it. Like I said.'

'Not if he went home with Eunice and Amelia, Dave.'

Dave frowned. 'He must have done. How else could he have got to Boggins Leap?'

'But wouldn't that mean your Land Rover would still be at Boggins Leap?'

'Maybe he abandoned it.'

An odd feeling of dread settled in the pit of my stomach. I cut the engine and got out.

'Where are you going?' Dave demanded.

'I want to talk to Arthur,' I said. 'Stay here and don't go messing about with Jack's Land Rover, otherwise you and I will fall out.'

I left Dave in the car, making sure to crack open the window – as one would for a pet – and headed over to the pub.

It always surprised me how different these establishments were in the cold light of day – a feeling of dampness coupled with the smell of stale beer.

I found Arthur wiping down the counter.

'It's allergies.' I said pointing to my face, but instead of the lewd joke I was expecting, Arthur turned to me grim-faced.

'Bad news travels fast. I only just heard myself five minutes ago.'

The knot in my stomach grew tighter. 'What's happened?'

'Lower Rattery way. Terrible. Terrible news. Happened on that blind corner, I reckon. Mown down like a pheasant, he was. Terrible.'

'Who was?'

'Webster,' said Arthur. 'Some dog walker found him this morning.'

'Is he all right?'

'No, my lovely,' said Arthur quietly. 'He's dead.'

To say I was shocked was putting it mildly. 'How can that have happened?' I asked. 'What was he doing on the road to Lower Rattery? I thought Eunice and Amelia came here and drove him home.'

'I never saw them.'

'But I did,' I said. 'They were arriving as I was leaving with Dave.'

Perhaps Amelia had a change of heart and decided that an inebriated Jack was best left alone to stew, but then I remembered. Weren't Elaine and Keith supposed to meet up with Jack?

197

'The Grim Rip-Off?' Arthur said in answer to my question. 'Yeah. After you left with Randall, they left the bar with Webster.'

'They *left* with Webster,' I said. 'You mean, they all left the pub together?'

Arthur nodded. 'And then it got busy. Vicky,' he hesitated for a moment. 'I like you, you're a good kid, but be careful.'

'What do you mean?'

'You don't know, do you?' Arthur looked at me in astonishment. 'Dave Randall. It was Dave Randall's Land Rover that knocked Jack down.'

Chapter Twenty-One

'But how could I have done it?' Dave said for the umpteenth time as we sped towards Lower Rattery. 'You took me home.'

My initial shock at Dave being guilty soon disappeared. Of course he couldn't have done it. Not just because I'd left him at Cricket Lodge practically unconscious, but because it meant he'd have had to cycle back to the pub to pick up his Land Rover. No, this had something to do with Elaine and Keith and wretched Angel's Rise.

'And I only remembered I had the bike this morning–'

'Be quiet, Dave,' I said for the umpteenth time. 'I need to think.'

If Amelia had decided to let Jack find his own way home, why would he have walked the long way round? Lower Rattery – a narrow winding road with a series of hairpin bends that climbed up the hillside and opened onto Ponsford Ridge – was a circuitous route taken by inebriated souls hoping to avoid the breathalyser. It was definitely not a route to take on foot.

We took three hairpin bends and, on the fourth, the road widened to include a grass verge and large oak tree flanked by Devon hedge-banks – and Dave's Land Rover.

'Bloody hell!' Dave gasped.

It had slewed off the road and been abandoned, with the nose partially buried under some low-hanging branches. Even so, the logo Jump Azberjam 2016 emblazoned on the driver's side was impossible to miss. Three orange traffic cones and blue crime-scene tape stretched from one side of the narrow road to the other.

'Where is he?' said Dave. 'I can't see Webster.'

I couldn't either. 'I think you should stay here,' I said for the second time that morning. 'Let me go and find out what's going on.'

'Do you think my equipment is still in the back? Those loppers cost me a fortune.'

'That's the least of your problems.'

Dave grabbed my arm. 'You've got to tell them about Webster cutting down Boggins Leap, Vicky.'

'Dave,' I said, trying to remain patient, 'don't you see that it gives you a motive?'

'Oh.'

I set off on foot. Two other vehicles – a police Panda car and an unfamiliar black Suzuki Kei hatchback – hugged the hedge further along. I heard voices and some rustling in the undergrowth. There was a flash of white nylon and a cry of, 'That's the wrong hole, Kelvin.' A white three-panel screen emerged from the bushes, neatly shielding the front of the Land Rover from the road.

For a moment, the enormity of what lay beyond made me hesitate. I had seen a dead body before and it wasn't pleasant. But, reminding myself I was a professional, I took a deep breath and whipped out my notebook.

DI Probes poked his head out from behind the screen. 'Oh, Ms Hill.'

'Morning officer,' I said. 'I just heard the news.'

Probes held up his hands as if stopping traffic. 'Come no further if you don't mind. This is a crime scene.'

I noticed that Probes hadn't had time to shave and had just thrown on whatever clothes he had to hand – a rather flimsy pair of sweat pants, which I always thought looked unflattering even on the most attractive of men.

Probes regarded me with curiosity that rapidly turned to distaste. 'Your face...?'

'Allergy,' I said desperately. 'Nuts.'

He shook his head and muttered something under his breath. 'Presumably you've seen Randall this morning?'

'He didn't do it,' I said. 'You told me to drive Dave home and I did.'

'Yes, of course you did,' said Probes bitterly. 'Before you went on to your next conquest.'

I was taken aback, but before I could comment a tall man with a button nose and domed forehead joined us. He reminded me of a character from the *Coneheads*.

'This is Coroner Bailey from Plymouth,' said Probes. 'Coroner Cripps is on a fishing trip in Canada. This is Vicky Hill—'

'*Gipping Gazette*,' I interrupted, taking his outstretched hand. Cold, firm fingers grasped mine.

'Nasty business back there.' Coroner Bailey beamed. 'The human body is an extraordinary thing. It tells us exactly what happened. Mr Webster suffered a compression of the chest as he was pinned up against the oak tree. It's a form of asphyxia. It leaves the face swollen and congested, with fascinating haemorrhages scattered across the skin.'

'Oh.' I was relieved I hadn't eaten breakfast, after all.

'You see, facial discolouration is caused by the overfilling of blood above the level of the heart,' the coroner continued cheerfully. 'The shattered legs signify that he was hit from behind—'

'I think we get the idea, Ray,' said Probes.

'Can you estimate the time of death?' I asked.

'I would say between ten and two.'

And since I'd already left Cricket Lodge by ten, Dave's only alibi was five pints of scrumpy.

'Can you confirm that you were with Randall all night, Ms Hill?' said Probes coldly.

'I didn't do it!' Dave hurried towards us.

'Ah, Randall. We need to talk to you.'

'I didn't do it,' said Dave again. 'Vicky was with me all night.'

Probes regarded me with open dislike. 'May I remind you that providing a false alibi is a criminal offence?'

'Actually, I returned to The Three Tuns.'

'Oh yeah. That's right. She went back to The Three Tuns. I left my Land Rover there, but that bastard Webster—'

'Shut up, Dave!'

'By the time I returned to The Three Tuns, officer,' I said. 'Dave's Land Rover had disappeared.'

'Perhaps you made a little stop on the road to meet a *friend*, Ms Hill?'

I felt my face redden as I remembered rolling around with Steve on the bonnet of my Fiat.

'Eh?' said Dave. 'But you promised to go back to the pub.' Dave looked confused. 'Where did you go if you didn't go straight there?'

'I did go back to the pub, Dave.'

'So you have no alibi, Randall,' said Probes. 'Where were you between the hours of ten and two?'

'Asleep,' said Dave. 'But in the morning, I got up and went to see Webster's missus.'

'If you didn't have a Land Rover, how did you get to Brooke Farm?' said Probes.

'I've got a bicycle. I left it in Factory Terrace.'

'That's right,' I said. 'Dave came to pick up his keys, but of course I didn't have them because they were still in his Land Rover, so anyone could have taken it from the car park.'

'I see,' said Probes slowly. 'But you could easily have cycled back to The Three Tuns, say, at midnight, collected your Land Rover, seen Jack Webster walking home on foot and decided to run him down. You would then have removed said bicycle and cycled back home.'

Dave shook his head vehemently. 'No. No.

That's not true.'

I had to admit that the exact same thing had crossed my mind. 'I think Dave needs a solicitor.'

'And what made you cycle to Mrs Webster so early in the morning?' Probes went on. 'Was it a disgusting attempt at pretending you hadn't just mown down her husband like a pheasant?'

Dave gasped. 'No! No! I went there because ... because ... Webster massacred Boggins Leap.'

'Boggins Leap?'

'He destroyed my dream, the bastard! I'm glad he's dead!'

'Dave, shut up, please,' I exclaimed. 'Officer, let me explain–' but Probes put his traffic hand up again. 'I think we should continue this conversation down at the station. I must warn you, Randall, that anything you say may be used in evidence against you. You have the right to remain silent–'

'What? You're arresting me!' he shrieked. 'You can't! I'm innocent.'

Another Land Rover came round the bend with John Reeves in the driving seat. To my dismay, Amelia Webster was beside him.

'Oh crap,' muttered Probes. It was the first time I'd ever heard him cuss. 'Kelvin! Where the hell are you?'

'Here, sir.' DC Bond emerged from the undergrowth, took one look at John Reeves, who was now striding towards us, followed by Amelia, and sprang into action: 'Stay back, sir! I say, stay back!'

'Jack!' she shrieked, breaking into a run. 'Where's my Jack!'

Both John and DC Bond made a grab for her,

but she fought them off with extraordinary strength. 'Jack! Oh God! *Jack!*' Amelia stamped hard on John's foot and kneed poor DC Bond in the groin. He fell to the ground and curled into a ball, groaning. Probes tried to stop her, and even Dave made a futile swipe at her coat-tails, but Amelia was too fast and darted behind the white screen.

We heard screams of distress and then, 'Mrs Webster, you can't take that. It's evidence.'

Probes nodded at DC Bond, who staggered to his feet, rolled up his sleeves and joined Coroner Bailey behind the white screen. There were sounds of a scuffle and then the young officer returned bearing Amelia in an armlock.

It was very upsetting, especially when she finally caught sight of Dave.

'You murderer! You killer,' Amelia spat at Dave. 'You killed my Jack. Oh, my Jack. You killed him!' She continued to struggle as the officer held on tight.

'You'll hang for this Randall,' John said.

Rather dramatic given that hanging was abolished as a capital offence in 1965.

'But I didn't do it,' Dave cried. 'Tell them, Vicky.'

And then, suddenly, Amelia's knees buckled and she collapsed in a heap onto the ground, dragging DC Bond down beside her.

'She's not breathing!' he exclaimed.

'Quick, get an ambulance, she's going into shock,' said John. '*Do* something!'

'I called for an ambulance fifteen minutes ago,' Probes said, checking his watch.

Fortunately, we heard the welcoming sound of

a siren drawing near. Steve's ambulance raced around the corner and stopped just inches from where we stood.

Steve and Tom tumbled out, raced round to the rear, then charged towards us holding an empty stretcher between them.

'Coming through. Medics coming through,' Steve shouted.

Moments later, Amelia was borne away into the rear of the vehicle, with John trailing the trio.

Probes turned to Dave. 'David Cyril Randall,' he said gravely as he snapped on a pair of hand-cuffs, 'you are under arrest for the murder of Jackson Bernard Webster.'

Dave dug his heels in. 'I won't go! I didn't do it!' he shrieked. 'I'm being framed! You've never liked me.'

As Dave broke down again, his cries of grief faded as I was transported back in time to Dad's last arrest. I remembered how Dad had stood proud and strong and how he'd winked at me as he allowed himself to be led away and put into the back of the waiting police car. He was not a snivelling twit like Dave.

'Oh for heaven's sakes, shut up, Dave,' I said far more harshly than I intended to. 'One minute please, officer.'

Probes gave a curt nod and stepped away.

I put my arm around Dave's shoulders. 'Now listen here,' I said urgently. 'This is what you do. You ask for a solicitor to be present when they question you, OK? Mr Trickey is really good but most of all–' I thought back to the after-dinner games of my childhood, like Quiz the Copper.

'Control the interview,' I said. '*You* control the interview. Understand? Answer a question with a question. Remember that.'

Dave nodded. 'Please show the cops Boggins Leap. *Please!* Show them what Webster did to me. And what about next Wednesday! What about Azberjam? What about *me?*'

Probes returned. 'Enough. You've had your minute.'

'Promise me, Vicky! Promise me!' shrieked Dave as DC Bond manhandled him into the back of the waiting Panda. 'I love you!'

'Very nice. Very cosy,' said Probes coldly.

DC Bond slammed the rear door, but was boxed in by Steve's ambulance, so we had to endure Dave pulling anguished faces through the rear window until, finally, Steve moved the ambulance and Dave was driven away, the Panda's blue light flashing and the siren on full blast.

Steve and John Reeves strolled over to join us.

'Amelia is stable,' said Steve. 'We're going to take her home. John said he could keep an eye on her. When should we come back for Webster?'

'We'll call you,' said Probes and vanished behind the white screen.

'What's wrong with your face?' said John. I quickly raised my scarf to hide the blotches.

'Yeah.' Steve studied my features with curiosity. 'Reminds me–'

'Ruth had those blotches to start with,' said John.

'Are you certain?' Steve said sharply.

'Yes. She complained that her throat felt tight and her hands were tingling.'

'You never told me that,' Steve said crossly.

'Because they went away.'

'What time was that?' Steve asked.

'That was – let me see – around five in the afternoon.'

'Did you tell the doctor?' he demanded.

John shook his head. 'No. Oh, and her lips were swollen.'

'Swollen?' Steve and I exchanged looks.

'I get that when I eat nuts,' said Steve.

'So do I,' I added quickly.

'Ruth wasn't allergic to nuts,' said John. 'She had a stomach like a cast-iron tank.'

'Mr Reeves?' Tom called out and waved from the ambulance. 'Mrs Webster is asking for you.'

'Excuse me, I'd best go to her,' said John and walked away.

Are you thinking what I'm thinking?' said Steve.

'What are you thinking?'

'Something fishy is going on here – and I'm not just talking about Webster being pinned against a tree.' Steve tut-tutted. 'I like old Cripps, but he's been a bit sloppy recently; Mrs Reeves's death is not the first time he hasn't bothered with an autopsy. Do you know who's standing in for Cripps?'

'Someone called Bailey,' I said.

Steve's jaw dropped. 'Ray Bailey is *here*? He's actually *here*?'

'Behind the white screen.'

'You *do* know who he is, don't you?' Steve seemed about to expire with excitement. 'Ray wrote *The Dummies Guide to Suspicious Deaths*. If anyone can order an autopsy, it's him. I mean,

207

he's like *God* in the forensic world.'

'Who is God?' said Probes.

Quickly, Steve shared his thoughts, and minutes later, Probes escorted Steve behind the white screen. I could just make out the words, 'fan', 'autograph my copy', 'another case' and 'Cripps got sloppy'.

This was exactly why Steve was an excellent resource and had been worth kissing on the bonnet of my car.

As I waited impatiently for Steve to reappear, a horn signalled yet another arrival.

Annabel raced towards me, flapping her note-book.

'Vicky! What the hell are you doing here?' she cried.

'I could ask the same of you. Wait, did Steve call you?' I was seized with irrational jealousy.

'No. Why? Did he call *you?*'

'No,' I said. 'I *do* have other informers, you know.'

'Omigod. Webster really is dead!' Annabel's eyes were as wide as saucers. 'I can't believe Dave killed him.'

'Allegedly,' I said.

I saw him in a police car,' she said excitedly. 'And look!' She pointed to Dave's Land Rover. 'Photos!' She whipped out her iPhone and began clicking away.

'I thought I heard your voice, Ms Lake.' Probes popped out from behind the white sheet.

'Oh, what a stroke of luck!' Annabel gushed. 'I must discuss an *international* case with you im-mediately. It concerns the Spat urns–' Annabel

208

threw me a triumphant look – 'and that silver chappy everyone is looking for: The Fog.'

'It's hardly the time,' I said, trying to still my pounding heart. 'Poor Jack Webster is dead behind that sheet and you're talking about–' I shrugged '– something trivial like theft.'

'*Trivial?*' Annabel gasped.

'Ms Hill is correct,' said Probes, uncharacteristically springing to my defence. 'Murder takes priority, Ms Lake, and deserves some respect.'

Annabel reddened. 'Yes. Of course, of course.' She flashed him a bright smile. 'So, what happened here?'

'The police will be issuing a statement,' said Probes. 'We cannot provide any comment at this time. I suggest you go back to your office and wait until we call you.'

'Oh.' Annabel seemed deflated. 'But ... but I need this for tomorrow's front-page exclusive and I've only got until noon.' Annabel batted her eyelashes. 'Please? Pretty please?'

'That's not my problem,' said Probes gruffly.

Annabel gave an impatient sigh. 'Can you at least confirm that Randall has been arrested for murder?'

'No comment,' said Probes. 'As I said, the police will be issuing a statement. Ms Hill, can I have a word?'

'Is this about the murder?' said Annabel. 'Only we're on the same side, Colin sweetie.'

Probes looked taken aback. 'Actually no,' he said coldly. 'This is about something completely different.'

'Oh.'

'Right,' I said, shooting him a brave smile, though my stomach was in knots. He was going to bring up the silver urns – or worse, Dad. Probes had hinted at it before and now he was going to ask me straight out.

'Let me escort you to your car,' he said, shooting me a shark-toothed smile. He took my elbow and steered me away from Annabel.

It was only when we were out of earshot that he said, 'Coroner Bailey has agreed to conduct an autopsy on Ruth Reeves.'

I stopped dead, stunned. 'That's brilliant.'

'Steve Burrows has good instincts,' he said, albeit grudgingly. 'As do you. And he's right. This isn't the first complaint we've had about Cripps being sloppy.'

'There's been something else?'

'Oh, nothing suspicious. Just not bothering to fill in forms correctly, that kind of thing. Look...' He paused for a moment. 'Forensics will be here for quite some time this morning, as will your friend Annabel, so why don't you and I go and look at Boggins Leap.'

'Dave Randall is innocent, officer,' I said. 'He's got too much to lose.'

At this, the warmth disappeared from Probes's voice. 'Not everyone deserves your protection, Vicky.'

'He does.'

'Get your car. I'll follow you.'

Chapter Twenty-Two

En route to Boggins Leap I managed to track down Pete and give him a quick recap of the morning's drama.

'Stop right there,' said Pete. 'Annabel is on it.'

'What?' I exclaimed.

'Conflict of interests. Randall's your friend. You took him home last night–'

'Dave isn't the only suspect,' I said, hotly cursing the town gossip. 'What about Elaine and Keith? They had a meeting with Webster in the pub afterwards.'

'Yeah. As I said, a conflict of interests. Annabel told me you'd a date with Keith. Blimey Vicky–' Pete gave a dirty laugh – 'you're really playing the field now. Anyway, Randall's vehicle was involved, so of course he did it.'

I was furious. 'Dave's got too much to lose. The Inter-Continental selection committee for Azerbaijan is coming–'

'They're coming here? When?'

'Wednesday. I thought you knew,' I said as I fell into the hole I'd dug for myself. 'It's not common knowledge.'

'Not common *knowledge!* Not common knowledge!' Pete screamed on the other end of the phone. 'Reporters don't wait for common knowledge! They look for breaking news – and this is breaking news.'

'I know. I'm sorry.' Maybe Probes had a point when he told me to question my loyalties. 'Dave wanted Boggins Leap to be kept quiet.'

'Boggins Leap? *Boggins Leap?*' I'd never known Pete so angry, and it was about to get worse. Where the bloody bollocks is Boggins Leap?'

For a moment I couldn't answer as the enormity of my mistake hit me. Even though Dave and I were definitely not a couple – nor would we ever be – I had let my personal feelings towards his ambitions get in the way of professional judgment.

'I messed up,' I said, the moment Pete stopped ranting to draw breath. 'I've seen Dave's secret hedge-jumping course at Boggins Leap–'

'Photos?' Pete snapped.

'Yes. Before and after,' I said. 'I'm on my way there now.'

'I want you back at the *Gazette*. Put Annabel on it, do you hear me?'

'Yes, sir.' I had no intention of doing any such thing – at least, not until I'd been there myself. 'But there's something else.'

'What?'

'We've got a new coroner. Ray Bailey–'

'Bloody hell! Not Ray Bailey? He's here? In Gipping-on-Plym?'

'It would appear so.'

'He's bloody famous.'

'Well, new facts have come to light and Ruth Reeves's burial has been cancelled tomorrow. There's going to be a full autopsy. My informer – that's Steve Burrows–'

'I thought he was Annabel's informer?'

'I'm afraid that was a case of wishful thinking,'

I said, wincing at the lie. 'Anyway, Steve suspects foul play.'

'From whom?' Pete said. 'I get that no one cares about Webster, but everyone loved Ruth.'

'What about Elaine Tully?' I'd seen her at John Reeves's house the night Ruth had fallen ill. I'd seen her hanging about Honeysuckle Lane and the Ponsford Ridge phone box, too. 'Don't you think it odd that she comes back to Gipping-on-Plym after forty years and suddenly there are *two* deaths?'

'You're saying there's a connection?' said Pete.

'I saw her in the pub last night flirting with John Reeves. She's had five husbands, maybe she wanted a sixth and Ruth was in the way.'

'Go on,' said Pete.

'Maybe, just maybe, there was rivalry between John Reeves and Jack Webster over Elaine Tully?'

'A bit of swinging going on,' said Pete with another dirty laugh. 'I like it. And you think it went sour.'

'Apparently Jack had been acting very suspiciously before he died.' I told Pete about the non-existent blackberries and the broken bottle of Asti Spumante near Dave's byre. '*And* he was trespassing. It bears all the signs of a secret rendezvous.'

'But you're missing something,' said Pete. 'Randall's Land Rover. How did that come to be at the scene of the crime?'

'Dave had left his keys in the ignition,' I said. 'Everyone knows that the cutters and jumpers despise one another. Maybe John Reeves took Dave's vehicle, deliberately ran down his rival and tried to frame Dave in the process.'

'I like it. *I like it!*' Pete shouted. 'You're a good reporter, Vicky.'

'You'll keep me on the case?'

'Get me something before noon, otherwise we'll run with Annabel's lead,' said Pete. 'Sorry, but that's the deal.'

Tap, tap, tap!

I looked up to see Probes rapping on my window. I must have driven to Honeysuckle Lane on autopilot because I couldn't remember pulling into the side of the road and cutting the engine.

I smiled and got out. He'd parked right behind my Fiat.

'This way,' I said.

We walked down the hill to the byre in silence. There was no one around. We'd never been alone together, and when I led the way over the stile, moving the branches aside to reveal the entrance of Boggins Leap, I began to feel nervous.

As we wove our way through the trees I could sense Probes following closely behind me. I could even hear his breathing. He only spoke once and that was to ask the meaning of the blue painted dots on the trees.

Finally we broke into the clearing.

'Oh, my God,' I whispered.

Dave had not been exaggerating. Boggins Leap had been completely destroyed with a chainsaw. The beautifully shaped hedges and splendid topiaries Dave had so lovingly cultivated were now no more than misshapen jagged pieces of wood. Calling it a massacre was accurate in every way. It was utterly shocking.

'How bad is this?' said Probes. I realized he had

no idea what Boggins Leap looked like before.

'I took photos.' I retrieved my iPhone and showed Probes.

'Bloody hell,' he gasped. 'Well, there's your motive.'

For the first time I doubted Dave's innocence.

'So, talk me through the landscape here?' Probes went on. 'Where is Randall's place and the Webster's Farm in relation to Boggins Leap?'

'We're here.' I set down a large stone then picked up a long stick. Scraping some leaves aside, I began to draw a rough map of the area. 'Access to Boggins Leap is either through the field we took and over the stile, or along this narrow bridleway that drops down from Honeysuckle Lane and passes Hugh's Folly.' I pointed to the tower that was just visible above the treetops.

'Got it.'

I went on drawing. 'This line *here* is Honeysuckle Lane. On either side we have Brooke Farm and Reeves Roost,' I set down two more stones, 'and Dairy Cottage, of course. *This* footpath from Dairy Cottage cuts across *this* field and down to Hugh's Folly. That's where Eunice said she heard Dave and Jack arguing.'

'And Randall's place?'

I drew another line from Dave's byre to Cricket Lodge. 'That bridleway is accessible by Land Rover.'

'The Grange?'

'Quite far from here.' I picked up another stone and placed it quite a distance from my crude little community.

Probes, arms akimbo, studied my map. 'Every-

215

one is closely linked by bridleways and footpaths,' he mused. 'And John Reeves, Jack Webster and Eunice Pratt don't like Randall.'

I nodded agreement. 'The cutters and jumpers have been feuding for years.'

'So it could be any one of those three who had access to Boggins Leap.'

'And who knew where to find it,' I said. 'But Dave took a lot of precautions. He made sure to cover the entrance with branches–'

'And mark the way with large daubs of blue paint,' said Probes drily.

'Well, yes.'

'I'll be honest, Vicky,' said Probes. 'It doesn't look good. Dave's got the perfect motive. He might face a charge of aggravated manslaughter, but the fact that he had to return to get his car from The Three Tuns car park makes it pre-meditated murder.'

'But how would Dave have known that Jack would be walking home on foot?' I said.

'Maybe you drove Dave back to the pub to pick up his Land Rover,' said Probes.

'But I didn't,' I said. 'I went back to get the keys and his Land Rover was gone when I got there.'

'Can you prove it?'

'Um. Well,' I swallowed. 'I did see Steve on my way back to the pub.'

'I presume you're talking about Steve Burrows,' said Probes. 'Where was this?'

'In a country lane,' I said wearily. 'He flagged me down.'

'Now, why would he do that?'

'He thought there was something fishy about

Ruth Reeves's death.' I met Probes's eyes and saw a flicker of amusement there. 'But you know that,' I said crossly, 'because it was *you* who drove past.'

'I just wanted to hear you admit it,' said Probes.

'Can we talk about something else? There are two people lying dead!'

'I am aware of that,' said Probes quietly. 'Why was Dave Randall in your car this morning?'

'When I left Factory Terrace, I saw Dave on a bicycle. He was very distressed and told me he'd discovered that Webster had cut down Boggins Leap.'

'This isn't Jack's work!' came a voice.

We spun around to find John Reeves emerge from the undergrowth.

'What the hell?' John roamed around the clearing, unable to stifle his horror at the carnage. 'This is barbaric! Amelia told me about Dave's accusations. Jack would never do this.'

'Good morning again, Mr Reeves,' said Probes, all politeness.

'He knows about Boggins Leap!' I exclaimed.

'What exactly are you implying?' John demanded.

'Why are you here?' I said.

'When we took Amelia back to Brooke Farm I saw your cars parked in the gateway,' said John. 'I heard the rumour about Dave's secret course and guessed you'd be looking into it, but I can tell you now, this is not the work of Jack Webster, one of the best hedge-cutters in England.' John Reeves was filled with such indignation that his walrus moustache quivered with fury.

'How can you be so sure?' said Probes.

'I know what this is!' He turned to us, eyes flashing with anger. 'This is a set-up. Those jumpers know they're losers and don't stand a chance at Azberjam–'

'It's pronounced Azerbaijan,' said Probes.

'I don't care how it's pronounced,' John fumed. 'They decided to sabotage their own course.'

'That's ridiculous,' I said.

'Do you own a chainsaw?' Probes asked.

'Of course I do,' said John Reeves. 'We all do.'

'And where were you between the hours of ten and two last night?'

'It's none of your damn business,' said John hotly.

'Just answer the question.'

'I was at home.'

'Can you prove it?'

'My wife has just died – have you no respect at all?'

'Did you hear a chainsaw last night?'

'A chainsaw? No. Why would I hear a chainsaw?'

Probes and I exchanged glances. 'You said someone had used a chainsaw here,' I pointed out. 'And given the proximity of your farm and that this is a valley, surely you must have heard something in the middle of the night.'

'I took a sleeping pill,' said John hastily. 'I've not been able to sleep since...'

'I'm sorry for your loss,' Probes said.

'But wait a minute...' John marched up to a fallen branch and studied it closely. Dropping it to the ground, he then marched to another and inspected that, too. 'This is utter nonsense!'

'Excuse me?' said Probes.

'Take a look,' said John. 'There are two basic types of saw teeth on modern handsaws–'

'You're saying it's a handsaw?'

'It would explain why no one heard a chainsaw in the night,' I pointed out.

'No, no!' said John impatiently. 'Whoever did this could have used a variety of saws and equipment. Look,' he said again. 'Crosscut teeth, as the name implies, are used to cut a piece of wood *across* the grain. Rip teeth are used to cut a piece of wood *along* the grain. See?'

I didn't.

'And then you've got your fleam tooth or bevel angle.' John seemed to be getting worked up. 'I would stake my reputation on it. This was done with shoddy equipment. None of my men are responsible for this. Randall is your man.'

'Presumably, whoever cut this down had to have lugged heavy equipment through the forest,' I said, 'or at least lived close by.'

Or used Dave Randall's carefully stowed equipment in the byre. But I wasn't going to tell either of them about that quite yet. I needed to check it for myself.

'What's that supposed to mean?' said John Reeves. 'Are you accusing me of being involved?'

'No. I'm just being logical.'

'Perhaps I could take a look at your hedge-cutting equipment?' said Probes smoothly.

'Be my guest,' said John.

'And Jack Webster's, too?' Probes added.

'Jack's Land Rover is still in The Three Tuns parking lot,' I said.

'Yes. His keys were still in his pocket,' said

219

Probes. 'We'll be taking the Land Rover down to the police station for examination.'

'Good,' said John. 'All right then. Let's go back to Reeves Roost, officer. I'll make us a cup of tea.'

I was about to say 'what about me?' but decided I'd rather stay behind. A lot of information had changed hands here this past hour and my mind needed to sift through it. I also wanted to check on Dave's byre and take a look at his equipment. Hopefully his chainsaw was as new as he'd claimed.

'Ms Hill,' said Probes, all business once more. 'I'm afraid I'm going to have to ask you to vacate the area.' He miraculously withdrew a roll of blue plastic crime-scene tape from his jacket pocket. 'This is now a potential crime scene and must be treated as such.'

'Of course,' I said brightly. Did he seriously think a piece of blue tape would keep me out?

All the same, I trooped after the men and ended up back at the byre. Spying the brass padlock still snapped shut, I said. 'I think I'll to do a spot of blackberry picking.'

'Blackberry picking?' said Probes.

'That's right,' I said. 'I'm moving house and I'd like to give my landlady a parting gift. According to Jack Webster, there are a ton of blackberries around here, isn't that right, John?'

John's expression darkened. 'There are no blackberries around here.'

'I've always thought that blackberries taste delicious with a glass of Asti Spumante.'

'I don't know what you're talking about,' John said coldly and stormed off, leaving Probes trying to keep up.

As I watched the pair climb the hill to pick up their vehicles in Honeysuckle Lane, I felt distinctly uneasy.

John's unexpected presence at Boggins Leap seemed a little too much of a coincidence. I also noticed his reaction when I'd mentioned Jack Webster, the blackberries and Asti Spumante. My earlier suspicion that Elaine was somehow involved deepened. Pete was onto something when he suggested a ménage à trois.

In my business as an investigative reporter, it was said that people got killed for four reasons: they have something, they heard something, they know something or they said something. If that was the case, maybe Dave was in danger, so it was just as well he was safely incarcerated at Gipping Police Station.

Right now, however, I needed to inspect Dave's equipment.

Chapter Twenty-Three

Picking the lock was easy. I pushed open the byre door and stepped inside. Thanks to the light coming from the small window in the gable end, I could make out Dave's tools arranged neatly across one wall on various brackets and hooks. He'd also made a little seating area with an old armchair and coffee table. There was no electricity, but there was a small primer gas stove set on top of an orange crate and two old-fashioned gas lamps. I spotted a kettle, mug, box of tea and sachets of Coffee-Mate and sugar. A square cake tin revealed a store-bought ginger loaf.

My tummy grumbled. I didn't need an excuse to make myself a cuppa and help myself to a slice of cake. Checking there was water in the kettle, I put it on to boil, lit the gas lamps and took a look around Dave's man-cave. It was actually quite cosy.

Fastened to the cross beam on one wall was an enormous sheet of paper showing detailed drawings of Boggins Leap. Dave had gone to a lot of trouble to build this course, and I couldn't imagine him sabotaging his own efforts, though it would definitely have given him a motive for murder.

I inspected Dave's tools – billhooks, loppers, a selection of axes, rulers and measuring sticks. There was a sawhorse and a long workbench next to one wall, upon which sat pots of paint, paintbrushes and coloured bunting, as well as a safety helmet with a visor.

In the corner was a huge canvas bag sporting the Husqvarna logo. Inside was Dave's chainsaw, its teeth protected by a hard plastic snap-on cover. The safety leaflet bore the copyright stamp of 2014. Whilst that discovery might put the chainsaw in the clear, it wouldn't necessarily help Dave.

The kettle boiled, and I made myself a passable cup of tea and ate a large slab of passable cake. Lounging in Dave's armchair I could see why Dave had been worried about Jack Webster stealing his tools. But why would Webster defy a court order when he had his own? Why would Webster want to break in *here*? I played the flashlight from my Mini-Maglite over the walls and that's when I saw it.

Tucked high on a wooden ledge was an upturned clay flowerpot. Dave had kept a spare key to Cricket Lodge under a flowerpot, maybe he kept another one here.

Curious, I stood on the sawhorse to reach the flowerpot. Yes! Underneath was a small key that could easily fit a padlock – only it didn't fit the padlock on Dave's byre door.

Why would Dave keep the wrong key under the flowerpot?

As a flock of birds flew overheard, I saw Hugh's Folly and had one of my epiphanies.

Moments later I had unlocked the padlock to the turret and was standing inside the empty circular room on the ground floor. I hadn't been in Hugh's Folly for over a year.

Whether it was the way the light shone through the gun-loops or the memory of what had transpired up top, the place gave me the creeps. I knew that Dave had had access to Hugh's Folly in the past, but why would he feel the need to padlock the empty turret now – unless he was hiding something.

I regarded the wrought-iron spiral staircase with trepidation. Taking a deep breath, I climbed the stairs, pausing to catch my breath at the top in front of the red velvet curtain. Was it possible that the love nest frequented by my former landlady, Mrs Poultry, was still there?

Slowly, I pulled the curtain aside and gave a

shudder of disgust. It was still there all right. I took in the deep purple cushions strewn over the floor and the circular mirror on the ceiling. There were half-burned candles but no signs of the sort of accessories that usually accompanied an illicit affair, such as wine glasses or vino – and then I remembered.

Jack Webster and his bottle of Asti Spumante! Jack Webster had been having an affair with Elaine Tully and John Reeves was jealous. My love-triangle theory was right!

No wonder Jack Webster had needed to get the key from Dave's byre. No wonder Dave had found him snooping around. But it wasn't about Boggins Leap, it was about getting the key to Hugh's Folly.

No – that didn't make sense. I sank down onto a purple cushion and thought hard – unless Jack had left something incriminating up here.

And then I saw it – tucked between two cushions was a black object. I leapt up and retrieved a Motorola disposable phone.

Unfortunately, the battery was dead, but I knew I could easily buy a power cord from This-and-That Emporium. Dave had his own mobile, so I had to assume that the one in my pocket belonged to Jack Webster, and that he didn't want anyone to know about it. I remembered when Mum found out that Dad had two mobile phones – one for his mistress. If I needed proof about his affair with Elaine, this was it.

Popping the mobile into my pocket I was startled when my iPhone rang and an unfamiliar number flashed up.

Vicky Hill,' I said. 'Who is this?'

'It's Topaz,' came a breathy voice.

'Your ladyship,' I said. 'Where are you calling from? This isn't your home number.'

'I've got a new mobile, and I'm undercover today,' said Topaz. 'I must see you immediately. Something terrible has happened.'

'Why?'

'It's *frightfully* important,' she said. 'It's about Jack Webster and that Elaine Tully woman.'

I was streets ahead of Topaz on that score. 'What's so important?'

'I met with her this morning and I want to show you something. It's made me very, *very* cross.'

'I can be at The Grange in twenty minutes.'

'No. Meet me outside Hugh's Folly.'

'Oh. Right. Great! I can be there in ten minutes.'

'I'll be there in five.'

I rang off, hurried downstairs, snapped the padlock back into place, popped the key in my pocket then sat on the stile to wait for Topaz to arrive.

I loved it when I was right. Jack Webster and Elaine Tully had been having an affair. But I didn't feel as excited as I should have. I checked my watch – it was gone noon. Too late for whatever revelations Topaz was about to share to make this Saturday's edition.

Minutes later, she was rattling the padlock on the door to Hugh's Folly. She'd discarded her lady-of-the-manor attire and was wearing leggings and a black sweater. I was always surprised at how skinny her legs were under all the ridiculous padding she insisted on wearing as her upper-class 'disguise'.

'How infuriating!' she exclaimed. 'Who padlocked this door? Now we can't go inside!'

For a moment I thought about mentioning the spare key I'd found under the flowerpot but decided it would only complicate things.

'I can pick the lock,' I said.

'Oh goody!' Topaz clapped her hands with glee. 'I must say I've missed all this excitement. I'm thinking about getting back into the game. It's frightfully boring running a country estate. All I do is open fetes and give trophies to Morris dancers.'

As I deftly picked the lock, Topaz droned on about her 'tenants' and how she hated feeling 'needed'.

'And everyone is complaining about my decision to cancel the reception after the worm festival,' she grumbled on. 'Annabel Lake says she knows the Spat urns are still in Gipping-on-Plym.'

'She's not still going on about *that?*' I said.

'Apparently she's been talking to criminals who know The Fog very well.'

'Honestly, Topaz,' I said. 'You don't want to believe everything Annabel says. Those urns are probably in America by now.'

'We're going to do this house-to-house search,' said Topaz. 'Rather like a treasure hunt.'

'Good luck with that,' I said. 'And where are you going to do this so-called treasure hunt?'

'Well, Annabel claimed the urns are near Uncle Hugh's old wool and textile factory in Factory Terrace.'

'Factory Terrace,' I squeaked. 'Why would Annabel say that?'

'Because she used to live around there, too,' said

226

Topaz. 'She made me promise not to tell anyone but I thought, since *you* still live in Factory Terrace, you might have heard something?'

'I think she's delusional,' I said firmly. 'Believe me, if anything was going on in Factory Terrace, I'd know about it.'

'That's what I thought,' said Topaz. 'I told her if she could locate the Spat urns by midnight tomorrow–'

'The search starts *tomorrow?*' Shocked, I instantly dropping the lock pick set.

'Oops, butterfingers,' said Topaz. 'As I was saying, I would still hold the post-festival reception at The Grange.'

I hoped Topaz couldn't read the horror on my face. 'What a great idea.'

I had to move the urns tonight! I had to! 'Are you sure you can do that search – legally, I mean?'

'Annabel said she'd take care of that. And, of course, with Amelia Webster's silver being stolen as well, we'll hunt for that, too,' said Topaz. 'It'll be super fun.'

'There, done it,' I said and removed the padlock from the door.

We stepped inside. I had to remind myself that as far as Topaz was concerned, I'd never been there before.

'Yes, my Great-Uncle Hugh had this built,' Topaz was saying. 'I used to play here with Cousin Colin when I was a girl. We decorated it as an Arabian tent. It was *frightfully* good fun in the school holidays. Colin used to dress up as a sheik and I was in his harem. He looked quite dashing, actually.'

'Isn't that illegal?' I said. 'First cousins and all that?'

Topaz hooted with laughter. 'Honestly, Vicky, everyone in the Royal family is related. I told you Colin and I had a thing for each other.'

I had suspected that, but even so I was surprised to feel a stab of jealousy.

'Come on. Up we go.' I followed Topaz up the spiral staircase. She stopped at the top and gazed out of the mullioned window. 'Well, what do you think?'

'Whatever's behind the red curtain?' I said, feigning innocence.

'Oh, nothing much. Just cushions and stuff,' said Topaz impatiently. 'Look! Can't you see them?'

'What am I supposed to be looking at?'

Topaz grabbed my shoulders and steered me over to the window. 'There! *There!*'

My stomach did a funny flip as I looked out on a spectacular view of a sparkling river running through a field of wild flowers. Five turbines stood on the horizon and, although the almond trees weren't in blossom, I knew. 'That's Angel's Rise.'

'Exactly!' Topaz exclaimed. 'Angel's Rise! Angel's *Rise!*' She pulled Elaine's photograph out of her leggings and handed it to me. It felt unnervingly warm.

'See?' Topaz demanded.

'The photograph must have been taken from up here,' I said. 'But I don't understand.'

'I'm going to prosecute, you know.'

'What did Elaine say when you confronted her?' I asked. 'Presumably that was why you met with her this morning?'

228

'She said she bought the field from Jack Webster based on this photograph.'

It certainly explained why Jack hadn't wanted to show Elaine and Keith the real location of the field.

'But Jack must have known he'd be found out.'

'That's what I said, but apparently she thinks Jack didn't know who he was selling the field to.'

'How could he not have known?'

'Apparently,' said Topaz, 'The Green Reaper advertised in *Farmers of Fortune* magazine, but under Elaine's married name of DiCaprio.' Topaz thought for a moment. 'I wonder if there is any relation to Leonardo?'

'I doubt it,' I said. 'So Jack never made the connection?'

'Not at first.'

'But *she* did when she recognized his name and Gipping-on-Plym,' said Topaz. 'And it was because of that connection that she trusted him.'

So that was why Jack had freaked out over Elaine's return to Gipping-on-Plym. He realized the cat would soon be out of the bag. Maybe there *was* no affair.

'When did Elaine find out that the land belonged to you and not to Jack?'

'This morning,' said Topaz. 'She was *frightfully* upset. She cried. It was so embarrassing. She said she'd already sold off some burial plots to a family from Romford in Essex.'

'But why would Jack Webster try to fob off your land as his own?' I said. 'It doesn't make sense.'

'Well, it is prettier,' said Topaz. 'But it doesn't matter. They still *bought* a field – only it isn't mine.'

It certainly gave Elaine and Keith a reason to be angry with Jack Webster, but was it enough of a reason for murder?

'I told her to go straight to Brooke Farm,' said Topaz.

'You haven't heard, have you?' I said.

Topaz frowned. 'Heard about what?'

'Jack Webster's dead,' I said. 'He was hit by a car.'

'Oh. How infuriating!' Topaz folded her arms in a huff. 'I'll have to talk to Amelia myself now and sort this mess out.' Topaz paused and then said, 'Whose car?'

'The police are still looking into it,' I lied.

As we parted ways and Topaz walked back to The Grange, I returned to my car deep in thought. Jack had risked prosecution by trespassing on Grange land; he'd even bought a padlock for Hugh's Folly and kept the key in Dave's byre. What had prompted him to take a photograph of something that didn't belong to him? He must have been paid a fair sum for Angel's Rise, and much as Amelia's diamond eternity ring looked like a good one, it definitely didn't equate to the going rate for agricultural land, which was about £6,000 an acre.

On the telly, detectives are always told to 'follow the money', and that's exactly what I intended to do.

Chapter Twenty-Four

Friday afternoons were always slow at the *Gipping Gazette*, and they usually included dandelion wine and some nibbly things accompanied by a bit of Frank Sinatra on Barbara's portable CD player – but not today.

When I entered reception the dandelion wine hadn't been opened and there were no snacks lined up on the counter.

'Are you all right?' I asked Barbara, who was immersed in a book. 'What are you reading?'

'*Fifty Shades of Grey*,' she said. 'I must say there isn't anything new or original in it.'

'How is Amelia?' I said. 'Have you spoken to her?'

'No. But John just called and said she's resting.' The reception doorbell dinged. 'Oh God help us. Here comes Olive.'

Olive entered carrying a Tesco shopping bag in each hand. Today, her bottomless 1970s wardrobe had produced a pair of plaid trousers, a matching polo neck sweater and a Tam o'Shanter cap perched on top of her sleek silver bob.

'Is it true that Jack Webster was mown down like a pheasant?' she blurted out.

'I'm afraid so,' I said.

'Do you have to say it like that?' Barbara cried.

'Isn't it sad,' said Olive. 'Still, at least Jack gave her the eternity ring before he got run over.'

231

'Do we have to talk about it?' said Barbara. 'It's very upsetting.'

'Although Eunice told me the ring was too large.' Olive paused to think. 'I wonder where he got the money from? They were strapped for cash, you know.'

'You're a terrible gossip, Olive,' Barbara snapped.

I hadn't considered Olive as a source of information.

'Maybe he sold something?' I said slyly. 'A piece of land, perhaps?'

'Oh no,' said Olive. 'Amelia would never agree to that. *Never.*'

'I think we should stop talking about Jack and Amelia Webster,' Barbara declared. 'Let's talk about something else.'

'I heard that it was Dave Randall who did it,' Olive persisted. 'Mowed him down then crushed him against a tree.'

'Olive, if you don't stop gossiping I'll make sure you get the sack.'

'Barbara!' I exclaimed as Olive gasped in dismay. 'What's the matter with you?'

'I told you I don't want to talk about it.' She flung the flap of the counter up, passed through and let it go with a crash. 'Excuse me. I need to be alone with my grief.' Then she flounced off to the nook and ducked behind the star-spangled curtain.

Tears welled in Olive's eyes. 'I didn't mean to upset her.'

'Have you brought some nibbly things?' I asked.

Olive nodded.

'Let's get this set up on the counter, shall we?' I suggested and took the plastic bags.

With painstaking slowness, Olive retrieved white paper plates followed by a red fluted pie dish with a raised chicken head. It was filled with pineapple, ham and cheese cubes on cocktail sticks.

I stared at the dish. A peculiar feeling swept over me. 'Where did you get that?' I said sharply.

'Pardon?' Olive turned red.

'Really, Olive!' Barbara materialized behind us. 'It's cracked. The dish is *cracked* right down the middle. You found that at the tip, didn't you?' Barbara rolled her eyes and pulled a face. 'She's always going through other people's rubbish.'

'Ronnie brought it home,' Olive faltered. 'Every day he brings me home a present.'

'Other people's cast-offs, you mean.'

The dish belonged to Amelia Webster, I was sure of it, and the last time I'd seen it was in Ruth Reeves's kitchen. I distinctly remembered Amelia saying that she'd had a set of fluted pie dishes and that they had belonged to her mother, so it was hardly something she'd have thrown out deliberately.

Why had John Reeves not returned it? Why had he thrown it out?

Before I could dwell any longer on the pie dish, Elaine swept into the office with a face as black as thunder.

'Ah, Elaine,' I said. 'Excellent timing. You're just the person I want–'

'Where's Wilf?' she asked. 'I must talk to him.'

Barbara bridled. 'Why?'

Elaine slapped a brown manila envelope down

on the counter, making Olive jump. 'Because I want this story on page one tomorrow. I've been ripped off! That's why!'

'It's too late,' said Barbara somewhat smugly. 'The paper's done. It'll have to go into next week's edition.'

Olive started to titter; it was an annoying habit she had whenever tension was rife.

Elaine shot her a furious look. 'I don't know what you find funny, Olive.'

Olive tittered all the more.

'I suppose you were in on it, Barbara,' Elaine exclaimed, 'as usual.'

Barbara stuck out her jaw. 'I don't know what you're talking about.'

'Is this about Angel's Rise?' I said, quickly sensing a catfight. 'Topaz – I mean, her ladyship – told me there had been some confusion about the photograph you used at the Women's Institute for the burial field.'

'No. I was not confused,' Elaine snapped. 'Jack Webster posted that photograph to me and told me it was the field I'd purchased. It was a deliberate misrepresentation.'

'So what did you purchase?' I asked.

'Apparently, I've purchased Black Crow Dell.'

'Oh dear.' The words were out before I could stop them. 'I am so sorry.' Olive's tittering had reached fever pitch.

'Black Crow Dell!' Barbara exclaimed. 'Yes, you've definitely been ripped off.'

This put a different spin on things. Black Crow Dell was a useless plot of land that was part marshland, part field and covered in ragwort,

234

stinging nettles and dock leaves. Jack had tried to rent it out to neighbouring farmers on more than one occasion. Twice he'd been hauled over by the local magistrate following incidents of cows getting stuck, and once a rambler had nearly drowned.

'Maybe it wasn't Dave Randall who ran poor Jack over,' Barbara cried. 'Maybe it was *you!*'

'What's wrong with Jack?' Elaine cried.

'He's dead,' Olive burst out. 'Mown down like a pheasant.'

Elaine's jaw dropped. She turned so white that I thought she was going to faint.

'I think we should take this conversation somewhere private,' I said. 'Elaine? Shall we go outside?'

'Jack Webster is dead?' Elaine said again. Her face crumpled and she sank into the ugly brown leatherette chair. 'Oh God no.'

My ears pricked up. Elaine seemed very upset – almost too upset. Maybe I'd been right about their affair, after all.

'So the rumour was true?' Barbara regarded her with disgust. 'Amelia suspected Jack was having an affair. She wrote to my column.'

'Don't be ridiculous. It was *years* ago!' Elaine shouted. 'I know you don't like me, Barbara Meadows. You never have. You're nothing but a horrible, mean-spirited cow.'

Barbara gasped.

Olive tittered.

'How dare you say that about me!' Barbara snatched up a handful of pineapple, ham and cheese cubes and threw them at Elaine. Olive

235

screamed and scurried into the nook. There was a crash as worm-charming paraphernalia clattered to the ground.

'Ladies! Ladies!' I shouted. 'Please! This is not a school playground.'

'I'm finished with the lot of you,' Elaine said coldly. 'I hope you all have miserable lives.' And she swept imperiously over to the counter, picked up her envelope and stormed outside.

'Elaine – wait!' I raced after her, but she had already scrambled into her Audi TT Quattro and sped off, oblivious to the cacophony of enraged motorists sounding their horns.

Seconds later, Keith's Tercel pulled into her vacated space. He leapt out and ran towards me, shouting, 'Where's Mum?'

'Been and gone,' I said. 'I suppose you've heard.'

'About Jack Webster. Yes, just now. Vicky, you and I need to talk.'

Chapter Twenty-Five

'About last night,' I began as we took a table by the window at The Warming Pan.

'Forget it,' said Keith with a dismissive wave. 'I told you, we've all got pasts – just don't play games or lie, that's all I ask.'

'But it was about work,' I protested. And it had been. Hadn't Steve told me all about Ruth's dying words?

'What the hell is going on?'

236

'I could ask you the same question,' I said. 'You saw Jack Webster last night.'

'If you think we had anything to do with his death, you're wrong.'

'Tell me what you know.'

'After you left with Dave–'

'I am sorry. Truly.'

'Mum and I went outside with Jack to the beer garden.'

'Whatever for?'

'He didn't want to be overheard in the pub – and now we know why.'

'And then what happened?'

'Mum and I went back inside.'

'Leaving Jack outside?'

'He went to the Gents',' said Keith.

'Did you see Amelia, his wife, at all?'

Keith shook his head. 'I waited for you. You didn't show up. I left.'

'So you went home.'

'No. I went out.'

'Out? Out *where?*'

'Just out,' said Keith.

'And Elaine? Where did she go?'

I have no idea. I left Mum talking to John Reeves about the celebration of life–'

'Which is no longer happening because there's going to be an autopsy.'

'So I heard. Mum's upset about that, too.'

'The autopsy? Why?'

'Well, we've spent a lot of money,' said Keith. 'Mum wanted it to be really special so that her old friends could see what The Green Reaper can offer.'

'So you don't know what time Elaine came home?'

'Nope.'

'I thought you shared the same house.'

Keith just looked at me. 'We do.'

'The police will definitely want to know your alibis.'

'Well. We don't have any,' said Keith. 'That's what I wanted to tell you.'

I looked at Keith who looked stonily out of the window. Was he involved in Jack's death, after all?

'How did you find out about Black Crow Dell?' Topaz had already told me that Elaine had no idea until this morning. 'From Jack?' It was a trick question.

'I found it in the contract,' said Keith. 'When Mum spoke to her ladyship and learned that the field in question was not the one she'd purchased, we looked up the topographic coordinates on an ordnance survey map. Mum went to look at it this morning.'

'Oh.'

'I *told* her not to buy anything sight unseen,' Keith said with despair. 'But she wouldn't listen. She *trusted* Jack Webster. Said they were old friends.'

'The Green Reaper is registered in your mother's married name of DiCaprio, isn't it?'

'So?'

'Perhaps Jack hadn't realized who he'd sold the land to,' I said. 'He never expected to see Elaine again.'

Keith nodded slowly. 'You're right.'

'How did he hear about the company?'

'We advertise online and in farming magazines. We had a big spread in *Farmers of Fortune* – that's when Jack Webster contacted us. Mum recognized his name and got all excited about moving back to Devon. Then she met Herman Whittler at Disney World and he told her that "home is where the heart is".'

'How did the money change hands?'

'He called me on a payphone,' said Keith. 'We arranged to rendezvous at Taunton cattle market. I met him there and gave him cash.'

'Can I ask how much you paid him?'

'Fifteen thousand pounds for two acres of land.'

'Fifteen *thousand*.' I felt a rush of adrenalin. I was right. It was far more than the diamond eternity ring.

'I told you. He was buying a houseboat.'

We sipped our tea in silence. My mind was working overtime.

'People are always ripping Mum off,' said Keith suddenly. 'They see her coming. She tries these get-rich-quick schemes and they always fail. Then she goes and marries someone, thinking that's the answer.'

And I thought my parents were bad!

'Do you think your mother ran down Jack Webster, Keith?' I said. 'Honestly, I'd understand if she had.'

'She's got a temper but...' he shrugged, 'she couldn't have done it last night. Just take my word for it.'

'And what about you?'

'Don't be daft!' Keith bent down and kissed the inside of my wrist, sending shivers up my arm. I

239

snatched my hand away and he laughed. 'Before all this drama happened this morning I was on my way to give you some good news.'

'I could do with some good news.'

'Yes. Let's forget about all this for a while.' Keith gestured for the waitress to bring the bill. 'We're going on an adventure.'

'Where?'

'Go and get your car, you silly thing. I've got a surprise for you.'

Chapter Twenty-Six

The moment Keith's Tercel turned into Mudge Lane my heart began to pound. Commonly known as 'smooch' lane, it had earned its romantic reputation because of a kissing gate that stood on a raised pedestrian walkway over a ford.

I couldn't believe that Keith was making his intentions so blatant – and in broad daylight, too – or was there an ulterior motive?

I stopped my car at the top of the drop. Was I being a fool? Was I committing the most stupid mistake of all: following a stranger into an isolated spot? Was I being TDTL too dumb to live? What did I really know about Keith Calloway – or whatever his real name was?

If he and his mother had been involved in Jack Webster's demise, Keith would hardly admit it to me.

As I hummed and hawed about whether or not

to follow him down the hill. Keith's brake lights flared and he reversed towards me. He got out and waved.

'It's not too steep,' he called out. 'Just take it slowly.' He pointed to the two triangular road-warning signs that flanked the entrance – one showed a vehicle being submerged in water; the other a cyclist being knocked over by a car. Of course, I already knew the dangers along this stretch of road as I'd been here before, but even so.

'When you get to the bottom,' Keith went on, 'whatever you do, don't stop. Drive through the water quickly and up the other side, OK? Look out for a hidden farm track on your right.'

'Drive *through* the ford?' So we weren't stopping at the kissing gate after all? Look out for a farm *track?*

'Don't look so scared!' Keith grinned. 'It's easy.'

Keith got back into his Tercel and plunged over the brow of the hill.

Once I started the descent I was committed. There was no turning back. I could only continue down. Keith reached the bottom, tore through and up the other side, and disappeared around a hairpin bend.

I continued to follow and floored the engine to make the climb out. Water mushroomed up the windows on either side, but I got through and sped up the opposing hill. I almost missed the farm track, but yes, there was the Tercel sitting waiting for me – like a praying mantis. Get a grip Vicky!

Keith gave the horn a few cheerful beeps and

sped off again; this time the track had grass running through the middle of it. I followed closely behind, wondering where on earth we were going.

We rounded yet another bend and stopped in front of an old farm building containing bales of rotting straw and the usual assortment of rusting farm machinery.

Now I was really worried.

I liked to think that I knew all the farms in Gipping-on-Plym, but I had never been here before.

I had made the most terrible mistake. I reached for my iPhone and groaned. Of course there wouldn't be a signal!

Keith jumped out of the car and hurried towards me, smiling like a Cheshire cat – hardly the expression of a killer – and wrenched open my car door. He was trembling with excitement. 'Come on, come on!'

I was reluctant to get out. 'Where are we?'

'We took a short-cut.' He grabbed my hand and dragged me out. 'This way!'

He pulled me behind him at a fast walk around the side of the old barn. I tried hard to yank my hand away.

'Vicky!' he said. 'What's wrong with you? It's a surprise.' He gave a snort of disgust and dropped my hand. 'Have it your way,' and promptly stomped off and out of sight.

Unsure what to do, I found myself following, but paused at the corner of the old barn.

'Oh,' I whispered.

He was standing in the middle of a very smart courtyard surrounded by beautifully renovated farm buildings, all with matching green stable doors and window boxes filled with winter pansies. We'd entered from a farm track. On the opposite side of the courtyard was a grand driveway, and beyond that stood a large farmhouse.

Keith regarded me with annoyance. 'Well?'

'Why are we here?'

'We're here because this is where I live,' Keith said, exasperated. 'These are holiday cottages.'

'Oh.' It was only now that I took in the names, neatly painted on green placards: The Piggery, The Bullpen, The Chicken Coop and The Hayloft.

He began to laugh. 'Seriously, Vicky. What did you think I was going to do? Get out my chainsaw and chop off your head?'

'Not funny,' I said tightly. To be honest, I felt foolish.

'Don't ever do that again. Jack Webster was killed last night–'

'You think ... oh...' He began to laugh.

'I'm leaving.' I turned on my heel and set off back down the path.

'Vicky! Wait!' Keith raced after me and grabbed my arm. 'Look, I'm sorry, OK. I didn't think. Don't spoil the surprise. Please?'

Reluctantly, I let him lead me to a small two-storey square building tucked behind The Piggery. A flight of stone steps ran up the outside of the structure to a wooden hatch above. 'This is The Granary because ... guess...'

'It used to be a granary,' I said drily.

'Correct.' Keith removed a key from under a flowerpot on the front step. Did *everyone* in the countryside leave keys in such obvious places?

'After you.' He unlocked the door and threw it

open. 'I'd carry you over the threshold if we were married.'

My stomach began to churn again. So this was it. The big seduction at last! After all these years of wishing and wanting and hoping, now the time was really here. It wasn't exactly how I imagined it would be, but all the same.

'Take a look around,' said Keith, who just wouldn't stop grinning.

Downstairs was open plan. It was small, but light and sparsely furnished with a sofa, Victorian pine table with four matching chairs and a bookcase filled with worn paperbacks and a small flat-screen television. A narrow counter separated the area from a galley kitchen with pine cabinets, a built-in refrigerator, washing machine and a four-ring gas stove. Beyond an open door I caught a glimpse of a white bathroom.

There was a wood burner stove in front of an L-shaped cream sofa, and in the corner was a wrought-iron spiral staircase leading to a mezzanine level.

The bedroom.

'Go up and take a look,' Keith said with a wink.

'It's OK. I'm fine here.' I was changing my mind about this seduction lark. It seemed so calculated. Where were the candles? Where was the soft music? And I definitely needed at least a bottle of champagne for Dutch courage.

'Do you have anything to drink?' I said.

'Not here, but I've got some wine at The Gables?'

'The Gables?'

'Yes. Mum and I live at the main house. It's

called The Gables,' said Keith. 'This is The Granary. *You're* going to be living here.'

I was stunned. 'But ... I don't understand.'

'I told the landlord that a friend of mine needed somewhere to stay for the winter.'

'I don't know what to say.' Then reality hit me: I couldn't afford it.

'It's free, Vicky,' said Keith, as if reading my mind. 'You'll have to move out in the spring, but for right now, this place is yours. It would have been left empty otherwise.'

'I don't know what to say,' I said again. No one had ever done such a nice thing for me ever. The Granary was adorable. I couldn't believe I was swapping Sadie's room with her tacky black satin sheets for somewhere so sophisticated; there was even a washing machine and flat-screen TV!

'There has to be a catch,' I said suddenly. In Dad's book, no one does this kind of favour without expecting something in return, but if it was sex, then maybe it wouldn't be so bad. He was nice. He was kind. He liked his mother and he didn't have a prison record. 'Why are you doing this for me?'

'Because I like you,' he said simply. 'We're kindred spirits. There aren't many people in the world like us, Vicky Hill.'

I found myself blushing and only just managed to stop myself from blurting out, *I think I love you.* 'Thank you.'

Keith pulled me into his arms and kissed me gently on the lips. I felt a rush of pleasure – not the mind-blowing dizziness that came from Steve's kisses, but I quite liked it, even though his hands were cold and his lips rather thin.

Keith broke away. 'Mum knew you and I would get on,' he said happily. 'It's hard to find someone who really understands you, don't you think?'

'Yes.' I wanted to kiss him again, but he shook his head. 'No. Later. Why don't we go back to your place now and pack up your stuff?'

'Definitely,' I said, but then I remembered. I had to take care of the Spat urns. 'Tomorrow is better.'

'OK. Tomorrow for that, but tonight we're going to go out celebrating.'

'Let's celebrate tomorrow as well,' I said quickly. 'I need to... I'd like to spend my last night with my landlady. She's been so kind to me.'

'Yeah, I get it. I can wait.' Keith gave a big happy sigh. 'But at least let me show you something.'

'Right now?' I said. 'I need to get back to the office.'

'It'll just take a minute.'

It was gradually sinking in. I had place of my own and I was beginning to get excited. In fact, I was so excited I thought I'd burst. 'Yes. Of course.'

'But it's at my place – The Gables.'

'Yes. Great. Wonderful. Let's go!'

We walked across the courtyard. I looked back at the little house and just couldn't believe my luck. Who would have thought that this time last night my life had been practically over? I'd had betrayals all round, was about to be evicted and my frenemy had stolen all my informers; now life was almost perfect. Mum always said that you never knew what was around the corner and, as usual, she was right.

Hand-in-hand we strolled up the path to The

Gables. It bore the same green-painted doors with window boxes full of winter pansies. As its name implied, the house was heavily gabled and reminded me of The Grange with its gargoyles and leaded light windows. 'Was this part of The Grange estate at some time?'

Keith shrugged. 'No idea.'

I pointed to the long drive that vanished over the horizon.

'Where does the drive come out?' I asked.

'Ponsford Cross,' said Keith.

Which was why I'd seen Elaine in the area so often.

Keith opened the front door and waved me inside.

'It's really nice,' I said, taking in the simple interior with the same colour scheme as The Granary only a bigger version. It had that same sterile feel with no homely touches or family photographs, although there was a beautiful floral wreath lying on the kitchen table.

'We've got all our furniture in storage,' said Keith, yet again showing an uncanny knack for reading my thoughts. 'That wreath would have been the centrepiece for tomorrow's celebration of life. Mum had to donate all the food she'd made to Gipping Hospital.'

'That was good of her.'

'She put a lot of work into it.'

'Who owns this place?'

'Someone with a lot of money.'

Of course I knew that Devon was a tourist destination and many farmers had converted outbuildings to holiday cottages, but I was still surprised I didn't know the owner.

'Four bedrooms. Three bathrooms. Place sleeps ten,' Keith went on. 'I'll show you my room.'

Keith took my hand and we went up the stairs. His room was the first on the right. I started to feel nervous again.

The first thing I noticed was a large bed with the most curious headboard ... until I realized what it was: a mock lichen-flecked headstone inscribed with the words *Here Lies Keith Calloway: Truth to Your Own Spirit.*

Seeing my look of surprise Keith said, 'Yeah. I wasn't going to put *that* into storage. I found it at one of those flea markets in Somerset.'

'It's great,' I said, but to be honest I found it a bit disturbing.

'I stole the epitaph from Jim Morrison's grave,' Keith went on. 'Have you been to Père Lachaise in Paris?'

'I don't know that restaurant.'

'Very funny.' He laughed. 'You're kidding me, right?'

'No I'm not,' I said. 'I've never left England.'

'Then you're in for a treat! We've got so much to see together.' Keith swept me into his arms and spun me around in a happy dance. 'Let's go to Europe together.'

'Seriously?' Keith's enthusiasm was contagious. 'I love travelling, don't you?'

'I've been to London – and to Edinburgh, once.'

'Highgate, yeah?' said Keith. 'And Greyfriars Kirkyard?'

'Um. Where?'

'Because they're two of the coolest cemeteries

in the whole of the United Kingdom!'

I smiled and nodded as he talked about his obsession for cemeteries. He seemed to exhibit the same passion for his hobby as Dave Randall did for his hedge-jumping dream. For a split-second, I remembered that poor Dave had been accused of murder, but it was hard to think about Dave's plight when I was being treated to a litany of Keith's favourite graveyards. I had a sinking feeling as it started to dawn on me why the gallant, chivalrous, kindly Keith was still single and living with his mother.

'So I'm writing a book,' Keith gushed on. He steered me over to the opposite wall, which was covered by a black curtain. I'd thought it hid a window, but apparently not. With a quick swoosh, Keith swept back the curtain to reveal a collage of coloured photographs of tombstones, headstones and mausoleums. Some had been taken during the daytime; most at night.

'Guess what my subject is?' He grinned.

'Cemeteries?'

'Correct!' He clapped his hands. 'The title is *Cemetery Crawlers.* It's a taphophile handbook – you know, for tombstone tourists.'

'Wow!'

'Do you belong to the A.G.R?'

'I don't think so.'

'The Association of Graveyard Rabbits. "Among the graves in the gloom and gleam, content to dwell where dead men dream." Frank Lebby Stanton said that,' Keith rambled on. 'I want to get in the *Guinness Book of Records.* I want to photograph every single churchyard in England.'

'Oh.' Could my disappointment get any more acute?

'That's where I was last night,' he said. 'St Winifred's Church in Branscombe. Dates back to 995.'

I had a sudden thought: 'And you say when you go cemetery crawling that you're there *all* night?'

'I should have been a vampire.'

I laughed with fake heartiness. 'You took photographs?'

'Yep. They're still in my camera. I've got to upload them.'

'So you can prove you were there?'

'Of course. All my photos are date-and-time stamped.'

'So you do have an alibi,' I said. 'Why on earth didn't you tell me?'

Keith looked sheepish. 'I had to be sure that you wouldn't think I was a freak.'

'Oh.'

He slipped his arms around my waist and began nuzzling my ear. 'It takes a special woman to understand a man like me.'

'It sure does.'

'I think we're soulmates.'

'Oh,' I said again, but to be honest my ardour was rapidly fizzling out. I was also having second thoughts about my new living arrangements, but as things stood, I didn't have another option – at least not right now.

I wriggled away from his grasp, but Keith frogmarched me to the other end of the room, where another, smaller noticeboard had squares of tracing paper covered in charcoal markings.

'I really must get back to the office,' I said. 'In

case you've forgotten, there was a murder this morning.'

'Gravestone rubbings,' he said, 'And that–' he gestured to a huge leather album on the dresser. 'In there are details of famous people and how they died. I've got a section on serial killers.'

'Sounds lovely.'

'And this.' Keith opened a drawer and pulled out *another* leather-bound book with the ghoulish title, *Death Masks*. 'My Victorian death-mask postcard collection.'

'I really have to go,' I said, edging my way to the door. He grabbed me again and kissed me gently.

'I promise I'll let you go if you do one tiny thing for me.'

'Fine.'

'Will you just lay on my bed and pretend you're dead?'

I was struck dumb. For a full minute all I could do was force one of Barbara's cartoonish smiles. 'Maybe tomorrow?'

'Yeah. Yeah, tomorrow,' said Keith. 'Sorry. Was I moving too fast? You're not freaked out are you? Oh, you are.'

He seemed so childlike in his enthusiasm that I felt a pang of guilt. 'Not at all.' I flashed another Barbara smile. 'As I said, got to go.'

A car roared up the drive and screeched to stop outside. I heard the car door slam hard.

'It's Mum!' Keith dashed to the window. 'Must talk to her.'

'Go ahead,' I said quickly. 'Don't worry about me. I'll see myself out.'

Keith tore down the stairs, leaving me alone in

251

his mausoleum. I knew now without a doubt that whatever relationship I'd fantasized about having with him was – no pun intended – well and truly dead.

Given that St Winifred's Church in Branscombe was a good twenty miles from Gipping-on-Plym, at least he was in the clear regarding the murder of Jack Webster. His mother, however, was not.

I tiptoed down the stairs and headed towards the sound of raised voices coming from the kitchen.

'Black Crow Dell is nothing more than a bog,' I heard Elaine say. 'Ragwort, dock leaves and stinging nettles. Poisonous plants everywhere – and don't you *dare* say I told you so.'

I couldn't hear Keith's response, but judging from his tone he was trying to placate her.

'I went to see Amelia but she refused to answer the door,' Elaine raged on. 'I even saw her hiding under the kitchen table! That's typical of her. Typical. She was always so stuck up; always thought she was better than the rest of us because she went to Cheltenham Ladies' College.'

'We still have a field, Mum,' said Keith.

Elaine blew her nose. 'I know. But who wants to get buried there? It's awful. I'll have to give those people in Essex their money back.'

'Mum, it's not the end of the world,' said Keith.

'We can never use it. It's useless.'

But I could.

Black Crow Dell would be the perfect place to bury the Spat urns! And no one would think to look for them there.

Thank you, Elaine!

I was just about to go when I heard Keith say,

252

'Have you spoken to the police yet?'

'Why?'

'Because there's a murder investigation, mother, that's why. They'll want to know where you were last night.'

'I thought they had someone in custody,' said Elaine. 'That hedge-jumping chappy.'

'They want to eliminate everyone from their inquiries.'

'So? We were together.'

'But we weren't, Mum, were we?' There was a long pause. 'Vicky knows I was at St Winifred's.'

'Why did you tell her?' Elaine seemed horrified.

'Because she asked and I was...' There was another long pause. 'Where were you, Mum?'

'It's none of your business!'

'I knew it! You did it, didn't you?'

'I don't have to answer questions from you!'

'Don't run away from me!' Keith yelled.

Heavy footsteps thundered towards me. I took off, raced to the front door and out into the drive. I didn't look back – just ran down the path and back to my car.

As I headed back to Factory Terrace my mind was spinning. Elaine Tully was guilty and Keith knew it. She'd as good as admitted it. She must have stolen Dave's Land Rover to mow Jack down and frame Dave in the process. Now all I had to do was prove it.

I stopped at the police station on my way home, but was told in no uncertain terms that Dave Randall – who was due to be arraigned first thing Monday morning – was not allowed to receive any visitors.

However, I did manage to give Dave a message, telling him not to lose hope and to keep fit enough for his meeting with the Inter-Continental selection committee on Wednesday – Boggins Leap or no Boggins Leap.

DC Bond snagged me, however, and insisted on taking a full statement regarding my movements on Thursday night and early Friday morning.

'Detective Inspector Probes wants *all* the details,' he said with a meaningful wink. 'He told me to tell you he would be verifying your story.'

I put in a call to Pete as well to tell him about my findings but, just as I'd expected, he said that without proof, it was all just hearsay.

Meanwhile, I had far more important matters to attend to.

Having packed up my bedroom I climbed into bed fully clothed and set my alarm for 2 a.m.

Chapter Twenty-Seven

'A special fry-up just for you,' said Mrs Evans as I walked into the kitchen bleary-eyed. I hadn't got to bed until gone four. 'Sausages, mushrooms, fried eggs, fried bread and fried tomatoes.'

'Sounds perfect.' The stuff of heart attacks, but I didn't care. The urns were safe in Black Crow Dell and my night-time manoeuvres had gone off without a hitch. Of course, I had a black plastic bin liner full of filthy clothes – Elaine hadn't been exaggerating about it being marshy – but I'd soon

254

be able to wash them in my very own washing machine!

During the long dark hours of muddy manual labour, I had thought about how Elaine could have done away with Jack Webster.

Lower Rattery, the scene of the crime, was miles from The Three Tuns – quite a walk for anyone to make, be they inebriated or otherwise, especially a woman in high heels. Elaine had to have had help.

Something didn't add up. If Keith was telling the truth and the pair had left Jack Webster outside the pub, wouldn't Elaine have assumed that Jack had simply driven home under his own steam? Did she know that Dave had left the keys in the ignition of his Land Rover? On the other hand, if Elaine had recognized Jack's Land Rover in the car park, how did she know which direction he'd walked home? He could have taken any one of a dozen routes. He could even have cut across open fields.

Mrs Evans set the plate down on the kitchen table, bringing me back to reality with a jump. 'And I brewed a fresh pot of tea just for you.'

'This looks delicious, Mrs E.' I was really touched.

'Well, I should be owing you two weeks' rent because you're leaving before the end of the month, but I thought you'd prefer a decent breakfast.'

Two weeks' rent was two weeks' rent and not the equivalent of a fried breakfast, but I let it go. Today was my last morning at Factory Terrace. Why go and spoil it by being petty?

Mrs Evans hovered over me in her floral apron. 'You just let me know if you need anything.

You're looking a little peaky.'

'Thank you, Mrs E.' A wave of nostalgia swept over me. I'd grown fond of my landlady and our funny routines – our evening viewing of reality television and our Saturday habit of pouring over Barbara's 'No-Frills Babs' advice column and guessing who the anonymous contributors were. I'd even warmed to her husband.

'Where is Mr Evans?'

'He's already out in the garden getting the ground ready for the terrarium.'

I almost choked on my tea. Thank God I'd moved those urns last night.

'Where's the *Gazette?*' I said, deftly changing the subject. 'We should have a look at "No-Frills Babs" one last time.'

'It's not yet nine,' said Mrs Evans. I heard the clatter of the letterbox. 'There's your paper now. I'll get it. You just sit there and finish your tea.'

Mrs Evans returned holding the newspaper close to her chest. Her expression was grave.

'What's the matter?' I said.

'You won't like it.' She put the newspaper on the table. 'Our Annabel is everywhere.'

Splashed across the front page was:

ACCUSED!
HEDGE-JUMPING CHAMP RANDALL
FACES MURDER CHARGES
INTER-CONTINENTAL DREAM IN
TATTERS
AN ANNABEL LAKE EXCLUSIVE!

Annabel had managed to get a thumbnail photograph of herself put beside her byline. A second photograph showed Dave Randall's Land Rover, with the logo Jump Azberjam 2016 clearly visible, at the crime scene. An arrow had been added that pointed to the front of the vehicle with the caption 'Mown down like a pheasant' and a second angled with 'Webster is under here!'

A third photograph showed Dave downing a pint of scrumpy at the recent scrumpy-drinking marathon. Other than a damning report of the fight seen at The Three Tuns, Annabel's story was nothing but fluff, with 'alleged' this and 'alleged' that.

But it wasn't Dave's predicament that I found disconcerting. It was her second big story on the front page that turned my blood to ice.

NET CLOSES ON THE FOG
LADY ETHEL RAISES SPAT URNS
REWARD
CITIZENS' PATROL JOIN SEARCH FOR
LOOT
AN ANNABEL LAKE EXCLUSIVE!

Annabel had got her hands on a photo of Dad. He wasn't looking his best, given that it had been taken at the time of his last arrest and showed him surrounded by police officers. With his sapphire-blue eyes wide, teeth bared and fists raised, Dad looked highly dangerous and, I hated to admit it, a bit insane.

Annabel went on to insist that The Fog was responsible for the spate of silver thefts at the Webster residence, Brooke Farm. This neatly

257

segued into a third exclusive on the front page, with yet another byline from Annabel, that said:

NOT QUITE A RUBY
WIDOW GRIEVES: TOWN MOURNS ICON
AN ANNABEL LAKE EXCLUSIVE!

Readers were encouraged to turn to page 5 for the 'Wedding Anniversary Round-Up' and find out about Jack and Amelia 'in happier times' where, to my extreme annoyance, Annabel had completely rewritten my interview.

'I've been written out of my own newspaper this week,' I grumbled. 'Look!' Even 'On the Cemetery Circuit With Vicky' had been replaced with Elaine Tully's feature on The Green Reaper.

The word 'Cancelled' – in bold, 36 font – had been slashed across the headline, RUTH REEVES'S CELEBRATION OF LIFE TODAY!

It was all in extremely bad taste.

Elaine had gone on to list what would have happened had the service been held. It would appear that John Reeves had selected Celine Dion's 'The Heart Will Go On', a flock of pigeons was to be released as the mourners left the church and miniature bottles of Asti Spumante, 'Ruth's favourite tipple', were to be given out as party favours.

Elaine managed to promote her company with a quick recap of the burial fields available: Heavenly Meadows and Celestial Comforts – not Angel's Rise, I noted – with the tagline, 'Always wanted to travel but never had the time? Get buried on the Isle of Man!', a phone number for potential investors who had a 'field to spare' and

258

links to The Green Reaper Facebook page.

'Do you remember Elaine Tully?' I asked.

'I'd heard she was back,' said Mrs Evans. 'Lenny used to call her the village bike.'

I felt my face grow hot. 'Oh, I see what you mean.'

'That's right,' said Mrs Evans with a nod. 'Everyone wanted a ride. She did the rounds all right, even had a go at my Lenny, though he swears nothing happened. I know she and Ronnie Binns had a fling.'

I must have looked disgusted because Mrs Evans laughed. 'You youngsters just see grumpy old folk past their prime, but remember, our menfolk were lusty boys back in the day. People used to say my Lenny looked like Paul Newman.'

'Do you think there was anything going on between her and Jack Webster?'

'Before Amelia married Jack there were rumours.'

'But not since Elaine came back?'

'She wouldn't dare, not if she wanted to keep her eyes.'

'What do you mean?'

'Amelia would scratch them out if Jack so much as looked at another woman, God rest his soul. I'm not one to speak ill of the dead, but Amelia kept him on a short leash.'

'What about John Reeves?'

'They always had a soft spot for each other,' said Mrs Evans. 'Mark my words. Now he's available, there'll be no shortage of women bringing him pies.'

'Thanks, Mrs E,' I said. 'Shall we look at "No-

Frills Babs"?' I turned to Barbara's column. 'How about this, "Dear Babs," I read, "I'm in love with a beautiful woman with sapphire blue–"'

Tap, tap, tap!

We turned to see Mr Evans with his nose pressed against the kitchen window.

'Open up!' He looked furious.

Mrs Evans scurried to the window and threw it open. 'What's the matter?'

'Millie, you've got to come outside and take a look at this,' he said. 'Someone's been out here. Someone's been digging up my garden.'

I hurried outside with Mrs Evans and took in the mess. The mounds of earth that I'd replaced last night with so much care had grown to towering mountains this morning.

Blast! I'd done my best to cover my tracks, but it had been dark and I'd been in a hurry.

'Perhaps it's rabbits – or moles,' I said desperately.

'Rabbits and moles don't leave ruddy big holes like this,' Mr Evans fumed. 'No, someone was here last night. I can tell. My snails are all upset and restless. Bullet didn't even touch his breakfast.'

'Oh no.' Mrs Evans's dentures clicked away in sympathy. 'Did you try him with a leaf of Romaine?'

'Yep. He turned his nose up.'

'Lenny!' Mrs Evans exclaimed. 'Do you think ... remember Amelia was burglarized? We're going to be next, Lenny. I can feel it in my water.'

'We already have been,' said Mr Evans grimly. 'Someone's stolen my shovel.'

All too late, I remembered I still had Mr

Evans's shovel in the boot of my car. I'd been so tired when I'd got home that I had completely forgotten to put it back in the shed.

'I'll call the police,' said Mrs Evans.

'Wait!' I suddenly remembered the front-page call to arms. 'I bet I know what's happened. Be right back.'

I dashed inside and grabbed the *Gazette* from the kitchen table, then tore back into the garden. 'Front page. See that – CITIZENS' PATROL SEARCH FOR LOOT? – that's what's happened!'

Mr Evans's eyes widened. 'Bloody hell. That Fog chappy is in Gipping-on-Plym. Millie.'

'I bet they started digging here,' I said.

'Well, I'll be blowed,' said Mrs Evans.

'My informer told me that the Citizens' Patrol was starting their search in Factory Terrace.'

'Whatever for?'

'No wonder poor Bullet went off his lettuce,' I said. 'He must have been frightened.'

Mr Evans folded his arms. 'I'm not happy about this. We should have been told.'

'I agree,' I said. 'Excuse me. Better go and finish my packing.'

I made my escape, congratulating myself on my quick thinking.

I gave my old bedroom a final once over and, in all the excitement, almost forgot to take the disposable Motorola phone I'd found in Hugh's Folly and which I'd left to charge in the corner behind my bedside table.

There was still five pounds left on it. I tapped open the contacts page but it was empty. Next I

261

opened the phone log and stared. How odd. There was only one phone number recorded – and this one number was called over and over again.

I dialled it.

It rang. In fact, it rang for a very long time. I was about to give up when I heard a click, then silence, though I knew someone was there.

I counted to ten. 'Hello?'

There was a long pause. 'Hello.'

It was a female voice.

'Elaine?' I said. 'Is that you?'

'Vicky?' came a familiar voice.

'*Topaz?*' I exclaimed. 'What on earth–?'

'How did you get this number?' she demanded.

'Am I ringing your *mobile?*' I was completely thrown.

'Why?'

'Wait a minute – don't hang up!' I retrieved my iPhone from the dresser and flipped to the list of incoming calls. 'Is your phone number 07755 43129?'

'You know it is,' she said crossly. 'You've just dialled it.'

'Just double-checking.'

'Why? Did someone report me?'

'Report you?' I was confused. 'About what?'

Topaz gave a heavy sigh. 'I found it. I was going to hand it into the police but I didn't see the point now that she's dead.'

'What?' I exclaimed. 'Who?'

'Ruth Reeves, silly,' said Topaz. 'I found this phone in her bicycle basket. It's only a cheap one and there was tons of money left on it.'

I sank onto the bare mattress – the sheets had

already been stripped, ready for Mrs Evans to wash them for Sadie.

'Can you tell me what numbers have been dialled from that phone?' I asked.

'Is this for a case?'

'Yes, yes.' I was getting impatient. 'Ring off and take a look.'

'How do I do that?'

'Just look at the incoming and outgoing call log.'

'OK. I'll try.' Topaz sounded doubtful and disconnected the line.

Three long minutes passed and then my iPhone rang. 'Topaz,' I said. 'Well?'

'Vicky?' came a voice in a low whisper. 'It's Steve.'

'Steve!' I exclaimed. 'Can I call you back?'

'Can't. Sadie's in the bathroom,' he said. 'It's important.'

'Go on.'

'Ray Bailey ran a toxicology report on Ruth.'

'Already?'

'Told you he was amazing.'

'And?'

'He found something. There were traces of Amanita Phalloides in her stomach, doll – death cap mushrooms.'

My heart began to thunder in my chest. 'Wait, so let me repeat this. You're saying that Ruth Reeves died from mushroom poisoning?'

'She must have eaten it by mistake, poor love.'

'When?'

'It's hard to tell with mushrooms,' said Steve. 'Ray gave me the lowdown. The symptoms are slow and don't appear for at least ten or sixteen hours after eating. It's often confused with gastro-enteritis.'

'John had mentioned that she had an upset tummy, but I put that down to drinking champagne on an empty stomach,' I said.

'If only I'd know earlier about her swollen lips,' Steve said with dismay.

'You wouldn't have been able to save her, Steve. Death cap mushrooms are fatal.'

'She died of liver failure, doll,' Steve went on. 'That's why her face went a funny yellow – oh, hey Sadie!' The line disconnected.

Before I could think any more about Ruth, my iPhone rang again.

'I did it!' Topaz cried.

'And?'

'Just one phone number called. And you'll never guess what...?'

'No time for guessing games, Topaz.'

'OK. OK, boss.' Topaz paused then screamed with excitement. 'It's that funny number you just called me on!'

Just as I had thought! Secret phones – secret, non-traceable phones used by lovers since the beginning of caller ID. It was all falling into place. The Motorola phone I held in my hot little hand definitely belonged to Jack Webster, and yes he'd been having an affair with Ruth Reeves and they'd meet in Hugh's Folly. Jack had put a padlock on the door and left the key under the flowerpot in Dave's byre. When Dave mistakenly believed Jack Webster had been stalking him, Dave had put a padlock on the byre door. Jack must have accidentally left his phone in Hugh's Folly. No wonder he'd been desperate to get it back! No wonder he hadn't wanted Amelia to find out about his illicit visits to the folly. He'd wanted to keep his eyes.

'Where did you find Ruth's bicycle?' I asked Topaz.

'I saw Ruth riding her bicycle on my land lots of times,' she grumbled. 'She'd always hide it under a pile of leaves.'

'You didn't think to ask what she was doing?'

'Oh, she never saw me. I used to watch her through my binoculars.' Topaz gave a snort of laughter. 'She looked quite funny. Have you ever tried cycling on grass? It's *frightfully* difficult.'

The broken bottle of Asti Spumante also gave the game away. Up until Ruth's tastes had changed and she'd moved on to Bollinger, Asti Spumante had been her favourite beverage; that was why it was going to be offered at her celebration of life. I also recalled how nasty Ruth had been about Jack Webster to Amelia's face that Wednesday afternoon – a sure sign that they were embroiled in an affair. Dad had been unkind about Mum's friend Pam Dingles, too, saying she had a face like the back of a bus, just to throw Mum off the scent.

How could I have been so blind?

The question was, had Amelia known about the affair? Steve had said that Ruth had eaten death cap mushrooms. Amelia had brought over a tart a couple of days earlier.

I'd never thought to ask what kind of tart it was. I just knew that anything Amelia made was inedible. But if it had been a mushroom tart, surely Amelia wouldn't have deliberately poisoned her best friend. Hadn't Steve said that even the most experienced mushroom hunters could mistake a death cap for the edible kind?

That didn't explain how the pie dish ended up in Olive's kitchen, though. If Amelia had done it, wouldn't she have disposed of the evidence and kept her beloved dish?

I needed to talk to John Reeves.

'What do you think, boss?' said Topaz, breaking into my thoughts. 'Shall I come over?'

'Not right now,' I said. 'But I'll be in touch, I promise.'

I rang off.

It still didn't explain how Jack Webster ended up crushed against a tree under the wheels of Dave's Land Rover, or how Boggins Leap came to be destroyed, or where Elaine Tully fitted in.

I found Mrs Evans in the kitchen, putting the finishing touches to Sadie's favourite egg and bacon flan.

'I've come to say goodbye,' I said.

'Oh, you were right about the Citizens' Patrol loot search,' said Mrs Evans. 'Mrs Stannard at number twenty-four had her garden dug up about an hour ago, but she called the police.'

'So the police didn't know about this so-called search?'

'No,' said Mrs Evans gleefully. 'And now Lenny's thinking about pressing charges for trespassing. I wonder why anyone should think the Spat urns would be buried in Factory Terrace?'

'I know. It's silly, isn't it?' I said.

Piling the last plastic dustbin liner that held my muddy clothes from last night's adventures into the back of my Fiat, I spied Mr Evans's shovel in the boot of my car.

I trooped back to the house and handed it back to my now former landlady. 'It was lying in the front garden,' I lied.

'Give us a hug.' Mrs Evans threw her arms out and I allowed myself to be smothered. 'I'll miss you, Vicky.'

'I'll miss you, too.' But to be honest I didn't think I would, and besides, I wouldn't have time to miss anyone.

I had to act fast.

Chapter Twenty-Eight

As I headed for my Fiat for the second time that morning, a minivan crammed with 1st Gipping Cub Scouts, with Scout leader Simon Mears at the wheel, sailed by. The sight of a troop of youngsters in Factory Terrace was so unusual – especially since the road ended in a cul-de-sac – that I stepped out into the street and watched it pull into the gated entrance to the abandoned wool and textile factory further down.

It was then that I recognized Eunice's silver Ford Fiesta.

Puzzled, I trotted over to the parked vehicles, where I found Eunice Pratt, Mary Berry and Simon Mears – in full-on Akela gear and sporting a Citizens' Patrol badge – standing on the pavement engaged in lively conversation.

'I told you. It's been called off,' I heard Eunice say. 'Legal reasons.'

'The boys will be very disappointed.' Simon gestured to the faces pressed against the glass of the minivan behind him. 'They'd been so looking forward to the dig. Didn't Annabel Lake think to check with the police first?'

'Morning all,' I said. 'Is something wrong?'

'Oh Vicky,' said Simon. 'Mrs Pratt says the search has been cancelled. Do you know anything about it?'

'I'm afraid not,' I said.

'Apparently, your colleague didn't realize digging up someone's garden was an invasion of privacy,' said Eunice.

Simon nodded gravely. 'I'm afraid she didn't adopt our motto: "Be Prepared".'

'Be prepared for a disappointment, you mean,' Mary Berry put in.

'We'll be lodging a formal complaint,' Eunice went on. 'I shall be writing a letter to the editor the minute I get home.'

The minivan began to rock violently and a few of the boys hammered on the windows. Simon cast an anxious glance over his shoulder. 'Right. I'd better go. I don't know what to do with them now. The parents had expected to have these lads off their hands for the day and now...' He shrugged.

'Perhaps a nature ramble?' I suggested.

'Good idea,' said Mary Berry. 'My son Robin always enjoyed pulling legs off beetles when he was a boy. Remember, Eunice?'

Upon hearing her nautical nephew's name, Eunice gave a wistful smile. 'He'd collect them in an old jam jar. He was such a sweet little boy.'

'A nature ramble is just the thing,' said Simon hastily. 'But we don't encourage boys to harm God's creatures in this day and age.'

And with that, he bade us all a good day, climbed back into the minivan, executed a perfect three-point turn and sped off as the raucous sounds of 'Ging, Gang, Goolie' echoed around Factory Terrace.

'I told you this was a waste of time,' said Mary Berry.

'Why would the stolen silver be around here anyway?' I said.

'That's what we were told,' Eunice exclaimed. 'Annabel Lake said that her ladyship's urns were buried in someone's garden in Factory Terrace–'

'And Amelia Webster's junk,' Mary Berry put in.

'Given that The Grange and Brooke Farm are miles away from Lower Gipping,' I said, 'don't you think that odd. I mean, why here?'

'Annabel was adamant,' Eunice went on. 'Said she'd got a tip-off from a couple of chaps in prison.'

'Wayne Henderson and Nigel Keeps,' Mary Berry declared. 'That's what she said.'

'Never heard of them.' I hoped my face didn't betray my shock at hearing the names of two of Dad's rivals, both of whom were currently guests of Her Majesty at Wormwood Scrubs. This was seriously bad news.

'But why dig up number twenty-four?' I managed to say.

'That's what Annabel told Mary. She wrote it down.'

'No, I didn't need to write it down.' Mary Berry tapped her head. 'Mind like a steel trap.'

'Where is Annabel this morning?' I asked.

'She didn't turn up,' said Eunice. 'And now we know why.'

I deftly changed the subject. 'How's Amelia holding up?'

'Devastated,' said Eunice. 'Jack was the love of her life.'

'Maybe I'll pop by with some flowers.'

'I shouldn't bother,' said Eunice. 'She doesn't want to see anyone. Refuses to answer the door or eat. Randall should hang for this.'

'I always liked him,' said Mary Berry wistfully. 'Especially in his moleskins.'

I had a sudden thought. 'Did you see Jack Webster in the car park on Thursday night?'

'Why are you asking?' said Eunice.

'Didn't you bring Amelia to The Three Tuns so she could take Jack home, given that she doesn't have her own car?'

'Yes she does,' chipped in Mary Berry. 'The parts I ordered for Amelia's Hillman Imp are on back order.'

'I drove Amelia to the pub.' Eunice paused. She licked her lips and appeared to find something fascinating about her shoes. 'But she changed her mind.'

'No she didn't!' Mary Berry cried. 'You said–'

'She changed her mind, Mary,' Eunice shouted. 'You weren't there. Jack was drunk so Amelia said, "Let him walk home."'

'So you *both* saw Jack on Thursday night?'

'No, we didn't see him,' Eunice said quickly.

'Jack's always drunk on market day. Amelia decided she didn't want an argument, and, as I said, we went straight home.'

'That's not what you told me,' Mary Berry mumbled.

'Well it's the truth. Ignore her, Vicky.' Eunice turned her back on her sister-in-law. 'Jack's dead. What does it matter if we saw him in the car park or not?'

It mattered a great deal. Dave Randall was in a cell accused of murder, and if Eunice was lying and had dropped Amelia off, I needed to know. Someone must have taken Amelia home and maybe – just maybe – that someone had been John Reeves.

'I already told that red-headed copper,' Eunice went on. 'We can't stand here all day. Mary's got the farm to see to. Come on.'

'One more question,' I said. 'Did either of you hear a chainsaw in the early hours of Friday morning?'

'I did. It was three forty-five exactly,' Mary declared. 'My alarm goes off at four and I distinctly remembered being cross that I'd missed out on that extra fifteen minutes.'

Three forty-five and, according to the brilliant Coroner Ray Bailey, that would have been hours after Webster was dead – and time enough for Dave to have returned to Boggins Leap.

But wait! John Reeves was a chainsaw expert – maybe too much of an expert. If he'd discovered that his wife had been having an affair with his best friend and wanted to get rid of him, *he* could have cut down Boggins Leap in an effort to frame

271

Dave Randall.

Thanking the ladies and promising them that yes, I'd be at the worm festival the following day, I headed back to my Fiat.

As I drove to my new abode, I called John Reeves, but had to leave a message on his voicemail asking him to ring me back. Next, I called Barbara in reception.

'I thought you were supposed to be taking the day off so you could move out,' she declared. 'You must give me your new address for our records.'

'I *am* taking the day off and I will give you my new address,' I said. 'But I just wondered if you'd heard anything about the aborted Citizens' Patrol search in Factory Terrace this morning.'

'Annabel is in the doghouse,' said Barbara. 'Wilf is livid. Furious. I've never seen him so angry. She went home in tears. I don't know what she was thinking.'

'Do you want me to come in today?'

'No. Tony and Edward are here, and what with Ruth's celebration of life being cancelled, we can manage.'

Twenty minutes later I stopped outside The Granary. I still found it hard to believe this was my new home.

Inside, a bouquet of flowers stood on the kitchen table, along with a loaf of bread, a box of eggs, a packet of PG Tips and a handful of sugar sachets. I opened the fridge to find a bottle of orange juice and a carton of milk. A note said, 'welcome to your new home', signed by Elaine and Keith.

They seemed so nice. I really hoped they weren't

involved in Jack's demise. I also hoped that I could extricate myself from any romantic liaison with Keith without losing my new home.

While the kettle boiled, I made forays back and forth to my Fiat, collecting the possessions I'd stuffed in black dustbin liners.

Although I had yet to solve the mystery of Ruth's death and Jack's murder. I was getting close. I could feel it.

Things were looking up. I had my own place at last. I'd averted a huge disaster with the Spat urns; Annabel had made several SNAFUs and had gone home in tears – she really should have checked her facts – and I was convinced now that Dave Randall was innocent. All I had to do was prove it.

As I poured water into the Brown Betty teapot – a brand-new one, I noted with delight – there came a knock on the door and Keith and Elaine stepped inside.

'Excellent timing,' I said happily. 'I've just made a pot of tea. I can't thank you enough. I love it here.'

Neither replied. In fact, Elaine looked as if she was going to cry and Keith's expression was grim.

I steadied myself for bad news. I knew it had all been too good to be true. 'Is something wrong? Do I have to move out?'

'Tell her, Mum,' said Keith.

'I spent the night with John Reeves,' Elaine blurted out. 'There. Are you happy now?'

'Yes,' Keith said tightly. He looked furious.

To say I was shocked was putting it mildly. I was *so* disappointed. Ruth couldn't have been dead for more than twenty-four hours. Was no relationship sacrosanct? Unless ... Elaine and John Reeves had been having an affair all along.

'It was a mistake,' said Elaine desperately. 'It should never have happened.'

'That's what you say every time, mother,' said Keith bitterly. 'So you see, Vicky, Mum has an alibi.'

'You spent *all* night with John Reeves?' I finally managed to say.

Elaine nodded. 'I can't expect you to understand–'

'She won't and neither do I,' said Keith.

Elaine began to sniffle.

'And those tears won't work on me either,' Keith snapped.

'Tea anyone?' I said desperately. 'Do go and sit down.'

I set out cups and saucers, milk and sugar in the most horrible silence. The atmosphere was so tense between mother and son you could cut it with the proverbial knife. I returned to the table with my notebook open. 'It's important I take notes,' I said. 'I hope you don't mind.'

Elaine made a listless move with her hand but started sniffling again.

'You were with John Reeves *all* night,' I said again. 'He didn't slip out at all? The police are going to ask you this.'

'I'm positive. You could say that we didn't sleep much,' Elaine said ruefully. 'John told me that he and Ruth didn't have sex any more and–'

'Really. I don't need the details,' I said quickly. 'Did you hear a chainsaw at all?'

'Oh yes,' said Elaine.

'Any idea what time?'

'I wasn't really paying attention to the clock, dear.'

'So let me get this straight,' I said. 'You went home with John from The Three Tuns.'

'Yes,' she said. 'He left first–'

'In whose Land Rover?'

'How would I know,' she said. 'They all look the same, apart from Randall's, of course, with its silly logo on the door. John told me to wait twenty minutes and then follow him.'

'Why twenty minutes?'

'Why do you think?' Elaine said. 'John didn't want us to be seen leaving together.'

'And whose idea was it to go back to Reeves Roost?'

'I don't remember,' she whispered. 'Mutual really. I was starving and John said to come back for a nightcap and that he had a mushroom tart–'

'You're certain it was mushroom,' I said sharply.

'Yes, but once I knew who'd made it, I didn't touch it.' Elaine pulled a face. 'I've always remembered Amelia's cooking.'

I tried to keep my voice steady but I was getting excited. 'Do you know what happened to the pie dish?'

Elaine laughed. 'Oh yes.' She shot Keith a look of defiance. 'We got carried away in the kitchen and, in our excitement, the dish fell on the floor and broke.'

'That's disgusting,' muttered Keith.

'Can you describe the pie dish?'

'It was red with a raised chicken head. It was the most hideous thing I've ever seen.'

'So, the pie dish broke – what happened to the tart?'

'John put it down the disposal unit and threw the pie dish in the recycling bin.'

Which was why it ended up at Gipping County Council rubbish tip and, from there, made its way to Olive Binns nèe Larch's kitchen, only to be lovingly mended with a spot of superglue.

I had a sudden thought. 'You mentioned that Black Crow Dell had some poisonous plants.'

'Don't remind me,' Elaine said. 'It's riddled with them. I know quite a lot about poisonous plants–'

'Dad was a botanist,' Keith put in.

'I know,' I said. 'You told me.'

'Solanum Nigrum, Atropa Belladonna,' Elaine ticked them off on her fingers. 'Conium Maculatum and, of course, Amanita Phalloides.'

'Amanita Phalloides,' I said. 'Death cap mushrooms.'

'Kiddies can easily mistake them for the edible kind,' said Elaine. 'That's why I was so upset. It's another reason why Black Crow Dell is a disastrous location for a green burial. Wait!' Elaine clutched at her throat in horror. 'Omigod. You don't think there were death cap mushrooms in that tart do you?'

'Since it was thrown out,' I said. 'We'll never know.'

'Omigod,' she said again. 'That stupid bitch could have killed me.' Elaine gasped. 'She must have poisoned Ruth!'

'Bloody hell,' said Keith. 'What do you mean? *Poisoned* Ruth? You mean *deliberately?*'

'We're looking into it,' I said carefully. I still wasn't sure if I trusted Elaine Tully's story, and I definitely didn't know either of them well enough to share my theories.

'Tell Vicky the rest, Mum,' said Keith.

Elaine gave a heavy sigh. 'I left the pub twenty minutes after John, but when I got to Reeves Roost, he wasn't there.'

'What do you mean, wasn't there?'

'In fact I almost gave up,' said Elaine. I must have waited at least half an hour and then, when he finally did turn up, he was very out of sorts.'

My heart began to race again. I'd been right. John Reeves *had* been involved.

'I tried to cheer him up and one thing led to another and—'

'I get the picture.' But something didn't make sense. 'What time did you leave the car park?'

'About eleven fifteen. After closing time.'

'And were there any other Land Rovers in the car park?'

'Just one.'

'Was that Dave's Land Rover – the one with the logo on the door?'

'No. I would have remembered,' she said. 'I'd parked next to his when I arrived. How can you miss that stupid logo? Azerbaijan is spelled wrong. Why?'

'So John definitely took his own Land Rover?'

Elaine shrugged. 'I suppose so. He was driving it when he came back to Reeves Roost. I was sitting in my car in his yard, waiting.'

Even if John Reeves had taken Dave's Land Rover, he could never have walked back to The

Three Tuns in the twenty minutes he'd told Elaine to wait behind.

'I feel just awful,' said Elaine.

But not *so* awful that she didn't seem to have a conscience about sleeping with Ruth's husband.

As if guessing my thoughts, Elaine said, 'John and I go way back. We'd had a fling in the past, so it hardly counts as being unfaithful.'

Keith snorted with disgust.

'Presumably John will back up your story?'

'He will. So you see, Vicky,' said Ruth. 'Dave Randall is guilty. I know you want to protect him, but he killed Jack Webster.'

'And Ruth?' said Keith. 'What happened to her?'

'Why, it's obvious,' I said smoothly. 'It was just a horrible accident.' Or was it?

'We'll leave you to unpack.' Keith forced a smile. I could see he was very upset about these new revelations. 'Mum and I have some important decisions to make.'

The moment they left I flung myself on the sofa, deeply perplexed. I wasn't sure who or what to believe.

I didn't want to believe that Dave Randall was guilty of running Jack Webster down, but I couldn't see who else could have done it – or why. Elaine and John were giving each other alibis, but maybe they were lying. And what about Keith? Yes, he was weird, and his time-coded photographs from St Winifred's seemed to provide him with a believable alibi, but how could I know for sure? Were mother and son trying to throw me off the trail?

And yet, the mushroom tart changed everything.

278

Picking up the flowers that Elaine and Keith had given to me as a housewarming gift, I wrapped them in a bag.

It was time to pay the grieving widow a visit.

Chapter Twenty-Nine

By the time I pulled into Brooke Farm, it was pouring with rain and the farmyard was slick with mud and manure.

Grabbing the flowers I headed to the back door. It was open, so I stepped inside and stopped in my tracks.

The kitchen was in a surprising state of disarray. The coloured recycling bins were in the proper places but were overflowing with rubbish, and stacked on the kitchen counter were boxes of spaghetti and rice. There were cans of soup and baked beans, pots of jams and marmalade and boxes of tea sitting on the trestle table. A note was propped against a cake tin that said simply, 'John'. On impulse, I opened the refrigerator. It was completely empty.

It looked like someone was leaving town.

On the dresser sat Amelia's open handbag. Tucked inside was a wallet emblazoned with the Qantas logo – the flag-carrying airline of Australia. Inside was a one-way ticket to Darwin that left that night. I also found Amelia's passport and was surprised to see that she was six years older than she claimed. Not only that, her passport had been renewed only three weeks earlier.

This trip had been planned, and if she'd planned the trip, perhaps she'd deliberately planned to poison her best friend and it hadn't been an accident, after all.

I became aware of footsteps padding back and forth overhead and the distant sound of music.

For a moment I hesitated. I'd watched enough television shows to scoff at the stupid girl who went into the attic knowing there was a killer on the loose, but even if Amelia proved to be such a one, she was old and frail. She'd be no match for me – and she was about to get away.

Even so, I decided to zip off a text to Steven as he was the only person I could think of who I could rely on – and whom I trusted.

Just as I left the kitchen, I noticed that the bill-hook that had hung above the Aga had disappeared. Would Amelia have taken it upstairs? Again, I hesitated, but time was running out. Somehow I had to stall for time.

Quietly, I took the stairs and the sound of Frank Sinatra got louder.

I reached the landing and took in the ancient burnished oak floor with an Indian runner that stretched the length of the corridor. It was gloomy, with the only light coming from an open door at the far end of the corridor, where Amelia, dressed in pale blue, passed back and forth in the doorway. As I drew closer, I could hear Frank singing 'Fly Me To The Moon' with Amelia screeching along at the top of her voice.

So much for a widow prostrate with grief.

Amelia paused in the doorway, giving me just

seconds to dart into a linen cupboard. I braced myself for discovery, but instead heard the door opposite open and close, followed by the click of the lock. It was probably the bathroom. Old habits died hard.

Quickly, I raced along the corridor and into Amelia's bedroom.

It was exactly as I had suspected.

On the bed was an open suitcase filled to the brim. On top of the neatly folded clothes was a photograph of Jack and Amelia on their wedding day – the same one that had appeared in this morning's *Gipping Gazette*.

I took in the bedroom with the patterned wallpaper showing the telltale squares of paintings that must have hung there at one time. The inglenook fireplace had been boarded up and replaced with a cheap three-bar electric fire. There were a few expensive antiques – a court cupboard, a four-poster bed and a nice pair of chairs. A kidney-shaped dressing table – identical to the one I had at number twenty-one Factory Terrace – had been cleared of knick-knacks, brushes and perfumes. Of the two night tables that stood on either side of the bed, one held *Farmers of Fortune,* the same magazine that The Green Reaper had advertised in. Save for a lamp, Amelia's bedside table was empty.

I heard the sound of a flushing loo and slipped behind the bedroom door. My hands were shaking. Far from being fragile, Amelia had seemed quite perky, although I was quite certain I could overpower her if it came to a struggle. I only hoped that Steve had followed my instructions and alerted the police.

Recalling Simon Mears's comment earlier that morning about being prepared, I retrieved my iPhone, switched on the voice record mode and slipped it back into my safari jacket pocket.

Still singing along happily to Frank, Amelia returned carrying a plastic drawstring washbag and pushed it into her suitcase.

I slammed the door shut and barred her escape.

Amelia screamed and spun around.

'Vicky! You startled me!'

'Are you going on holiday?' I said.

For a moment, Amelia didn't speak, but then she smiled. 'Yes,' she said sadly. 'With all this business with my darling Jack and poor Ruth, I decided to go and visit Robert for a while.'

'What did the police say when you told them you were leaving the country?'

'They wished me a pleasant trip. I gave them Robert's number, of course.' She sat down on the edge of the bed and held her hand to her heart. 'Sorry, you gave me rather a fright. I didn't hear you knock.'

'Perhaps I can take you to the airport?'

'How kind, dear,' said Amelia. 'But there's no need. I've ordered a car.' She gave another bright smile. 'Is that why you're here?'

Amelia's calmness was unnerving. I had fully expected her to panic, but instead she was acting as if everything was business as usual.

'I brought you flowers – they're downstairs,' I said. 'And some good news.'

'Oh?'

'I found your mother's pie dish.'

Amelia frowned. 'Pie dish?'

'Remember? You had a set of three with chicken heads on the rim and you only had one left?'

'Goodness!' Amelia exclaimed. 'I wondered what had happened to that. John told me he'd lost it. How kind and thoughtful you are. Where is it?'

'At the police station,' I lied.

Amelia blinked. 'I'm afraid I don't understand.'

'The police are very interested in the mushroom tart you made for Ruth.'

'Whatever for?'

'Ruth died from eating the mushrooms in your tart.'

Amelia clapped both hands to her mouth in horror. 'But ... that's not possible!' she exclaimed.

'Traces of death cap mushrooms were detected in Ruth's stomach, Amelia.'

'No. Oh no! John, oh *John.*' Amelia's face crumpled. 'I even asked him where he'd bought those mushrooms.'

I regarded Amelia with suspicion. I distinctly remembered her demanding her pie dish be returned. 'So you're telling me that *John* made the mushroom tart but he used *your* pie dish.'

'No. I made the tart but John gave me the mushrooms. He said he'd bought them at Gipping market. You hear about these things happening. Remember when that finger was found in a Chicken McNugget? We must alert the newspaper at once!'

This was going to be more difficult than I'd thought. Think, Vicky, *think!*

'I will, but for now forensics are on it,' I lied. 'Modern-day technology is amazing. Did you

283

know that they are able to pinpoint exactly where those mushrooms were picked?'

Amelia's jaw dropped.

'They were picked at Black Crow Dell, Amelia,' I bluffed.

Amelia's face crumpled. 'It was an accident,' she whispered. 'It was just a tiny pinch. I didn't mean to kill her.'

'Try telling the police that.'

'I just wanted to give Ruth a gippy tummy. Just something to put a damper on their naughty weekend away.'

'But how did you know that John wouldn't have had a slice? Or me, for that matter!'

'John hates mushrooms.'

'But I don't!'

'Ruth was my best friend.'

'Who was sleeping with your husband,' I pointed out.

'You're too young to know what true love means.'

'I know that Jack was your life,' I said. 'Just tell the police what happened. If you leave the country it will look suspicious.'

'Jack always wanted to be with Ruth,' Amelia said quietly. 'Always.'

'But he married *you.*'

'He married me because Ruth had gone off and married John. I got in the family way and I forced Jack to marry me. He'd been having an affair with Ruth for decades!'

'So why did you stay with him?' I asked, bewildered. 'I know Brooke Farm belongs to you. Why didn't you throw him out?'

'Because I loved him.' Amelia's expression hardened. 'Do you know what Ruth said to me once? I asked her if she thought he was having an affair, and do you know what she said?'

'No.'

'"You're the centre of his world, Amelia,"' she mimicked. 'She actually said that to my face! The centre of his world!'

'Did you know that Ruth broke off their relationship?' I said.

'She was always saying that,' said Amelia bitterly.

'This time she meant it,' I said. 'Those were her dying words.'

'She lied!' she shouted. 'She always lied. She wanted the best of both worlds. She wanted John's money but Jack's heart.'

Much as I didn't want to believe it, I had a feeling Amelia might be right. That's exactly what Mum used to say about Dad – that he wanted her cooking and Pamela Dingles' boobs.

'Oh yes,' Amelia went on. 'They used to meet at Hugh's Folly. I knew all about their Wednesdays in Dawlish. Jack would drive there and meet Ruth off the train. She would leave her car at the station car park, making sure it couldn't be spotted by CCTV.'

'How do you know all this?'

'I have friends – *good* friends.'

'You mean friends like Barbara?' I said, recalling the comment Barbara had made about an affair in "No-Frills Babs". No wonder Barbara had been acting cagey.

Amelia didn't answer.

'Eunice knew about the affair, didn't she?' I went

on. Eunice had claimed Jack was picking black-berries. 'But why would Eunice want to protect Jack?'

She wasn't protecting *Jack*,' said Amelia with scorn. 'She was keeping nosy people like *you* out of our business. I couldn't bear a scandal. Do you think I want to be on the front page of the *Gipping Gazette?* The shock would kill Daddy.'

'Is your father still alive?' I exclaimed.

'He's at the Sunny Meadows Retirement Home for the Elderly,' said Amelia. 'He's ninety-eight. The Brooke-Luscombes have excellent genes.'

'Amelia, please talk to the police,' I said.

'I've already told them my story.' She shot me a complacent smile. 'Now, if you'll excuse me, I really must finish packing.'

'I saw that your passport was renewed three weeks ago,' I said quickly. '*You* made the mush-room tart knowing that Ruth would eat it, but that it would take a few days to kill her, and by then you'd be on a plane halfway to Australia.'

'Really, Vicky,' Amelia sniggered, 'what a vivid imagination you have. You can't prove a thing.'

'But Eunice can.' It was another bluff and I wasn't sure if Amelia would take the bait.

Amelia went very still. 'What are you talking about?'

'Eunice admitted that she lied when she told me she'd driven you back to Brooke Cottage. She left you at the pub that night, didn't she?'

Amelia stared stonily ahead.

'You deliberately tried to frame Dave Randall by stealing his Land Rover,' I went on. 'It was *you* who ran Jack down. *You* killed him, and John

286

helped you. He obviously knew about the affair.'

'Leave John out of this,' Amelia snapped. 'He's a good man.'

'A good man who didn't waste time jumping into bed with another woman just two days after his wife died?'

Amelia seemed genuinely shocked. 'What are you talking about?'

'Elaine Tully,' I said. 'They spent the night together. She sure gets around. I bet John was furious with Jack for stealing his wife ... and then his new girlfriend. One minute Elaine's with Jack—'

'There was never anything between Jack and Elaine,' Amelia burst out. 'Never!'

'Jack even bought a diamond eternity ring,' I said. 'I wonder who it was for? Ruth or Elaine? It certainly didn't fit your finger.'

'The ring was for me!' Amelia shrieked. 'For our anniversary.'

'You kept Jack on a leash,' I said. 'He wanted his own money – money to buy his mistress a ring. That's why he sold Black Crow Dell.'

Amelia gasped. 'He couldn't have. The farm is *mine*. He can't sell anything without my permission.'

'He sold Black Crow Dell to Elaine Tully for fifteen thousand pounds.'

Amelia was trembling with rage. 'You're lying!'

'You're right. The ring wasn't worth fifteen thousand pounds,' I said. 'The rest of the money went towards a houseboat.'

All the colour drained from Amelia's face. 'No. No!'

'Jack was leaving you.'

'He couldn't. He could never leave me,' said Amelia harshly. 'He had no money of his own. Nothing. You see! You're *wrong!*'

And then I knew. Chuffy McSnatch had said that someone in 'my area' had been selling silver on the black market.

'You didn't guess that it was Jack who'd been selling off your silver and lining his pockets.'

Amelia slumped onto the bed. 'He wouldn't ... couldn't...' she whispered again.

All the anger seemed to drain from Amelia's body. I felt incredibly sorry for her.

'You did pick Jack up from the pub that night,' I said gently. 'But you took Dave's Land Rover by mistake.'

Amelia nodded slowly. 'I can't see very well in the dark.'

'Amelia, there are hidden CCTV cameras there,' I bluffed again. 'It's all on tape.'

'Yes. Yes. You're right.' Amelia gave a heavy sigh. 'I did pick Jack up. I did take Randall's Land Rover – the keys were in the ignition. They all look the same.'

'What happened?'

'Jack kept shouting at me and calling me a stupid fool for taking Randall's Land Rover. He was so drunk.' She fell silent for a moment. 'I told him I knew the eternity ring had never been meant for me, but he just laughed. I said... I said' – she swallowed hard – 'that with Ruth gone we could try again but ... but ... Jack told me he was leaving me anyway.'

'What happened next, Amelia?' I said, praying that my iPhone was picking up this entire con-

288

versation and wishing that Steve would hurry up and arrive.

'He said he wanted to walk home. So I let him.'

'He got out–'

'He was walking in front of the Land Rover. He was *drunk* and weaving all over the road. I just... I just...'

Suddenly, Amelia jumped to her feet and shoved me so hard that I fell over backwards and hit my head on the corner of the tallboy. My iPhone fell out of my pocket. For a split second, Amelia seemed puzzled, but then guessed I'd been recording our conversation. Quick as lightning she picked up a poker by the fireplace and, spinning round, brought it down on my arm with a crack. I yelped with pain and rolled away.

She snatched up my iPhone and stuffed it into her pocket.

'Amelia!' I shouted. 'The police will be here any minute!'

But she'd fled the bedroom. The pain in my wrist was excruciating. I managed to crawl out onto the landing and grabbed the end of the Indian runner, yanking it hard with my good hand.

The rug gave a violent jolt. Amelia lost her footing but picked herself up and raced down the stairs with surprising agility. I had completely underestimated the Brooke-Luscombe genes.

I staggered to my feet, clasping my arm as the numbness began to tingle so much I felt certain I'd broken it. Hurrying after her I burst outside and tore down the path to find her standing paralysed in the courtyard.

My Fiat was blocking her escape.

'Amelia!' I shouted. 'Stop!'

She took off again towards the barn. Outside was a large rain barrel and, to my dismay, she withdrew my iPhone and flung it in with a plop, then disappeared inside the barn.

I'd lost her taped confession. Damn and blast!

The power with which Amelia had struck me in the bedroom left me in no doubt that she was dangerous. I wasn't sure what to do, so I waited, nursing my injured arm and fighting waves of nausea.

Then I caught a glimpse of baby blue through the trees halfway down the hill. Amelia must have cut through the barn and had broken for cover.

I couldn't even call the police.

Where on earth was Steve?

I took off after her and, as I half-slithered, half-ran down the footpath, I realized exactly where she was going: Black Crow Dell.

I found her crouched under a bank of oak trees, snatching at plants.

'Amelia! What are you doing?' I shouted.

She spun around, holding one hand high with what I realized had to be poisonous mushrooms.

When I was ten feet away I stopped. Amelia was crying. 'He's not worth it,' I panted. 'He's just not worth it, Amelia.'

'Leave me be, Vicky.' She sank down onto the bank and studied the mushroom in her hand. 'I can't live without him,' she whispered. 'I don't want to.'

A watery sun broke through the heavy rain clouds, sending a shaft of sunlight down the valley. I saw a flash of silver and my heart turned over.

Oh no!

It was the Spat urns. I'd buried them deep, but the land was waterlogged and perhaps a wild animal had been at them.

'Vicky?' Amelia said.

I gazed at them in horror, then at Amelia who – with the mushrooms not quite touching her lips – was watching me with shocked surprise.

'Amelia!' I said suddenly. 'It's the Spat urns – over there, look. Jack must have stolen them. They've been there all the time!'

Distracted, Amelia looked away and I dived on top of her, knocking the mushrooms out of her hands. Amelia kicked and squirmed whilst I held on tightly, despite the terrible pain in my arm.

'Jack would never steal from her ladyship,' she shrieked. 'Never. *Never!*'

'He took your silver,' I said as I struggled to hold her still. 'Why not the Spat urns, too?'

'My urns!' Topaz burst through the woods 'My urns! My urns! You found them!'

Amelia seemed frozen to the spot, and as DC Bond snapped on the handcuffs, she stood there, mute.

Suddenly, Black Crow Dell was teeming with people: policemen, John Reeves, Errol Fairth-weather and some other cutters – and Steve. He had, indeed, called out the cavalry.

I heard a shout. John Reeves had been scavenging around in the undergrowth with his cronies. They held up a chainsaw and the billhook I'd seen hanging over the Aga.

'Did you slash Ruth's sunflowers?' I said to Amelia.

She held her head high. 'Yes.'

'And cut down Boggins Leap?'

'Yes.'

'Of course!' I exclaimed. 'John saw you walking home that night after you ran Jack down and abandoned Dave's Land Rover. He gave you a lift back to Brooke Farm.'

'Yes.'

'You set up the perfect motive for Dave to kill Jack.'

'Yes, I know,' she said. 'It would all have worked out perfectly if it hadn't been for that *tart* Elaine Tully. Goodbye, Vicky.'

As DC Bond led Amelia away, Probes took a look at my arm, which had now swollen to the width of a python – at least that's how it seemed to me.

'That's broken,' he said.

'You do your job and I'll do mine,' said Steve, brandishing an inflatable cast. 'Now, if you don't mind, I'd like to get this young lady to hospital so we can take a few X-rays. Are you OK to walk, doll?'

'Yes, I'm fine.'

'Another Vicky Hill exclusive, eh?' Probes regarded me with suspicion. 'Strange that Jack Webster had hidden the Spat urns in Black Crow Dell.'

'Yes, it is,' I said with false heartiness. 'They were under our noses all the time.'

Chapter Thirty

'Get to your plots!' shouted Errol Fairweather through his bullhorn. As worm master extraordinaire, Errol Fairweather was dressed in a white coat, red spotted neckerchief and bowler hat, complete with a giant rearing worm on the top. 'And ... GO!'

The five-bar gate was dragged open and, with excited screams of delight, hordes of contestants stampeded through the entrance and raced to their allotted three-foot squares.

'And remember,' the worm master continued. 'The world record for the most worms charmed still stands at five hundred and sixty seven! Today, let's make history!'

'What a load of idiots!' laughed Keith.

For some reason his comment bothered me. It was perfectly fine for me to criticize my fellow citizens, but not an outsider – although I felt like an outsider myself that day.

Steve had put a cast on my wrist and I'd been told to take a few days off work, which I didn't like one bit. And now that I lived in the middle of nowhere, I had to rely on other people driving me around.

'You know the rules,' yelled Errol Fairweather. 'Five minutes to worm up. *Five* minutes!'

'They take it very seriously,' I protested.

'Yeah. Right. Seriously?' Keith pointed to our

chief garbologist, Ronnie Binns, who had teamed up with Olive as 'official cheats'. Both wore top hats and tails and were drifting around, tempting contestants to buy worms from their Tupperware containers.

'And what are those wooden stakes for?' Keith went on. 'Looks like someone is trying to kill off a vampire.'

'They're called stobs, actually,' I said defensively. 'You drive them into the ground and wiggle them with a rooping iron. The correct term is worm grunting.'

'Well, Mum did mention that she charmed worms as a child,' he sniggered. 'But I didn't expect *this*.'

'Welcome to the countryside,' I said.

'Let's go and get a cup of tea,' said Keith. 'I've seen enough.'

'Don't you want to watch your mother competing for the Trewallyn Chalice?' I pointed to Elaine who was standing in a huddle with Coroner Ray Bailey and Pam Green. Elaine was holding Ruth's ocarina, Ray Bailey was making a meal of flexing his fingers and Pam Green cradled a large glass bowl, clearly anticipating a large haul.

'And see Mum make a fool of herself? No thanks.' Keith gave a snort of disgust. 'She's already getting her hooks into that coroner bloke.'

As I watched the coroner ruffle Elaine's short hair, I had to admit that Keith could be right. I regarded Keith with curiosity. He had dark circles under his eyes and he seemed paler than usual – and bad-tempered.

'Is everything OK?' I asked, but whatever he'd

been going to answer was drowned by the blast of the klaxon horn.

Other than a tangible tension, stillness descended on the field.

'Ladies and Gentleman,' Errol Fairweather cried, 'you have fifteen minutes to get worming.' He blew the whistle and there was a mass call to action. 'May the earth be ever in your favour!'

The Gipping Worm Festival had officially begun.

'There you are!' Annabel stormed towards us. 'You think you're so clever!'

'I'll meet you in the WI refreshment tent, Keith,' I said hastily and turned to face my attacker.

'Hi Annabel,' I said. 'Not competing today?'

Annabel was quivering with fury. 'You moved them!'

'Moved what?'

'The Spat urns,' she hissed.

'I honestly haven't a clue what you're talking about. They were discovered in Black Crow Dell – why you thought to dig up Mrs Stannard's garden is anyone's guess.'

Annabel stamped her foot. 'That stupid Mary Berry got the wrong address.'

'A professional journalist always double-checks her sources,' I said. 'And if you'd suspected the Spat urns were buried in Mr Evans's garden, why did you wait until now?'

'Believe me, I would have done, but I only found out on Friday,' she snapped. 'Does the name Chaffy McSnatch mean anything to you?'

'Chaffy Mc*Who*?' Although I burst out laughing, it was of the forced variety. In truth, I was shaken to the core. It was all I could do not to demand where she'd heard Dad's right-hand man's name. This was deadly serious.

'I have no idea who you mean.'

'I don't care if you do or if you don't,' Annabel gloated. 'I'm onto you, Vicky Hill. Just you see. I'm watching you. Your career will soon be *over* and you'll go to prison.'

'I think it's more a case of your career being over,' I said. 'Those front-page blunders are going to take some living down.'

Annabel gasped.

'Accusing an innocent man of running Jack Webster down?' I went on. 'Really? What an amateur mistake.'

'It's good publicity for Dave Randall,' Annabel protested. 'Have you seen the Jump Azerbaijan donation tent? It's packed with well-wishers.'

'And I'm surprised you, of all people, didn't realize that Ruth was having an affair with a married man.'

She gasped again, and I felt a twinge of guilt, but as my Dad always said, 'Attack is the best form of defence,' and her mention of Chuffy McSnatch had shaken me to the core.

'Urgh! With Jack Webster! Anyway, Ruth still didn't deserve to be poisoned,' she continued. 'And it was obvious that Jack wasn't satisfied in the bedroom. Men never cheat if they're satisfied.'

'You're the expert,' I said. 'But I really believe Amelia didn't mean to kill her friend. I heard she's going to face charges of manslaughter on both counts.'

'Nice try at changing the subject,' Annabel said. 'I've already talked to Colin. There is so much I know that you don't! You'll soon be *toast*.'

And without another word, she flounced off.

I needed to warn Chuffy McSnatch. I had to get word to him, but wasn't that exactly what Annabel was expecting me to do? What if she was having me followed?

Suddenly the festival's worm wizard blocked my path. 'Ah, there you are, Ms Hill. I've got something for the newspaper.'

I took in his ankle-length purple silk robes, pointed hat and fake long white beard, but there was something familiar about him.

And then I knew.

It was Chuffy McSnatch in disguise!

'This way. Follow me.' In a whirl of purple, the wizard strode off in the direction of the kids' bouncy castle.

I found him behind the generator.

'Thank God!' I exclaimed. 'What's going on?'

'You won't see me for a long time.' Chuffy's voice was urgent. 'My cover's blown.'

I felt a stab of panic. Chuffy McSnatch was the one connection I had to my parents. 'But ... what ... how...?'

'Just watch out for the classifieds in the *Gipping Gazette*, OK? Just for a while.' Chuffy McSnatch's eyes twinkled. 'Smart of you to shift the blame to that old farmer. Those Spat urns were hot property all right.'

I was beginning to get emotional. 'So Dad's not angry with me?'

'No. Relieved, more like,' said Chuffy Mc-Snatch. 'And that other matter – those silver thefts I told you about – we got to the bottom of that. A bloke called Jack Webster was flogging them on the black market. Nothing here that can be traced back to the boss.'

Of course, I already knew that, but it was a good feeling to have it confirmed, especially where the family reputation was concerned.

Annabel was wasting her time.

Chuffy McSnatch suddenly gave me a bear hug. 'I'll be seeing you, kid.'

And with that, he shoved me aside, pushed through the hedge and was gone.

By the time I had managed to compose myself and returned to the worming field, Topaz – dressed in her lady-of-the-manor garb – was in charge of the bullhorn.

'I have a few announcements to make,' Topaz declared. 'First of all, whoever purloined the worm wizard's costume from the changing tent, please return it. Secondly, do sign Eunice Pratt's turbine petition. We cannot allow such hideous machines to mar our Devonshire hilltops. Thirdly, registration is open for November's exhilarating tar barrel racing event – and let's try not to light too many spectators on fire this year. Lastly – and I do not wish to dwell on the recent tragedies – the traditional reception following the final competition continues tonight at The Grange, where I will announce the winners. Thank you.'

'Vicky!' a familiar voice called out. 'I've been looking for you everywhere.'

My stomach plunged into my boots as DI Probes came striding towards me. I had to escape. Quickly, I spied Keith at the same time as he saw me, and he hurried over.

'Where were you? You missed Gillian Briggs's excellent Victoria sponge.'

'I got held up.' Linking my arm through his I said, 'I think I'm ready to go home now.'

As we turned away I saw Probes watching. I waved but felt sick. Had he seen me talking to Chuffy McSnatch?

Keith seemed subdued on the journey back to The Granary and I was lost in my own problems.

'Vicky, there's something I have to tell you,' he said.

'I hate that phrase,' I said. 'It always means bad news.'

'It depends on how you look at it.' Keith pulled his Tercel over to the side of the road and cut the engine. He turned to me and reached for my good hand. I started to get nervous.

'I'm leaving town and I want you to come with me. Come and travel the world! We'll go to Père Lachaise in Paris, Zentralfriedhof in Vienna, Prazeres in Lisbon, the City of the Dead in Cairo! The world is our mausoleum! We can write my book together!'

'What about Elaine?' I said, trying hard to keep the 'hurrah' out of my voice. I hadn't the heart to end it, regardless of his peculiar bedroom aspirations. My prayers had been answered.

'I can guarantee that wedding bells will soon be in the air,' Keith said ruefully.

'So she'll be staying in Gipping-on-Plym?'

'Yes. And of course I'll be back visiting from time to time.' He gallantly kissed my hand. 'At least think about it.'

We continued the rest of the drive in silence. Of

course I'd already decided, but it would seem rude to turn him down so quickly, and besides, I still couldn't drive for another week.

As we pulled into the cobbled courtyard, I stifled a cry of alarm.

There, parked outside the door of The Granary, was DI Probes. He was waiting for me. Annabel had won after all. It was over.

Chapter Thirty-One

Keith flung open his car door and got out. 'Ah! Just the person I was hoping to see.'

So this was it. It was over. Probes had come to arrest me. I was sure of it. How else could he have known where to find me? I hadn't even given Mrs Evans my forwarding address, and I definitely hadn't told Barbara.

As Keith greeted Probes with a warm hand-shake, I wondered if the pair of them had been in cahoots from the beginning.

I couldn't believe it.

Keith returned to the Tercel and opened my door. 'Are you going to sit there all day?'

''Course not,' I said and stepped out of the car with my head held high. 'I'm ready.'

As Probes materialized by my side, I braced myself for the clink of handcuffs, but instead he said, 'For you,' and handed me a spider plant.

'It's a housewarming present,' he said stiffly.

'Hey, Colin,' said Keith, 'did my mother talk to

you about The Gables?'

'Yes, she did,' said Probes. 'I've just been up there. I told her that she's welcome to stay there until Easter – that's when the holiday season starts.'

'Wait a minute...' I looked from one man to the other. My stomach was churning with anxiety. 'What's going on?'

Probes looked startled. 'You haven't told her, have you?'

Keith just shrugged. 'I thought she knew.'

'Knew what?' I croaked.

'Meet your new landlord,' said Keith.

'*Landlord?*' I whispered.

'Colin owns the Mudge Estate – it used to be part of The Grange, isn't that right?'

'Keith mentioned you needed somewhere to live and the winter months are always quiet.' Probes gave a wolfish grin. 'Besides, someone has to keep an eye on you.'

'I don't know what to say.' And I really didn't. In fact, I was thoroughly alarmed. Keith had done me a huge favour, but why had Probes agreed. He had to have an ulterior motive.

'If you don't mind, Keith, I need to talk to Vicky about her...' he turned pink at the ears, 'the terms of her lease.'

'Sure thing, mate,' said Keith. 'And Vicky, think about what I said. There's a big wide world out there and I know we can make a go of things.' He blew me a kiss and exited the courtyard.

'Shall we go inside?' said Probes. 'I fancy a cup of tea.'

'It's your house,' I replied tightly and, carrying

301

the spider plant, went inside to put on the kettle. I stuck the plant on the windowsill. 'Thanks again for the gift.'

My knees were shaking and I was so nervous it was all I could do not to hyperventilate.

Probes didn't help. He walked around the room with his hands behind his back. Twice I saw him bend his knees and mutter, 'Well, well, well,' as if he were on the beat.

'You and Keith, then,' he said finally.

'It's not what you think, officer,' I said. 'We're just friends.'

'Yes. I know *your* kind of friends.'

'He's leaving the area,' I said. 'Going on a European cemetery crawl.'

The kettle began to boil, giving me an excuse to do something. 'Milk? Sugar?'

He didn't answer, and when I turned back to the kitchen table, he was just standing there, staring at me.

'Please, sit down,' I said.

'It's no good,' he cried, his face a picture of torment. 'I can't stand it any longer. I can't stand to see you with these ... *gorillas!* I love you.'

I was transfixed, unable to respond, and then, in two short strides Probes pulled me into his arms. I could smell his peculiar musky scent.

I felt a shooting pain race up my arm. 'Mind my wrist,' I squeaked, but he didn't seem to hear.

'Oh, Vicky, Vicky,' he cried. 'I know who your father is and I don't care.' His lips sought mine and he tried to kiss me but I pushed him away.

'I'm an orphan,' I protested weakly.

'Ah yes, the eaten-by-lions-on-safari story.' His

blue eyes looked deeply into mine and I saw only kindness there. 'I won't betray you, Vicky Hill.'

'Don't,' I protested.

'Isn't it time to start living for you? Take a risk? Follow your heart?' He lifted my chin with his fingers and kissed me again, gently. 'I know you care about me. Give us a chance, Vicky. That's all I'm asking. Just a chance.'

'I don't know,' I mumbled.

The truth was, I'd always fancied the redheaded copper – I just hadn't allowed myself to dream of going out on a date with him, let alone anything more. I knew it would devastate my parents. I would officially be thrown out of the firm.

But Probes was right. Maybe I should take a chance. Why not? It wasn't as if we were going to get married. We'd just keep things quiet. No one need ever know. I had to admit I quite liked the way he'd kissed me, and I couldn't remain pure and unsullied for ever.

It really *was* time.

I took a deep breath. 'OK.'

He broke into a wreath of smiles, exposing those little shark-like teeth I now thought rather endearing.

But then he frowned. 'There's just one thing.' He cleared his throat. 'It's rather embarrassing actually.'

'What?'

Probes flushed a violent red. 'I ... I ... I...'

I hadn't heard him stammer for months.

'I know that the physical aspect of a rel–rel–relationship is important to you and, call me old-fashioned, but–' he took a deep breath. 'I don't believe in sex before marriage.'

'You don't believe in sex before marriage?' I whispered. 'Not ever?'

'Frankly,' he went on, 'sex causes nothing but problems.'

'Oh,' I said.

'And I don't believe in this new-fangled dating nonsense either,' Probes went on. 'If you agree to be my girl, you're *my* girl and there can be no other men.'

I nodded.

'Well, what do you say?' Probes looked at me with so much hope I felt a bit funny.

Perhaps he had a point. You only had to look at the Webster-Reeves fiasco. I thought of my first landlady, Mrs Poultry, and those years she wasted as Sir Hugh Trewallyn's mistress. Then there was Eunice Pratt and her unrequited love for that cad Douglas Fleming; our receptionist Barbara's yearning for our one-eyed editor; Annabel's slew of broken romances with unsuitable men, and poor old Steve and his uncontrollable libido. And, of course, there was my own parents' love triangle with that tart Pamela Dingles.

Maybe sex *was* over-rated? Or was it? Given that it caused so many problems, there had to be something that made it worthwhile, and I didn't want to feel I was missing out.

Dad always liked to say, "Keep your friends close and your enemies closer", so I just smiled and said, 'Can I think about it?'

The publishers hope that this book has given you enjoyable reading. Large Print Books are especially designed to be as easy to see and hold as possible. If you wish a complete list of our books please ask at your local library or write directly to:

Magna Large Print Books
Magna House, Long Preston,
Skipton, North Yorkshire.
BD23 4ND

This Large Print Book for the partially sighted, who cannot read normal print, is published under the auspices of

THE ULVERSCROFT FOUNDATION